W9-BKL-221

OOLONG
DEAD

OOLONG DEAD

Tea Shop Mystery #10

LAURA CHILDS

BERKLEY PRIME CRIME, NEW YORK

THE BERKLEY PUBLISHING GROUP
Published by the Penguin Group
Penguin Group (USA) Inc.
375 Hudson Street, New York, New York 10014, USA
Penguin Group (Canada), 90 Eglinton Avenue East, Suite 700, Toronto, Ontario M4P 2Y3, Canada
(a division of Pearson Penguin Canada Inc.)
Penguin Books Ltd., 80 Strand, London WC2R 0RL, England
Penguin Group Ireland, 25 St. Stephen's Green, Dublin 2, Ireland (a division of Penguin Books Ltd.)
Penguin Group (Australia), 250 Camberwell Road, Camberwell, Victoria 3124, Australia
(a division of Pearson Australia Group Pty. Ltd.)
Penguin Books India Pvt. Ltd., 11 Community Centre, Panchsheel Park, New Delhi—110 017, India
Penguin Group (NZ), 67 Apollo Drive, Rosedale, North Shore 0632, New Zealand
(a division of Pearson New Zealand Ltd.)
Penguin Books (South Africa) (Pty.) Ltd., 24 Sturdee Avenue, Rosebank, Johannesburg 2196,
South Africa

Penguin Books Ltd., Registered Offices: 80 Strand, London WC2R 0RL, England

This book is an original publication of The Berkley Publishing Group.

This is a work of fiction. Names, characters, places, and incidents either are the product of the author's imagination or are used fictitiously, and any resemblance to actual persons, living or dead, business establishments, events, or locales is entirely coincidental. The publisher does not have any control over and does not assume any responsibility for author or third-party websites or their content.

PUBLISHER'S NOTE: The recipes contained in this book are to be followed exactly as written. The publisher is not responsible for your specific health or allergy needs that may require medical supervision. The publisher is not responsible for any adverse reactions to the recipes contained in this book.

First edition: March 2009

Library of Congress Cataloging-in-Publication Data

Childs, Laura.
    Oolong dead / Laura Childs.—1st ed.
        p.   cm.—(Tea shop mystery; #10)
    ISBN 978-0-425-22599-8
    1. Browning, Theodosia (Fictitious character)—Fiction.   2. Women detectives—South
Carolina—Charleston—Fiction.   3. Murder—Investigation—Fiction.   4. Tearooms—
Fiction.   5. Upper class—Fiction.   6. Charleston (S.C.)—Fiction.   I. Title.

    PS3603.H56O55 2009
    813'.6—dc22

                                                                              2008040616

PRINTED IN THE UNITED STATES OF AMERICA

10   9   8   7   6   5   4   3   2   1

For Virg—remembering our crazy ad days.

ACKNOWLEDGMENTS

Many thanks to Sam, Tom, Sandy, Bob, and Jennie—and to all of you who e-mail me with wishes for a real-life Indigo Tea Shop. I wish there was one, too. I would treat you all to a scone and a cuppa!

OOLONG
DEAD

1

Overhead branches slapped at Theodosia's cheeks, and a crisp breeze nipped and pecked tendrils of auburn hair from beneath her black velvet riding cap. Sitting astride Captain Harley, a dun-colored jumping horse, Theodosia Browning couldn't have cared less as she charged her mount toward the fifth jump in the annual Charleston Point-to-Point Race.

This pulse-pounding, exhilarating ride was part of a high-society weekend Theodosia felt lucky to participate in. The Wildwood Horse and Hunt Club, a club she'd ridden with before, had invited her to join them. One of their members, a regular steeplechase rider, had broken his collarbone a week earlier and she was riding in his place.

And wouldn't you know it? This was one of those amazing October days when the sky was a curtain of cerulean blue and every shrub and tree blazed red and gold.

Starting from the outskirts of Ruffin, where the horsy set

mingled with Charleston society over mint juleps and bourbon
and branch, the racecourse snaked alongside a country road,
headed into deep woods, and ended at a makeshift finish line
some six miles away. It was a challenging course, littered
with two dozen tricky jumps that included hedges, logs, fences,
and muddy ditches. Heady stuff for Theodosia, who spent
much of her time indoors.

Amidst the hiss and burble of teapots and the coming and
going of customers, Theodosia Browning served as owner
and proprietor of the Indigo Tea Shop in Charleston's historic
district. For the past four years, she'd served tea, catered
events, and dealt with the challenges of being a small business owner in a great big, ever-changing, free-market econ-
omy. No wonder, when it came to riding, she was also a fierce
competitor.

Pounding down a long, sloping trail, Theodosia was happy
to be far away from the viewing stand, hospitality tent, and
inevitable TV cameras. The air was cooler here and the mossy,
loamy scent of low-country soil filled her nostrils.

As brush swooshed against her leather riding boots, Theodosia charged toward the always-difficult in-and-out jump.
Easing back on the reins just slightly, she tried to gauge her
timing. At the last jump, Captain Harley had launched a
little early and his back hooves had ticked down hard on the
gate. Even though this in-and-out jump carried a greater degree of difficulty, Theodosia intended to take it cleanly.

Bending forward now, Theodosia felt the heave and shudder of the large horse beneath her and squinted intently as
the double jump came into view. Her hands slid forward to
grasp a fistful of the horse's rough mane to ensure she
wouldn't get left behind when the big horse launched. Then,
forearms aligned with Captain Harley's head, knees grip-

ping the horse's mud-spattered sides, they were suddenly airborne.

Skimming over the first split-rail fence with ease, they landed with a resounding thud that sent clods of mud flying. Captain Harley took one scrambling, bounding stride, then Theodosia felt his muscles gather again as they launched like a giant spring over the second fence.

Leaning back in her saddle, Theodosia prepared herself for the inevitable hard jounce when the big horse touched down. Felt a tingle of exhilaration mingled with accomplishment.

But Captain Harley suddenly stumbled, then lurched crazily, his landing completely off-kilter!

Bad landing, Theodosia thought as she was jerked rudely in the saddle, her horse slaloming left, sliding a few feet, then crab-stepping wildly off course.

What happened? she wondered. *Bee sting?*

Theodosia dug her heels into the horse's sides and jerked hard at the reins, fighting to regain control. But her quick efforts weren't enough. Something—some movement she'd also caught out of the corner of her eye—had spooked the big horse once again.

Leaning forward, Theodosia continued to jiggle at Captain Harley's bit, trying to simmer him down.

But Captain Harley, caught in his paroxysm of equine panic, was having none of it. Lips slicked back over long teeth, Captain Harley shook his great head from side to side, tossed his head back, and uttered a shrill, high-pitched whinny that sounded like a banshee's shriek as it echoed through the depths of the piney forest.

He's going to rear over backward, Theodosia thought. And just as Captain Harley flung his head back for the second time and his front hooves churned wildly in the air, Theodosia felt herself beginning to slip backward. Gradually, inescapably, she was going to go down.

Theodosia, who'd been riding since she could practically walk, who'd been in tight jams before, did what any seasoned rider would do to save their own hide. She did a tuck and roll.

Only in this case, it was more like a sickening, slow-motion summersault. First, Theodosia was staring at blue sky populated by airy puffs of clouds, then she had a view of sloppy mud, littered with pine needles. Back to a quick, dizzying image of treetops, then another terrifying view of dark earth spinning toward her.

Thud.

A rude, teeth-rattling landing jounced Theodosia the full length of her body. As her breath was punched out of her, her head reeled, and a cloud of darkness began to descend. Hovering on the edge of consciousness, Theodosia willed herself to keep breathing, even as her mind seemed to spin like a centrifuge.

Moments crawled by as Theodosia lay huddled on the ground. Captain Harley was long gone, his hoofbeats miniature thunder that echoed off the trees, then faded to nothing. Gradually, Theodosia felt dampness seep through her riding breeches, became aware of the rich, arboreal scent of forest floor prickling at her nose. She also felt a sharp stab of pain in her side.

Ribs cracked? Maybe broken?

And a raw, intense throb at the base of her neck.

Dear Lord, not my spine!

Theodosia's eyes peeped open. Landing in a semi-sprawled position, she found herself facing the second split-rail fence.

Her nose and the left side of her cheek tingled hotly and she vaguely remembered scraping up against a creosote-coated rail.

Staring at her boots, Theodosia gingerly tried to move her left foot. Though it felt strangely disconnected from the rest of her, the black riding boot bobbled to and fro just fine.

Feeling heartened, she tried the right foot. Again, a moderate amount of success. Deciding she might not be so badly injured after all, knowing she had to get to her feet before another horse and rider came charging through the jump, Theodosia let loose a slow groan and rolled over onto one side.

That's when she saw a fresh spatter of blood tingeing a small patch of grass.

Bleeding? Where?

Her addled mind still wasn't tracking properly. Theodosia peeled off her riding gloves and felt her face, but couldn't detect any major cuts or scratches.

She slid off her riding cap, really a fancy hard hat, and released her mass of curly auburn hair. She carefully patted her scalp. No dampness oozed; her skull seemed blessedly intact. So far so good.

Then . . . what? she wondered.

Twisting her neck slightly, feeling a rise of panic, Theodosia caught sight of more blood. And finally saw the body. Laying right there in front of her. A woman in a pale peach suit, crumpled horribly and slumped against the split-rail fence.

Theodosia's first panicked thought was that she'd run the poor woman down. Had crashed into her and unwittingly battered her with Captain Harley's lethal, steel-shod hooves.

That's what I saw. That's why Captain Harley freaked out! Oh, dear Lord.

Theodosia pulled herself to her feet, staggered slightly, thought for sure she was going to be sick. Then she somehow got it together.

Managing another step, she went down hard on her knees beside the woman.

Is she breathing? Theodosia wondered. She tried to recall the ABC's of first aid. Airway, breathing, circulation.

She touched two fingers to the front of the woman's throat, just above the cameo that was pinned to her blouse, but could detect no pulse. She scanned quickly for some sign of injury, but saw none.

Gently, cautiously, Theodosia pushed the woman's brown hair from her face. The woman's eyes were shut tight, blood smeared her forehead and all the way down to the bridge of her nose And, there, right between the woman's eyes . . . Theodosia leaned in closer to look . . . was a small black hole. The sort of entry hole a small-caliber weapon might make.

Shocked, Theodosia stared into the woman's slack face as the metallic, slightly cloying scent of blood wafted upward.

Theodosia squeezed her eyes closed, forcing herself to breath through her nose, willing herself to calm down. Not to panic.

She slowly opened her eyes and focused.

In the dim recess of her brain, something about the woman struck her as being strangely familiar.

Theodosia rolled back on her heels and studied the woman again. She noted the thrust of the woman's jaw, her high cheekbones, the spark of diamond studs in her ears. And was suddenly rocked to her inner core.

She knew this woman! Had seen her on TV just the other night. Had exchanged slightly unpleasant words with her a few months ago. Had . . . *ohmygosh, it can't be her!* . . . had dated her brother!

It came to Theodosia in a wild rush of recovered memory. The name popped into her brain with so much force she swore it made a cartoon bubble above her head.

"Abby Davis," said Theodosia, her voice rising as if it were a pleading, crying question. "Shot to death?"

She stared at the woman again as a sick feeling puddled in the pit of her stomach.

Last time Theodosia had come face-to-face with Abby Davis, they'd had a rather public disagreement. And now here she was, lying dead in front of her.

The coincidence, the irony, seemed almost too much for Theodosia.

Nerves on edge, she studied the body again. Noticed there was fresh dirt under the fingernails of Abby's left hand. As if she'd attempted to pull herself along.

Shaking, feeling somewhat repulsed, Theodosia reached out and carefully shifted the body. It rolled over and settled lifelessly into a sad heap. The fingernails on Abby's right hand were just as filthy.

Theodosia lifted her gaze to the bloodless pallor of Abby Davis's face. It was a shocking contrast to the cameo that glinted so hypnotically in the fading afternoon sun. Red, blue, and brilliant yellow stones shining brightly.

"What just happened here?" she muttered.

But there was no answer save the faint whisper and sigh of the forest.

2

"*I can't believe* you even came in today," said Drayton. Tall and dapper, sixty-something, and dressed impeccably in a Harris tweed jacket, white shirt, and trademark bow tie, Drayton Conneley focused his full attention on Theodosia.

She'd shown up early as usual this Monday morning to supervise the day's preparations at the Indigo Tea Shop. True, her ribs were taped and she was moving at reduced speed, but she was there.

Haley Parker, the tea shop's gifted young baker and kitchen savant, was also in scolding mode. "You should march right back upstairs to your apartment," she urged. "Crawl back in bed and take it easy. Let Dayton and me run the tea shop today."

"Lord knows, we've run it before," said Drayton. He stood ramrod stiff, obviously nervous and concerned about Theodosia's physical well-being.

"And we always do a terrific job," said Haley. She pushed

her stick-straight blond hair behind her ears and winked at Drayton, who answered by rolling his eyes and mouthing, *credible job.*

"I'll be fine, you two," Theodosia assured them. "I just won't be doing my usual scurrying and hefting of teapots." Besides sore ribs, her left knee was swollen and throbbing like crazy. And she still had the remnants of a headache. Just what she needed at the start of a busy workweek.

"But we already have everything well in hand," protested Drayton.

Gazing about the tea shop, Theodosia could see that Drayton was quite correct. Tables were draped in white linen, candles flickered enticingly in glass tea warmers, silverware was polished and carefully arranged. Fresh flowers, what appeared to be red and yellow zinnias, bobbed their shaggy heads in crystal vases. And with sunlight filtering in through lead pane windows onto the pegged wooden floor, the Indigo Tea Shop gleamed like the storybook cottage it was.

"Polished to perfection," murmured Theodosia. Her blue eyes crinkled in her broad, intelligent face with its peaches-and-cream complexion courtesy of English ancestry. Her Irish ancestors' DNA had gifted her with a mass of curly auburn hair that would've made a painter such as Raphael jump for joy.

"Thank you, ma'am," said Drayton, posturing slightly. As tea master and catering director, he managed his job with great dignity and prided himself on anticipating any problem.

"Helloooo!" called a high-pitched voice. "Anybody home?" This was followed by several sharp, insistent raps on the front door.

Oops. There was one problem the staunchly diligent Drayton hadn't anticipated.

"Delaine," said Drayton in a somewhat resigned tone, which elicited gentle snickers from Theodosia and Haley. Delaine Dish was the chirpy, upbeat owner of Cotton Duck, a clothing boutique located a few blocks away. Delaine's upscale shop specialized in both luxe and casual clothes, and Delaine fancied herself as one of Charleston's best dressed.

Haley scrambled to the front door, flipped the latch, and let Delaine in.

Dressed in a poppy-red cashmere sweater and skirt with matching four-inch stiletto pumps, Delaine clacked her way noisily across the tea room floor. With a determined scowl on her lovely, heart-shaped face, she made a beeline for Theodosia.

"I can't believe you're up and walking!" Delaine exclaimed in a strident tone that had to reach at least seventy decibels. "After all you've been through!"

"I'm feeling lots better," Theodosia lied. Delaine had been one of the volunteers at the point-to-point race yesterday and had probably picked up enough information mingled with rumors to make her dangerous.

"Is she *really* okay?" Delaine turned her violet-eyed laser gaze on Drayton as she shook back shoulder-length dark hair.

His eyebrows shot up. "Says she is."

Delaine slid into a chair across from Theodosia, then reached out and grabbed one of Theodosia's hands. "I've been so worried, Theo! There we were, having a perfectly *lovely* high-society event. And you go and stumble upon that poor woman's dead body!"

Drayton rolled his eyes toward the ceiling. "I hope you realize Theodosia didn't exactly go looking for trouble."

Delaine continued to pat Theodosia's hand as her words poured out. "Of course, I know that. But such a totally bizarre coincidence! Theo's former boyfriend's sister found murdered." She cocked her head, thinking. "Let's see, is that correct?" She nodded to herself. "Yes, that's it precisely. To think Abby Davis almost became your sister-in-law!"

Haley set plates of steaming hot oatmeal scones in front of everyone, then suddenly spoke in a high-pitched voice. "So, are you going to fill us in on what really happened?"

"Haley," chided Drayton. "You are sometimes woefully short on tact."

But Theodosia just nodded. She knew Drayton and Haley were secretly dying to hear every single detail. After all, the three of them had worked together for so long, they were almost family. When one of them was traumatized or hurt or landed in trouble, the ripples rolled out to the other two. And Delaine, of course, was always eager to glean the latest gossip.

"The thing is," said Drayton, trying not to appear overanxious, "we know some of it."

"Parker called last night," explained Haley. "From the hospital." Parker Scully was Theodosia's boyfriend and owner of Solstice Bistro. He'd been there, of course, when Theodosia was brought back to the clubhouse. Had stood by her, or at least outside the clubhouse door, while Sheriff Newton Clay questioned her at length.

"Parker rang us up while you were at Memorial Hospital having your various X-rays and CT scans," added Drayton. Now he looked worried again.

Theodosia saw they were both struggling to put words to

their concern and her heart went out to them. "How much did Parker tell you?" she asked, standing up to grab a jar of lemon curd from its display on a nearby highboy.

"Theo," implored Drayton, practically wringing his hands. "Please remain seated. I'm genuinely worried about you."

"You're treating me like a Dresden figurine." Theodosia laughed. But she eased herself down anyway. And when her back once again touched the fluffy cushion in the captain's chair, she did feel a smidgeon of tension ooze from her.

"Let me pour us all some tea," offered Drayton. He hustled over to the counter, grabbed a Brown Betty teapot, and was back in no time. Haley, in true Haley fashion, scampered into her postage stamp–sized kitchen and brought back footed glass dishes filled with Devonshire cream and raspberry jam.

"Just fill in some of the blanks for us," suggested Haley. "While we have a proper cream tea breakfast." Cream tea at the Indigo Tea Shop always consisted of scones, jam, Devonshire cream, and good strong tea.

"Where to start?" murmured Theodosia. She sighed, thinking she'd rather not relive yesterday's awful memory. But Drayton, Haley, and Delaine peered at her anxiously. And with more than a little curiosity, too.

"Your horse spooked at the fifth jump," prompted Haley. "And then you were thrown."

"Something like that," said Theodosia as she watched Drayton pour steaming tea into elegant bone china teacups.

"This is a Formosan oolong," he told them. "Lightly oxidized with a subtle peachy flavor. You won't need sugar with this one." He tugged at his jacket, then sat down. "And when you landed and came to . . . well, there she was," said Drayton.

"Abby Davis," said Theodosia. The name tasted strange in her mouth. The last time she'd seen Abby Davis was two months ago at the Charleston Film Festival. They'd met somewhat accidentally on the red carpet and Abby had managed to hurl a few choice insults at her. Theodosia could still see Abby the TV reporter, her face pulled into an unflattering mask of anger, as she nattered away. Since that strange encounter, Abby Davis had been promoted from investigative reporter to evening news anchor at Trident Media. Probably, Theodosia decided, the murder of someone who was that media prominent was going to garner lots of attention.

"And she'd been *shot?*" said Haley, still trying to pry details out of Theodosia, while managing to look horrified and intrigued at the same time.

"It sounds like Parker filled you in a lot," said Theodosia, taking a sip of tea. It was hot and fragrant, as promised. Excellent. She knew she was going to need something bracing to propel her through the morning.

"The thing of it is . . ." began Drayton. He stopped, bit his lower lip, then rubbed the back of his hand against his cheek.

"The fact that it was Abby Davis makes it doubly strange," said Delaine, jumping in.

"Since you *did* date Jory Davis for a couple of years," added Haley.

"True," said Theodosia, although the memory had faded some, thanks in no small part to Parker Scully.

"And, by your own admission, you and Jory had a messy breakup," said Delaine, brightly. She thought for a moment. "It does look rather strange, doesn't it? Two months after Abby Davis tried to goad you into a very public argument she turns up dead. Shot clean through the head." She looked around, wide-eyed. "Well, it was a clean shot, wasn't it?"

"Shot through the forehead," said Drayton, then moved his hand to cover his mouth, as if embarrassed by his rather gossipy remark.

"That's okay, Drayton," said Theodosia. "I'm finding this all a bit strange, too."

"A bizarre coincidence," said Haley.

"Kismet," proclaimed Delaine.

"I believe kismet is actually a *good* thing," corrected Drayton.

"Okay then," said Delaine. "Call it some weird synchronization between the two of you. That your paths kept crossing."

"They won't anymore," said Haley, in an ominous tone.

"The police don't think *you* did it, do they?" asked Delaine. She voiced the one terrible thought they'd all danced and jigged around.

Theodosia sighed. "I don't know. I hope not. Sheriff Clay asked a million questions all the while playing it fairly close to the vest. And he had a crime scene technician do some sort of gunpowder residue test on my hands."

"That must have been unnerving," said Drayton.

"And they told me not to leave town," said Theodosia.

"Sheesh," said Haley. "Just like in the movies."

"Only this is reality," Drayton pointed out, a grim look clouding his face.

"Why was Abby even out there?" asked Haley.

"From what I understand," said Theodosia, "she was doing some sort of film segment. Trident Media was one of the race's sponsors."

"Did she have a camera man with her?" asked Haley.

"Don't know," said Theodosia.

"But she was out in the woods," said Delaine. "Could she have been shot by a hunter?"

"A hunter who just happened to drag her body over to a jump where Theodosia would find it?" said Haley. "Sounds wacky."

"I wonder why someone else didn't find her first?" said Delaine.

Theodosia had pondered that herself. "It could have been deliberate," she murmured quietly.

Delaine's brows pinched together. "Huh? You mean somebody *knew* you were headed for that jump?"

"That's all I can figure," said Theodosia. "The names of all the riders and their start times were clearly posted."

"Somebody was trying to set you up?" asked Haley.

"Or Abby had hatched some diabolical plan to try to scare me or spook my horse," said Theodosia. "And something went terribly wrong."

"Abby wasn't that crazy, was she?" asked Delaine.

"Then who would stage the body like that?" asked Haley. "And why?"

Theodosia shrugged and her whole upper body seemed to ache. "Search me."

Drayton's face drooped as he stared unhappily into his teacup. "Oh, I'm sure they will."

3

Teakettles hissed and burbled, and the brass bell over the front door tinkled constantly as Drayton and Haley flew about the tea shop like winged warriors, greeting customers, seating customers, and making everyone feel welcome. As they kept up their frantic pace, pouring tea and serving oatmeal scones and pumpkin biscuits, they were determined not to allow Theodosia to budge from her table in the corner.

"Theo's catbird seat," Drayton had declared. "Where she can see and be seen, but is not required to lift her little finger."

"Unless she's holding a particularly delicate teacup." Haley laughed.

It wasn't long before most every table in the Indigo Tea Shop was filled with morning customers. There were the regulars, of course, who wandered in from neighboring shops on Church Street. Suzanne from Robillard Booksellers. Daria from the Antiquarian Map Shop. And Sabrina from the Cabbage Patch Needlecraft Shop. The Indigo Tea Shop was a special place for them, an Old World tea salon where time slowed down, tea drinking was elevated to a genteel art, and the aroma of fruity Darjeelings, malty Assams, and toasty Keemuns filled the air and imparted an almost aromatherapy-like effect.

And there were loads of tourists, too. Folks who'd been drawn to the romance and genteel beauty of Charleston and journeyed from all points of the globe. They explored the 250-year-old historic district, trod narrow cobblestone walkways, marveled at the Italianate, Georgian, and Victorian mansions that lined the Battery, gasped at the beauty of the Atlantic Ocean rushing in to meet the Ashley and Cooper rivers, and succumbed to the charms of Charleston's bountiful gardens that seemed to flourish anywhere and everywhere. And for some intriguing reason, a lot of these tourists ended up at the Indigo Tea Shop.

Haley carried Theodosia's thick black ledger out to her, so she could review and tally last week's receipts. But Delaine was still keeping Theodosia close company and seemed in no hurry to leave. In fact, Delaine hadn't budged for over an hour, except to signal, with an imperious wave of her hand and a clank of her chunky gold charm bracelet, for a fresh pot of tea.

"You know," Delaine told Theodosia in a languid drawl, "you still haven't decided which evening gown you're going to wear to the Masked Ball this Saturday night." The Masked Ball, named after the Verdi opera *Un Ballo in Maschera*, was a gala affair designed to kick off Charleston's much-heralded opera season.

"Mmm," said Theodosia. It was the last thing on her mind right now.

Delaine raised her perfectly waxed brows. "I'm still holding the green silk with the beaded bodice as well as the peachy gold vintage Perry Ellis with that amazingly full skirt. You're going to have to make a *choice*, dear. And fairly soon at that."

Theodosia shifted uncomfortably in her chair and decided she probably needed to gulp another Motrin. "I'm not sure how much dancing I'll be able to do," she told Delaine.

Delaine's eyes were suddenly burning with an almost religious fervor. "But the Masked Ball is shaping up to be one of Charleston's truly *major* social occasions! Everybody who's anybody is attending. The ne plus ultra of the upper crust. Frankly, I'd say it's almost mandatory you put in an appearance."

"Oh, I'll be there, all right," said Theodosia. "Drayton would be upset if I missed it." Drayton was a big wheel in the Charleston Opera Society and had made a special point of inviting her as well as having the catering contract awarded to Parker. "Plus, Drayton's tapped Haley to bake traditional Italian bread for the bruschetta appetizers." Theodosia hesitated. "And you know the tea shop is hosting the Bravissimo Club's luncheon tomorrow."

Delaine waved a hand dismissively. "Of course, I'm planning to attend. The date's in my Filofax, noted in *ink*."

"I take it the Bravissimo Club is trying to solicit money from donors?" asked Theodosia. The Bravissimo Club was a sort of women's auxiliary to the Opera Society. Besides being opera fans and boosters, they often worked to raise money to fund the various operas.

"You make it sound so crass," said Delaine. "But yes, the Opera Society happens to be woefully short on money right now. In fact, we barely have enough in our coffers to purchase costumes for the upcoming production of *La Bohème*. So the plan is to ask a few of Charleston's social doyennes if they might find it in their hearts to make a generous donation."

"Good luck to you," said Theodosia. "I know that most arts organizations are tight on funds these days. All nonprofits are, in fact." Theodosia was on the board of directors of Big Paw, Charleston's service dog organization. Big Paw rescued dogs from local shelters, then trained them to be service dogs and therapy dogs for people with disabilities. Last month they'd graduated two seizure alert dogs. And even though people seemed to love Big Paw's mission, the group was always scrambling for donations, be they monetary or in-kind.

"I just hope you're a lot more mobile tomorrow," said Delaine. "From what I understand, we have a fairly large group coming for lunch."

Theodosia opened her ledger and flipped to the back page. "Last I heard, the number of guests was set at twenty-four." She tapped her Montblanc pen on the wooden table. "Are you telling me there'll be more?"

Delaine waggled her fingers and her moonstone ring glinted in the sunlight. "I'm really not up on tedious details," she said, spitting out the word *details* like she was referring to horse manure. "To tell you the truth, I'm really more of a big . . ." Delaine's head pivoted suddenly and a strange look crossed her face.

"You were saying?" said Theodosia.

"Big problem," muttered Delaine, suddenly jumping up. "Ta-ta, must run!"

The big problem arrived by the pound today. A lot of pounds. Detective Burt Tidwell stood in the open doorway of the tea shop, virtually blotting out the sun. He was a bear-sized man with a strange bullet-shaped head and giant hands. Like many large men, he'd taken to wearing vests, and the buttons on Tidwell's vests always strained mightily. Head of Charleston's Robbery-Homicide Division, Tidwell was brilliant, shrewd, driven, and utterly neurotic. His homicide detectives detested him, complained bitterly about his exacting ways, and went so far as to mock him behind his back. They would have also, at the crook of his little finger, followed him unquestioningly across burning coals.

Theodosia was, alternately, mildly amused by Tidwell, grateful for his assistance with past problems, and a little in awe of this former FBI agent who, depending upon which way the wind was blowing, vacillated between blustering and coy.

Cutting through the tea room like a Greek supertanker headed for an oil port, Tidwell artfully dodged tables and slid past Drayton and Haley, who were ferrying luncheon plates to waiting customers.

Arriving at Theodosia's table, Tidwell gave a quick bob of his head, then eased himself into a chair. There was a mild groan, but the chair, thankfully constructed of fine Carolina pine, held steadfastly together.

"Detective Tidwell," said Theodosia. "What brings you here?" As if she didn't know. "Lunch perhaps?"

Tidwell arranged his mouth in the semblance of a smile, one a friendly barracuda might use to entice his own lunch. "Perhaps."

Looking across the tea room at the chalkboard, Theodosia squinted and rattled off the day's menu. "We can offer you cream of sweet potato soup, strawberry and cream cheese tea sandwiches, pineapple tea sandwiches, or a lovely vegetable egg strata."

"Soup would be lovely," purred Tidwell.

Seeing Tidwell settle in, Drayton was at Theodosia's side in about five seconds.

"Drayton, when you have a moment, could you bring us each a bowl of sweet potato soup and a couple of tea sandwiches?" asked Theodosia. "And maybe . . . let's see . . . are the chocolate sour cream scones out of the oven yet?"

"I'll check," said Drayton. "And might I suggest a pot of Dimbulla black tea? Its flavor is highly complementary to the soup."

"Lovely," said Tidwell, smiling again.

Formal pleasantries and two smiles in a row. Theodosia knew something was definitely brewing here besides tea.

"You're here because of yesterday," she said. There was no sense in beating around the bush. Might as well get everything out on the table, so to speak.

"Of course," said Tidwell pleasantly. "As you have probably surmised, Sheriff Newton Clay has asked me to lend a helping hand in the Abby Davis homicide investigation. Colleton County isn't all that . . . shall we say . . . *experienced* with homicides."

"And you've graciously acquiesced," said Theodosia, waiting for the other shoe to drop. She didn't have to wait long.

Tidwell leaned back in his chair and let loose a deep, almost regretful sigh. "So, Miss Browning, once again a dead body."

"Not my doing," she responded.

Tidwell's hands were clasped firmly across his ample midsection. Now he lifted them slightly and, in a gesture that was pure Tidwellian, spread his fingers apart as if to convey, *kindly enlighten me.*

Theodosia could provide no information that enlightened.

Tidwell decided to attempt a more direct approach. "The bereaved family is understandably upset and outraged." He allowed his mouth to twitch upward. "It probably won't be long before they take up pitchforks en masse and make rumblings about pressing charges."

"Certainly not against me," said Theodosia. Her heart skipped a quick beat, then settled back into its normal rhythm. After all, she had nothing to fear. Did she?

"This is clearly a homicide," continued Tidwell.

"A bullet in the head usually is," agreed Theodosia.

"You don't seem to be taking this very seriously," said Tidwell. He stared across the table at her with the bright, beady eyes of a magpie. He kept his gaze on Theodosia while Haley unloaded soup, sandwiches, and chocolate scones from a silver tray propped against her hip. Finally, she set out a dish of butter molded into a tiny beehive and a cut glass bowl filled with lemon curd.

"Anything else?" asked Haley. She stared silently at Tidwell, as if sending him a subtle warning to back off.

Theodosia shook her head. "Thank you, Haley."

Picking up a silver spoon, Tidwell slid it into the rich, creamy broth, then held it to his lips and took a delicate slurp. "Excellent," he pronounced. "Celery, cinnamon, and an appropriate hint of nutmeg."

"I'll be sure to tell Haley you're pleased," said Theodosia.

They ate in silence for a few minutes, spoons clinking against china bowls. Then Theodosia stared at Tidwell with all the earnestness she could muster and said, "You know I'm not guilty."

"I only know the facts," replied Tidwell. "And the fact is, you had a verbal and highly public disagreement with Abby Davis some two months ago. Then yesterday she turned up dead. At your feet, no less."

"Correction," said Theodosia, holding up an index finger. "Concerning that argument, *Abby* was the one who did the disagreeing." Was really the disagreeable one, she wanted to say. "Abby was the one who tried to provoke me with her nasty, sniping words."

"And you're telling me you didn't snipe back?" asked Tidwell.

"What would have been the point?" asked Theodosia. She pursed her lips, gave Tidwell a look of sublime disapproval. Really, the man could be such a male cliché. Did he honestly believe the two of them would show their claws in some sort of public argument? A catfight? Oh please.

The silver butter knife was dwarfed by Tidwell's big paw as he sliced off an ample chunk of butter and lathered it onto his scone. He bit into it, chewed slowly, closed his eyes as if savoring every nuance. When he opened them again he asked, "Any ideas?"

"Not really," said Theodosia. "And that's the problem. I turned the whole thing over and over in my head all night long, but nothing seemed to gel."

"Mmm," answered Tidwell, still nibbling at his scone.

"Given time," said Theodosia, "I might be able to come up with something."

Tidwell's faced clouded ever so slightly. "That would entail meddling."

Theodosia waited a couple of beats. "More like making a few discreet inquiries."

"Inquiries," repeated Tidwell, as though the word carried

an unfamiliar ring. "Among the deceased's family?" He popped the rest of the scone into his mouth and chewed viciously.

"Not sure," said Theodosia, gazing at him. She realized that this was the closest he was ever going to come to asking her for help. This was crunch time. "Maybe I could do that."

Tidwell reached for a second scone and a long silence spun out between them. Finally he said, "Perhaps you could."

4

"This is utterly spectacular," said Drayton, gently balancing a sweetgrass basket in his hands and giving it an admiring gaze. The basket was a classic fruit tray style, shallow with a large, swooping handle.

"Mm-hm," replied Miss Josette. She was an African American woman with bright, intelligent eyes and smooth skin the color of rich mahogany.

"You should, indeed, be classified as a fine artist," marveled Drayton, surveying the array of elegant, handwoven baskets she'd just delivered to the Indigo Tea Shop.

Miss Josette was probably in her late seventies, but could pass for early sixties. She wore a tomato-red dress with large glasses to match. A red-and-turquoise-fringed shawl was draped casually around her shoulders. "These are for Theodosia," she cautioned. "For her T-Bath products. Not to decorate the walls of your tidy little bachelor kitchen."

Drayton put a hand on his heart, trying his best to appear sincere. "I wouldn't . . ." he began. "It never crossed my mind."

"Of course, it did," said Miss Josette. "I know you covet my baskets. Haley told me you bought three from that last batch I brought in." She winked at him. "Kind of on the sly at that."

"You got that right," said Theodosia, pushing her way through the celadon-green curtains that divided the tea room from the kitchen and back office. "Our Drayton's suddenly become a collecting fiend for sweetgrass baskets. Or rather I should say *your* baskets, Miss Josette."

Sweetgrass baskets were unique to Charleston and the surrounding environs. Elegant and utilitarian, they were woven from long bunches of sweetgrass, pine needles, and bulrush, then bound together by strips from native palmetto trees. Over the years, sweetgrass baskets, crafted predominantly by African American women, had become celebrated pieces of art. A collection of low-country sweetgrass baskets was even on display at the Smithsonian in Washington, D.C.

Now Haley hurried out to exclaim over the baskets. "These are so gorgeous," she marveled. "I tried to weave one once but I was all thumbs."

"Takes lots of practice," said Miss Josette, knowingly. "Years, in fact."

"Wouldn't it be cool if we hung them on the walls?" asked Haley.

Miss Josette glanced around. The walls of the Indigo Tea Shop were already festooned with antique engravings depicting rice plantations and various views of Charleston harbor, as well as Theodosia's handmade grapevine wreaths decorated with teacups. Antique plates were propped on several wooden shelves along with collectible cup-and-saucer sets. A highboy held tins of tea, jars of DuBose Bees Honey, and Theodosia's selection of T-Bath products. All retail products offered for sale.

"Only if you can find room," chuckled Miss Josette. "But probably the best thing is to use them just like you planned— for your beauty products. After all, my baskets come directly from Mother Nature, just like your lotions and potions." Indeed, Theodosia had developed Green Tea Lotion, Chamomile Comfort Lotion, and Jasmine Rejuvenation Oil, to name a few.

"The T-Bath products always sell well," said Theodosia. "Here and on our website. But once we add a fluffy towel and a loofah, and arrange an assortment of creams and lotions in a sweetgrass basket, they fly out of here like hotcakes."

"Good," said Miss Josette. "That means these old fingers will be staying busy."

"Excuse me," said Drayton, pulling out a chair for Miss Josette. "Where are my manners? Please sit down and let me bring you a cup of tea."

"Better yet, lunch," offered Haley. "We've still got sweet potato soup. Oh, and I can do apricot jam and cream cheese on zucchini bread if you'd like. The zucchini bread just came out of the oven."

"Sounds lovely," said Miss Josette. "But I'm in a hurry today. Take a rain check for next time, though."

"Next time then," said Drayton, seeing her to the door. "For sure."

"You know what?" said Haley, quickly surveying the tea shop. "I'm gonna take these baskets in the back and start

filling them with products. Have them ready for that opera luncheon tomorrow." She shrugged. "Who knows, maybe opera lovers like to shop. Drayton . . ." She dropped her voice. "Can you take care of the three tables we have left?"

"I live to do your bidding," responded Drayton. "Although I just delivered fresh pots of tea so all our customers should be set for a while." He gazed at Theodosia. "Did you eat?"

She nodded. "With Tidwell, remember?"

"Then you probably have a nasty case of indigestion," grumbled Drayton. "I don't see how you tolerate that man. Such an abrasive manner."

"Just doing his job," said Theodosia. *And enlisting me to help*, she thought with a start. When had that ever happened before? She thought for a few moments. The answer was never.

"If you have a couple of minutes," said Drayton, "we should run through a few ideas for our holiday teas. After all, Thanksgiving is . . . what? Little more than a month away?" He looked slightly bewildered. "Isn't it dreadful how time just slips away?"

"Dreadful," agreed Theodosia. But she was thinking of something else.

They sat down at the corner table and Drayton pulled a small notebook from his jacket pocket. "I've made a few notes." He slid a pair of tortoiseshell half-glasses onto his nose. "Obviously, everyone looks forward to us developing tasty new blends."

Haley suddenly came flying out of the back room to grab more bottles of Chamomile Comfort Lotion. "You're just *start-ing* on holiday teas?" she asked Drayton. "You should have jumped on that project at least six weeks ago. People have been *asking.*" She grabbed six bottles of lotion, spread her fingers wider, and tried for two more.

"Well, I know that," groused Drayton. "You don't have to lecture me."

"We go through this every year," said Haley, suddenly dropping her bottles of lotion, watching them scatter, then hastily kneeling down to retrieve them. "You know what, Drayton? I'm so smart I can tell you exactly when Thanksgiving is. In fact, I'm so smart I can even tell you when Christmas . . ."

"We get the idea, Haley," said Drayton in a solemn voice. He ripped a slip of paper from his order pad. "Kindly deliver this to table five. They look as though they may be ready to leave."

"Got it," said Haley, suddenly snapping back into work mode.

"So," said Drayton. "The holiday teas."

Shaking her head to clear it, feeling a sudden spasm in her neck, Theodosia said, "I guess we should be thinking citrus and spice."

"And everything nice," added Drayton. As a master tea blender who'd earned his chops at the great tea auctions in Amsterdam, Drayton adored developing new house blends. His Summer Solstice Tea with lemon and vanilla had become a real classic, as had his Christmas Spice, a blend of Chinese black tea, cinnamon, and cardamom.

"By the mischievous look on your face I'd say you've got something offbeat in mind," said Theodosia.

Drayton nodded. "What would you think of blending black and green teas and adding a hint of vanilla bean?"

Theodosia peered at him thoughtfully. "That's a combo

I'd never have thought of in a million years. But I like it. I mean, it's unusual, but . . . have you tried it?"

"Of course," responded Drayton, "and I can assure you it's excellent."

"Got a name?"

"Hmm," said Drayton, thinking. "How about . . . Holiday Dream?"

"One down," said Theodosia.

"As long as you're open to something novel," said Drayton, "indulge me once more. Chinese black tea blended with citrus peel, rose petal, and almond."

"To be served with Chicken Almond Ding." Theodosia chuckled. She was laughing, suddenly feeling a whole lot better. Was starting to feel like the worst might be behind her when, suddenly, the bell over the front door tinkled insistently. She and Drayton glanced over, expecting to see one of their Church Street neighbors popping in for a midafternoon pick-me-up of tea and scones.

But it wasn't anyone from Church Street. In fact, it wasn't even anyone from Charleston.

Jory Davis, Theodosia's old boyfriend from three years ago, looking slightly older but quite dignified in a three-piece navy pinstripe suit, stood in the doorway, scanning the tea room with weary eyes. Upon seeing her, his expression changed. And, like a lightbulb suddenly being turned on, an enormous smile of relief flooded his face.

Theodosia pulled herself up slowly, one trembling hand going to her throat, the other resting on the table to help steady herself, and said in a small voice, "Jory?"

Drayton leapt from his chair and dashed across the tea shop, practically setting a new land speed record. He dodged left, then right in an attempt to block Jory's intended path. "I don't think you should be here right now," he said, a sharp, cautionary note rising in his voice. He sounded just this side of threatening.

"It's okay, Drayton," called Theodosia. She'd regained her composure in the few moments that Drayton had spent posturing, while Jory looked quizzical. "Let him by."

Jory Davis literally bounded across the tea shop. "I just flew in from New York," he told her. Now he looked flushed and a trifle apprehensive. "I . . . I came here first."

Holding out her hand to him, Theodosia said, "Jory, I'm so sorry for your loss."

5

~⚜~

The first few minutes were slightly awkward. Theodosia extending her condolences, Jory nodding soberly. They both seemed to be slowly acknowledging the fact that they were sitting together, talking calmly and rationally. It was a far cry from the angry words they'd hurled at each other some three years ago, all of which had led to an extended period of being incommunicado.

Finally, Jory said, "You were there. You found her."

"Yes," Theodosia murmured.

Jory leaned forward. "Was Abby able to say anything? Did she . . . ?" His voice faltered, then dissolved into a choked sob.

"I'm so sorry," said Theodosia, "but I'm afraid she was already gone."

"So you don't really have any sort of . . . uh . . . clue," said Jory.

"Not really," responded Theodosia. Abby Davis had made

no dying affirmation, had whispered no words that pointed to her killer.

"And the police?" asked Jory. His face reflected inner turmoil, but through sheer willpower, he had gotten himself under control. "I assume they questioned you at length?"

"The murder . . . homicide . . . occurred in Colleton County," said Theodosia. "So Sheriff Newton Clay, a fellow who actually seems like a decent enough sort, is in charge."

"But does he . . . ?" began Jory.

"However," continued Theodosia, "Sheriff Clay seemed to feel their law enforcement agency didn't have quite enough experience with homicides. So he has requested Charleston PD's Robbery-Homicide Division to lend a hand. Detective Burt Tidwell has taken, shall we say, a somewhat personal interest in the case."

Jory gazed at her earnestly. "That's good, right? I mean, Abby was kind of a media star here. So it stands to reason she should get some extra attention."

Theodosia hesitated for just a millisecond. "Yes, I think it's good Tidwell is handling it."

Jory suddenly looked around, as if only now realizing where he was. "I've got to go see my family," he said. "What little of them are left."

"You have an uncle and aunt here in Charleston," said Theodosia. "And cousins in Sumter."

Jory sighed deeply. "Yes. Do you suppose they've made any arrangements? Funeral arrangements?"

Theodosia bit her lower lip. "I don't think the police have released Abby's body yet."

Jory put a hand to his cheek and his eyes fluttered slightly. He suddenly look drained.

"Drayton." Theodosia raised her voice slightly, curled a hand.

Drayton, who'd been hovering at the counter, casting glances their way, appeared in an instant. "Yes?"

"Could you bring a pot of strong tea and some of those leftover tea sandwiches?"

Drayton nodded. "Of course."

Jory gazed at her. "You're being very nice."

Theodosia smiled faintly. "You want me to be nasty?"

Now it was Jory's turn to give a wan smile. "You don't have it in you."

Theodosia lifted a single eyebrow and let it quiver. "Don't be so sure about that. Besides, you're an attorney. You should know better than to underestimate people." She was going to say *underestimate your opponent*, but decided that sounded a bit harsh.

"Theo," said Jory, and now his voice was intensely serious. "I would never do that with you."

Wriggling her aching shoulders, Theodosia leaned back in her chair. "I heard you might be getting married."

Jory grimaced. "Yeah, well, that's been put on hold."

"What exactly does *put on hold* mean?" she asked. "Postponed or not happening?" Theodosia knew she was pushing Jory a little hard, but she was curious and rightly so. This was the man who, not that long ago, had asked her to marry him. Of course, there had been a big fat condition attached to his proposal. Leave her tea shop behind and follow him to New York.

"Probably not happening," muttered Jory. "But I can't even begin to deal with that relationship until this . . . this *thing* with Abby is cleared up. I've got to start doing some hard digging."

"You plan to get involved in the investigation?" asked Theodosia. Jory wasn't a criminal attorney or even a trial lawyer, but he was well versed in the law, investigations, and how to deal with the authorities.

A strange look descended on Jory's face. A little sad, with a smattering of optimism thrown in. "I was hoping you'd help me with that."

His words came as a complete surprise to Theodosia. "Me? You've got to be kidding."

Jory shook his head. "Never been more serious in my life."

"Your family will never buy it." Theodosia let loose a wry laugh, then thought, *Why should I buy it?*

"It's not up to them," said Jory. "This is what I want, what I'm asking of you."

"Tidwell said something about them picking up pitchforks."

"Never happen," said Jory. "Besides, I'm the persuasive sort. I can bring my relatives around. You've helped us all before so I'm confident they'll listen to reason."

"And you're the voice of reason?"

"Sure," said Jory. "I can be." He sounded a little unsure.

This was turning into another bizarre day, Theodosia decided. Requests for help from both ends of the spectrum. "So why ask me?" said Theodosia. "Really."

"Two reasons," Jory said, without hesitation. "One, you were right there. I can't get it out of my head that Abby had somehow struggled over to the racecourse." He drew a strangled breath. "That her poor, dying brain had figured out where to find you. And that, deep down, she *knew* you'd help her."

"I find that hard to believe," said Theodosia, gazing into Jory's earnest brown eyes, reminding herself how truly nasty Abby Davis had always been to her.

"Believe it," said Jory. Then, as if reading Theodosia's

mind, he said, "She didn't really hate you, you know. She was just awfully upset. About us."

"Okay," said Theodosia, deciding that conversational hot potato was best left to sizzle by itself for a while. "You said two reasons. What's the second one?"

Jory gazed at her with what could only be described as open admiration. A look that hadn't been so magnificently bestowed on her in quite some time. "Because you're still the smartest person I ever laid eyes on."

Drayton chose that exact moment to arrive with a tea tray laden with a pot of Darjeeling, cups and saucers, a plate of sandwiches.

"Flattery . . ." began Theodosia.

"Will get you nowhere," huffed Drayton. He deposited the tray with a clatter and spun on his heels.

Saying nothing, Theodosia reached for the teapot and poured out the steaming hot liquid.

"I see Drayton hasn't changed," said Jory. "Still quiet and reserved as always."

"He's just worried about me," said Theodosia. She was grateful for Drayton's concern. And knew that once Jory left, she'd have to reassure Drayton that any nervousness he had was completely unfounded. Picking up the plate of sandwiches, she held it out toward Jory. "Eat something. Keep your blood sugar up."

"Thank you," said Jory.

"No problem. We had plenty left over."

Jory stared at her earnestly. "That's not what I meant."

After Jory drank his cup of tea and wolfed down at least four tea sandwiches, Theodosia said, "Okay, fill me in."

"You're going to help?" Jory's tired eyes were suddenly lit with excitement.

"Depends," said Theodosia. She was treading cautiously. His request still felt a little like a minefield and she was undecided if she should venture on through.

"Depends on what?" asked Jory.

"On how much you can tell me," replied Theodosia. "I didn't really know Abby. I know nothing about her life and I'm certainly not psychic. So you've got to provide me with as many facts as possible. And then, just maybe, we can find a logical place to start probing." She hesitated. "Abby was married?"

Jory nodded eagerly. "Had been for four years. To Drew Donovan, a really terrific guy. We . . . all the relatives . . . think the world of him. He developed some condos last year down near Hilton Head and has become quite successful in his own right. I think he's even on the Charleston Board of Realtors."

"And they lived in Savannah," said Theodosia, "before moving here. Because Abby was on TV there, too." She knew that if she kept feeding Jory leading questions, she could count on him to give her a sort of running commentary, a free-word association.

"They moved up here a year ago," said Jory.

"So he . . . Drew . . . relocated for her. When Abby got her job at Trident Media."

"Yes," said Jory. He squirmed a bit at that one. After all, Jory had been the one who wanted Theodosia to give up her tea shop and move to New York. Marriage had been part of the package, too. But, in Theodosia's mind, it had been offered as an afterthought.

"Okay," said Theodosia. "You and Abby were close. You talked fairly often. Stayed in contact."

"Sure," said Jory. "We talked on the phone all the time."

"Anyone in her life who was giving her trouble?"

Jory considered Theodosia's question for a couple of moments. "Not really. Well, there's a fired Trident anchorman. You probably know him. Webster Hall."

"Web," said Theodosia. "Sure." Until Abby had been moved into the anchor position at Trident Media, Web Hall had honchoed their ten o'clock news for as long as she could remember. Web Hall was a born and bred South Carolina boy who delivered the news like he was chatting with neighbors across the back fence. Real folksy and friendly. Almost small town.

"So . . ." said Theodosia. "Abby forced him out?" She could certainly imagine a scenario where Abby Davis staged a power play.

Jory scratched his head. "I don't think it was anything that dramatic. Linus Gillette, the general manager, just wanted to, you know, update things. Whenever that happens, the old guys tend to get swept out the door."

"So he was fired," said Theodosia.

"According to Abby," said Jory, "newscasters don't retire. Their contacts just don't get renewed."

"Which, of course, is the kiss of death," said Theodosia.

"TV's a tough business. You ought to know that."

"Not really," said Theodosia. She didn't have a TV background per se. She'd worked at one of Charleston's major marketing firms. First as a media planner, then as an account executive for a number of technology clients. Helped them develop competitive strategies, PR campaigns, and marketing plans.

"Well," said Jory, "you're familiar with that whole industry."

"And Webster Hall was upset?" Theodosia asked.

"He was extremely bitter about his separation and apparently very vocal in blaming Abby."

"And you know that for a fact?"

Jory nodded eagerly. "Abby mentioned it just last month when I was down here for the Compass Point race."

"You were down here?"

"Yeah," Jory told her, not quite meeting her eyes. "I've been back quite a few times."

Theodosia dug in the pocket of her sweater until her fingers found another Motrin tablet. She palmed it, popped it into her mouth, and swallowed it along with a small sip of tea.

"I never realized Webster Hall had been fired," she told Jory. "I guess, like most viewers, I figured he just stepped down. Retired or something. Moved out to that old plantation home near Parkers Ferry that he always talked about. He even showed photos of it sometimes."

Jory shrugged. "Like I said, it's a tough business."

"Okay," said Theodosia. "Who else? Or *anything* else Abby might have been involved in?"

"There is another thing," said Jory. "Something my cousin Jimmy Joe mentioned when I spoke to him on the phone last night. Although Jimmy Joe tends to be a little vague."

"What?"

"Apparently Abby had continued with a couple of investigative reporting projects."

Theodosia leaned forward. Vague or not, this could be something. Could serve as a motive, perhaps, if Abby had dogged someone hard. As she was known to.

"Do you know what kind of projects she was working on?"

"I only know about one." Jory dropped his voice a touch. "Abby was looking into some kind of Charleston bigwig secret society."

Theodosia stared across the table at him. "Great. Abby teamed up with the Hardy Boys. Maybe even Nancy Drew."

"Tell me you haven't heard rumors," said Jory.

Theodosia shrugged. "Maybe a couple. But I've always dismissed them. Figured it was folks who'd been frozen out of Charleston's inner circle. Were jealous at not being asked to serve on the museum's board of directors, or chair the Symphony Ball, or join the Founders' Society." *Or the Opera Society*, she thought to herself.

Jory held up his hands, palms turned outward as if in surrender. "Suit yourself."

"Okay . . ." said Theodosia. She wasn't completely dismissing the idea. She'd maybe do a little research on her own. But she didn't think much would come from it.

"So you're going to help?" asked Jory.

"Maybe," hedged Theodosia. "I'll try."

"Because you're already involved," said Jory. "You were there."

Yes, there is that, thought Theodosia.

Jory pushed back his chair and stood up. "We'll talk tomorrow?"

"Give me a call." Theodosia pushed herself up, too. "Not too early, though. We've got a big group coming in for lunch."

"Later in the day then," said Jory. "Here?"

"Yes, call me here."

"Gee, it's good to see you," said Jory. They were wending their way through the empty tables, heading for the door.

"Mmm," said Theodosia.

Jory paused, his hand on the doorknob. "You still have your dog, Earl Grey?" Earl Grey was Theodosia's mixed-breed Dalbrador and the unofficial tea shop dog, who made occasional afternoon appearances when things were winding down. And also made visits to senior citizen homes in his capacity as official therapy dog.

"Of course," she told him. "He's still my best buddy."

"Talk to you tomorrow," said Jory.

Theodosia hesitated for just a moment. "Tomorrow then," she said as she closed the door.

There was a gentle swoosh as Drayton ducked out from behind the velvet curtains. "Well, *that* was interesting," he said in a slightly sarcastic tone.

"Jory's pretty torn up about his sister," said Theodosia.

"Funny," said Drayton, "I thought he seemed more focused on you."

"He asked for my help," said Theodosia. For some reason she felt the need to explain herself. Maybe because Drayton seemed to have hit the nail precisely on the head?

Drayton pulled himself to his full height and peered down his patrician nose. He suddenly reminded Theodosia of an old picture she'd seen of Charles de Gaulle. Pompous, effete, yet filled with nobility and courage. "He asked for your help," repeated Drayton. "With funeral arrangements?"

"No," said Theodosia, knowing Drayton had deliberately misunderstood her. "With Abby. With . . . you know . . . looking into her murder."

Drayton clapped a hand to his heart in a grand theatrical gesture. "And you said . . . yes."

Looking distressed, biting her lip, Theodosia whispered, "How could I not?"

6

~❧~

Snapping the leash onto Earl Grey's collar, Theodosia clattered down the back stairs with him, heading out for a short walk. As the day passed, she'd felt better and better. Her shoulders were a lot looser, the pain in her knee had subsided to a dull throb, the tension in her hip had magically disappeared. Maybe it was the power of ibuprofen; maybe it was just having Abby Davis's murder to focus on.

Whatever the reason, she was feeling good and Earl Grey could sense it. He strutted down Church Street, full of beans and vigor, tugging hard at his leash. They turned into the residential section of the historic district, ambled past gorgeous mansions that stood shoulder to shoulder like elegant, genteel dowagers. Snuck down a narrow cobblestone lane arched with trees where wrought-iron lamps glowed yellow in the purple gray dusk. When they were finally within shouting distance of White Point Gardens, the huge expanse of park that bordered the seawall, Earl Grey turned his big head to gaze at her. It was an eager look that said, *Come on, dear human, let's get cracking. Let's stretch our legs, maybe run down a couple of rabbits, and really blow out the carbon.*

"Sorry," Theodosia told him. "Not yet. Gotta watch it for a couple of days. But . . . I'll tell you what. You can have an extra dollop of yogurt on your kibbles for being such a good boy."

Tossing his head, always a little full of himself, Earl Grey seemed to acknowledge her trade-off. And they turned for home.

Theodosia's kitchen was warm and cozy. Walls painted a flat ivory, cupboards painted a pale peach, matching peach rag rugs on the floor, and ivory appliances that had been updated in the last couple of years—a lovely pale French palette. A fantastic brass-and-crystal chandelier dangled from the center of the ceiling. The countertops had been a drab vinyl, so Theodosia had employed a local carpenter, a guy Haley had dated a few times, to rework some reclaimed cypress that had once served as flooring in an old warehouse. The countertops he'd fashioned fastened right over the old countertops and the result had been instantly spectacular. Warmth, a nice touch of antiquity, and counters she could set hot pans directly on.

Because she lacked cupboard space, Theodosia had purchased an antique secretary at an auction over in Goose Creek. Once she'd stripped the black paint off, no small feat, the wood had fairly gleamed. And Drayton had carefully pointed out that, though not Hepplewhite in strict provenance, the carved cornice and pendant medallions on the glass doors certainly *suggested* a certain Hepplewhite influence.

A compulsive collector of teacups and tea towels, Theodosia's lovely objects seemed to have taken over her kitchen. So after she fed Earl Grey, who was eating a little early tonight, Theodosia puttered around, rearranging things. She'd picked up four new cup-and-saucer sets last week and still hadn't found a spare inch of space in which to display them. So maybe . . .

She glanced around, couldn't find a place to put them. Hmm. Looks like something would have to be de-acquisitioned and moved downstairs to the tea shop for sale.

Feeling a little hungry, Theodosia pulled open the refrigerator, scanned the shelves, but didn't come up with anything that readily tripped her trigger.

"Hey," she said to Earl Grey. "Want to go for a ride?"

He cocked his head as if you say, *You wouldn't be pulling my tail, would you?*

"I'm serious," she told him. "Let's go."

They trooped downstairs, piled into her Jeep, what she considered the perfect vehicle for zipping into nearby woods and swamps to gather dandelion greens and wildflowers, and headed down Church Street. When she hit Market Street, she hung a left, bumped down a narrow brick alley, and pulled up at the back door of Solstice Bistro. She eased herself out of her vehicle and held up a finger to Earl Grey. "Stay put, okay?" He settled down on the backseat, his long, elegant muzzle cradled on top of his outstretched paws.

Theodosia went to the back door, which was usually locked, and rapped loudly. A few seconds later, the heavy metal door creaked open and Jimmy Ray Tatum, one of Parker's sous-chefs, poked his head out. "Theodosia," he said in a long, languid drawl. Jimmy Ray was from Savannah, where they seemed to pride themselves on the art of the slow drawl.

"Hey, Jimmy Ray," she said. "Can Parker come out and play?"

Jimmy Ray grinned and opened the door. "C'mon in here, gal. I'll see where he's at."

Standing at the back of the kitchen, cloistered between the walk-in cooler and stacked crates of fresh produce, Theodosia watched the chefs in their endless ballet of cooking and plating. Reveling in the spicy aromas that hung redolent in the warm air, she detected fresh ginger from a fish dish that sizzled atop the gigantic commercial stove, as well as thyme and basil from pan-roasted chicken. And was that coriander she smelled as well? Sure it was.

"Theo!" called Parker, as he edged carefully through the busy kitchen to greet her. "What a terrific surprise." Then his exuberant smile faded to concern. "How're you feeling? Your back's better? And, hey, did we have a date or something that I forgot about?"

She put her hands on Parker's collar and pulled him outside into the alley. He was mid-thirties, a year or two younger than she was and very easy on the eye. Tall, broad-shouldered, with cobalt-blue eyes that peered out from beneath a tousle of blond hair. Tonight, as debonair restaurateur-about-town, he was dressed casually in gray slacks and black silky shirt.

"Whoa," Parker said, grinning and holding up his hands, "I'm being shanghaied." But he went readily along with her anyway.

Theodosia kissed him, long and lovingly, in that dark alley. To the tune of copper pots thumping and banging in the kitchen, strains of jazz free-floating out the back door of the nearby Club Bomba, and the hum of cars zooming past on Market Street.

"Hey," he said, smiling at her. "You *are* feeling better. I'm gonna have to escort you to that ball on Saturday night after all. Wear the dreaded monkey suit."

"You have to be there anyway," she replied.

"So I do," replied Parker. "Hey, why do I rate this surprise visit?"

A *reaffirmation*, Theodosia wanted to tell him. *Of our relationship. Make sure we're still cool, still together, still feeling it. That you're still feeling it.*

Instead, she simply said, "I missed you."

"Good enough," said Parker, putting an arm around her waist and scooping her toward him again, planting a kiss on her forehead, her cheek, and finally her lips.

They stood there in the dark for a few more moments, hugging, just holding each other, listening to the beat of each other's hearts.

"Come in and have something to eat," Parker finally said. "Chef Toby made quail tonight. Stuffed with country sausage." Toby Crisp was their executive chef who specialized in classic low-country dishes.

"Can't stay," said Theodosia. "There's a couple of things I gotta do."

"The police been all over you today? Asking more questions?"

"Not too bad," she told him.

"Well . . . that's good," said Parker, ever the upbeat optimist. "Hey, you're sure you can't stay? You gotta eat. Keep you strong and feisty."

Theodosia shook her head.

"Then let me pack something for you to take home. A meal to go. Meals on wheels."

Theodosia laughed. "Sure, okay."

"Go sit in your car, take it easy. I'll be back in a couple of minutes."

He was.

"Cadged one of the quail for you," he told her, "along with a side dish of southern corn casserole. Ten minutes at three hundred and fifty degrees. No more, no less." He handed her a tinfoil box with a cardboard top. "But take the top off first. Don't want to start a fire."

"Thanks," she said.

"And be careful, it's a little spicy. Well, the sausage is maybe more than a little spicy. Definitely got some heat."

She started her Jeep, leaned out the window, blew him a kiss. "As if I haven't had enough of that already tonight."

Back home, she put her quail in the oven, following Parker's instructions to the letter. The treat he'd sent home with her was slathered in a spicy red pepper puree. As it bubbled and hissed in the oven, the aroma wafted into her dining room, where she sat at her dining table, jotting notes on a large pad of white paper.

They were, for lack of a better term, her murder notes. She wrote *Abby Davis* in the center of a page and drew a circle around it. She jotted smaller notes around it. *Web Hall, fired anchor. Secret society—invest. story. Abby—friends? Abby—enemies?*

Theodosia tapped her Magic Marker against the pad of paper and gazed toward her living room. Comfy and cozy, it featured a blue-and-paprika-colored Oriental rug, squishy brocade sofa facing the small brick fireplace, two elegant sea-scapes hanging above the mantel. Antique lamps, Chinese vases, and a gilt French clock served as accent pieces. She sighed, happy and content with the Old World elegance she'd created for herself.

The bell on the stove dinged and Theodosia pushed her-self up and headed for the kitchen. As she did, she thought about what to do next. She should probably try to talk to some of Abby's friends and colleagues at work. They might be able to shed some light on possible enemies or enmities. Because, sure as shooting, Abby had certainly made enemies. She'd been tough and abrasive, had elbowed her way up fast in the TV business. So there must have been casualties along the way. Jory might not know who they were, but *somebody* had to. Hopefully.

7

"*Drayton,*" *said Theodosia,* first thing the next morning. "What do you know about secret societies?"

"Are you questioning me about Opus Dei, Skull and Bones, or the CIA?" replied Drayton as he deftly swirled warm water in a blue-and-white Chinese teapot, dumped it out, then added three heaping tablespoons of Fujian golden tip, followed by a half kettle of steaming hot water.

"I'm talking about right here in Charleston."

"I see," said Drayton, as he snugged a matching blue-and-white toile tea cozy around the teapot.

"Is there one?" asked Theodosia. She'd never heard definitive proof about a secret society's existence, but that didn't mean anything. She wasn't exactly descended from high society. Neither was Drayton, of course, but he did seem to hobnob with some of the more moneyed and noteworthy Charlestonians. The ones whose names and photos appeared regularly in the society pages. And Drayton *was* friends with

Timothy Neville, the executive director of the Heritage Society. Timothy seemed to exist in that higher firmament due to his enormous wealth, power, and a lineage that stretched all the way back to the early French Huguenots.

"I'm not exactly the one to ask now, am I?" said Drayton.

"You answered a question with a question," Theodosia pointed out.

"Ah," said Drayton, his mouth twitching. "I suppose that is a tad rude."

"So," said Theodosia, trying to get something, anything, out of him, "what do you know?"

Drayton removed a long black Parisian waiter's apron from a hook and draped it over his head. "Over the years I've heard rumors of a society," he said, then paused to fumble with the back ties. "Well, actually more than rumors. There is a group that supposedly calls themselves the Peninsula Club."

That tidbit of information seemed to knock Theodosia for a loop. "You mean like the Peninsula Grill?" The Peninsula Grill was an elegant, upscale restaurant located in the Planters Inn. Its steaks, chops, and champagne menu were unparalleled, and a good deal of Charleston's power lunches took place there.

"Not exactly." Drayton smiled. "Realize, please, the Peninsula Club was formed eons before our own lovely Peninsula Grill ever existed. The club probably stretches back maybe . . . a hundred and fifty years? Two hundred?"

Theodosia let loose a low whistle. "So this Peninsula Club is old. We're talking founding fathers."

"Bingo," said Drayton.

"You really do know about this stuff," said Theodosia excitedly. Maybe Drayton was her entrée after all.

"No, I don't. In fact I'm quite ignorant of it," said Drayton, and this time he sounded a little crabby. Crabby even for Drayton. "If you really want to learn more, you're going to have to speak with someone who might possibly be privy to a few of the group's secrets."

"You know someone?" asked Theodosia. She smiled reflexively as the door opened and a group of four women, all wearing elaborate red felt hats, strolled in. This would be the Dexter party, she decided, sneaking a quick peak at the reservation list. The tea shop had only accepted early reservations today, since the Bravissimo Club luncheon was scheduled for one thirty.

"Timothy Neville," Drayton whispered in her ear. "Talk to him." Then Drayton turned a bright smile upon the new arrivals. "Ladies!" he extolled. "Welcome. I have a lovely table for you right by the fireplace. Nothing like a crackling fire and a nice hot cuppa to take the chill off."

"Not too busy?" asked Haley. She was standing at the commercial stove they'd somehow managed to shoehorn into the small kitchen, stirring a pot of wild rice soup and keeping a watchful eye on two pans of scones that baked in the oven.

Theodosia leaned in the doorway, observing and marveling at Haley's skill and prowess in the kitchen. Someday, she figured, Haley would finish her business degree and strike out on her own. Probably become an executive in some techy-type company. Or maybe even open her own tea shop or chain of tea shops. Drive her out of business. Until then, Haley reigned supreme in the Indigo Tea Shop kitchen and Theodosia was more than grateful to have her shining presence.

"We've got maybe six reservations," said Theodosia. "Which should easily clear the tea shop by one o'clock, giving us enough time to push a few tables together and make everything gorgeous."

"Got it," nodded Haley, who thrived on scrambling. "And you're feeling okay? Not too creaky?"

"Lots better today," said Theodosia.

"Then you're a fast healer," said Haley. "But I still think it's good we asked Miss Dimple to come in and help serve." Haley looked at her watch. "She should be here any minute."

"Great," said Theodosia. She wasn't nervous about the Bravissimo Club luncheon, but she did want to make a good impression. After all, she'd be hobnobbing with the Opera Society folks come Saturday night. "Haley, why don't you run through the final menu, just so it's locked in my head."

Haley wiped her hands on the terry cloth towel tucked in the waistband of her apron. "Six courses. Wild rice soup, apricot scones, a fruit salad served in stemmed parfait glasses, sliver of zucchini quiche, and shrimp salad in mini croissants with champagne grapes."

"That's five," said Theodosia.

"And for the pièce de résistance," said Haley with a grin, "an opera cake. Four layers of chocolate sponge cake, three layers of buttercream, one layer of ganache, and a coffee glaze."

"How absolutely decadent," said Theodosia.

"I made plenty of everything, so obviously we're serving the scones, soup, quiche, and desserts to our six early parties, too."

"Smart planning," said Theodosia.

"When you're working in a kitchen this small"—Haley laughed—"you've got to double up on things. Oh, and hey, you're still gonna put together those floral arrangements?"

"As soon as this group is served, I'll jump on it," promised Theodosia. Hattie Boatwright from Floradora Flowers had delivered a couple of large buckets of flowers and greens first thing this morning. Theodosia's plan was to twine fresh green banana leaves around tall glass containers, then wrap thin gauzy ribbon around the containers to hold the leaves in place. Once those vases were completed—she figured she needed eight of them—she'd fill them with stems of lilies, orchids, and sweet peas.

"Theodosia!" Drayton suddenly loomed behind her. "Everyone's been served either the Fujian or silver needle tea. Time to bring out the scones."

"Hi, Drayton," Haley sang out as Drayton disappeared as fast as he'd appeared. "Bye, Drayton."

One o'clock brought a royal schism between Haley and Drayton.

"I planned on using the Pickard Rose and Daisy dinnerware," said Drayton. Tables had been pushed together and draped with fresh white linen, yellow napkins had been folded into bishop's hats, gold pillar candles rested in elegant, gold candleholders. Theodosia's floral arrangements were positioned carefully on the tables.

"No can do," said Haley, facing off against him. "We're doing six courses. The Pickard only has enough dishes for five."

"But if we switch now, the colors will be off," argued

Drayton. "We agreed upon red, yellow, and gold as our thematic colors."

"Drayton, do you want me to serve soup in their shoes?" Haley laughed. "Change it, for goodness sakes. Do your plans always have to be *carved in stone?*"

"Of course," said Drayton, agreeably.

Theodosia and Miss Dimple, their freelance bookkeeper and part-time server, glanced from one to the other as if watching a tennis match.

"You're impossible." Haley laughed again.

"Drayton's a tough old bird," added Miss Dimple.

"What if," said Theodosia, stepping in, "what if we mixed in plates from the Belleek porcelain? The lovely pearl luster certainly works within your color scheme."

Drayton stood with his arms folded in front of him. "For which course?" he asked.

"How about for scones?" asked Theodosia.

"They're awfully large plates," replied Drayton.

Theodosia knew she'd have to get creative. "Instead of putting bowls of Devonshire cream and jam on the tables, we'll arrange everything on the plates. Do individual servings of Devonshire cream and jam using those adorable little glass bowls you picked up at that tag sale down in Beaufort."

Drayton cocked his head, considering her suggestion. "Those are rather nice." He seemed to be nearing a compromise. "So then . . . the tiny bowls right on the plates."

"Tucked next to the scones," said Theodosia.

"Those glass bowls will be perfect," enthused Haley. "Then again, Drayton's always had a good eye."

Drayton pursed his lips. "I know when I'm being placated. I even know when I'm being *handled.* But my answer is yes, I do believe that solution is workable."

"Hallelujah!" cried Haley, dancing a crazy little jig and tossing her hands up in the air.

Thandie McLean and Claire Bouchon, the president and vice president of the Bravissimo Club, and the luncheon's organizers, showed up ten minutes later.

"We know we're a tad early," said Thandie, a petite blond who was pushing fifty but looked thirty-five, thanks to some very skillfully administered collagen injections. "So just shove us out of the way if you have to."

Claire was older, red-haired, a little giggly. "We just have a few items to set up." She hefted two shopping bags stuffed with gold-wrapped boxes tied with red gossamer ribbon.

"Oh, you brought presents," said Theodosia. "How fun."

"Favors," said Thandie.

"Wrapped in red and gold," commented Drayton. "Perfect." He was laying out the last of the flatware.

"The way we see it," said Thandie, "we need to pass out all the swag we can, since we're courting some serious mucketymucks."

"Don't you mean muckesses?" Claire giggled.

"Whatever," said Thandie, rolling her eyes. "Any way you look at it, the Opera Society is in need of a serious cash infusion." She put a hand on Theodosia's arm and said in a stage whisper, "We've spent a *ton* decorating the Corinth Theatre for Saturday night's Masked Ball."

"We're having real actors in costumes and authentic stage sets!" added Claire. "It's going to be shockingly marvelous!"

Drayton beamed. "I have it on good authority that the Masked Ball will be one of the seven wonders of the Charleston social season."

"My dear Drayton," said Claire with a giggle, "you just said a mouthful!"

As Theodosia carefully lit candles, Thandie pulled her aside. "Are you okay, honey? I heard about what happened at that horse-jumping race on Sunday. The tumble you took and, well . . . you know."

"It was all quite a shock," admitted Theodosia.

Claire overheard Thandie's words and edged over to join them. "We're just *so* sad about Abby's death . . . er . . . murder," she said. "It's been splashed all over the news like some sort of horrible scandal, even though not a lot of hard details have been released. Do you know, are they any closer to catching someone?"

"The Colleton County sheriff and Charleston police are working together," said Theodosia. "So hopefully they're hot on the trail."

"Well, good," said Thandie. "That's what we citizens like to hear. Cooperation among law enforcement."

"Abby was one of our members," said Claire. She turned a solemn expression on the sparkling tables lavishly laden with dishes, bouquets, candles, and presents. "She probably would have been here today," she added, her words catching in her throat.

"Abby got us a lot of publicity, too," said Thandie. "Even helped set up our photo shoots." Her face crumpled slightly as she gazed sorrowfully at Claire. "Now who's going to do publicity for the Opera Society?"

"No idea," said Claire. "That's something we're going to have to figure out."

They looked at each other and something seemed to pass between them.

"Would you have any ideas on that, Theodosia?" asked Thandie. "I know you've handled publicity for Spoleto Festival." Spoleto was Charleston's highly popular and ever-expanding music, opera, dance, theater, and literary festival that was held each May in venues all across town.

"They always get so much," added Claire.

"I can probably give you some names of marketing and media people," offered Theodosia. "I'm sure someone would be willing to step in and help."

As Thandie unsnapped her handbag and pulled out a CD, Theodosia noticed she was wearing a pink-and-cream cameo at the neck of her pink suit. A pin that was, in fact, strikingly similar to the one Abby Davis had been wearing.

"We'd like to play Verdi's *Un Ballo in Maschera* during the luncheon," said Thandie. She held up the CD and passed it to Claire. "Get everyone in the mood."

"Drayton," called Theodosia. "Will you pop this CD in the player?"

Drayton nodded and gestured for Claire to bring the CD to the front counter where their sound system was set up.

"I just noticed your cameo," said Theodosia. "It's really lovely."

Thandie turned back to her and her hand came up and sought it out. "Oh, it's just something I picked up at Vianello. You know, that shop down on King Street? They have an absolutely marvelous selection of antique jewelry, rings, beaded bags, and masks. It's run by that fellow, Julian Bruno."

"Don't know him," said Theodosia.

"Then you simply *must* stop by. He has utterly stellar

taste. Of course, I don't believe this cameo is particularly old. But he has some that are really quite incredible. Oh, and he's got a fabulous selection of Venetian masks. You'll need one for Saturday night, you know."

The front door flew open then and Delaine came charging in, followed by at least a dozen other women, all dressed in gorgeous fall suits and dripping with jewelry, the serious twenty-four-karat kind.

Some of them had to be potential donors, Theodosia decided.

And then they were off and running.

Theodosia, Drayton, and Miss Dimple ferried pots of tea, plates of steaming scones, and the rest of Haley's delicious offerings to their guests. The guests nibbled, chatted, giggled, and shrieked over small hilarities, sipped endless pots of tea, and appeared to be having a collectively marvelous time. Halfway through the luncheon, it got so warm inside the Indigo Tea Shop that Theodosia had to prop open the front door to let breezes from the Cooper River waft in and work their cooling magic.

"Drayton!" called Thandie. "I understand that, besides being a tea master, you're also a connoisseur of tea poetry. Would you please give us a quick poem?"

"Yes, yes!" The cry went up around the table. "A recitation, please!"

Fairly beaming, Drayton threw his shoulders back and lifted his chin. "It's a tea poem you'd like to hear?" He adored these requests. There was a reason he was a frequent guest lecturer at the Heritage Society.

More vocal encouragement followed.

"Well, then," said Drayton, "I do have a particular favorite that was penned by William Gladstone . . ."

When the world is all at odds
And the mind is all at sea,
Then cease the useless tedium
And brew a cup of tea.
There is magic in its fragrance,
There is solace in its taste;
And the laden moments vanish
Somehow into space.
And the world becomes a lovely thing!
There's beauty as you'll see;
All because you briefly stopped
To brew a cup of tea.

Haley had been spot-on about the shopping. In fact, it was fortuitous she'd stuffed the sweetgrass baskets full of T-Bath products, because once their guests finished nibbling their desserts, they began snatching baskets left and right. A fruit bowl basket carried an assortment of Earl Grey Grapefruit Lotion, Chamomile Bliss Bath Salts, and Lemon Verbena Oil. A cake basket held mini bottles of Green Tea Feet Treat, Darjeeling Lotion, and Assam Enchanted Evening Aromatherapy Lotion. In other sweetgrass baskets, Haley had made combinations that included scone mixes, jars of honey, jams, and mini tins of tea.

Once the baskets had all been snatched up, the women of the Bravissimo Club and their guests went on to grab grapevine wreaths, various antique teacups, and pieces of vintage sterling silver that Theodosia had picked up at tag sales around the county, as well as candles, tea infusers, and tins of tea.

One woman in a killer navy-blue Chanel suit, who'd just presented Thandie with a donation check that made her eyes cross, even tried to buy the highboy that held Theodosia's display of DuBose Bees Honey, cut glass bowls, and antique cake stands.

It was a good offer, but Theodosia held firm. After all, she *needed* that piece.

Theodosia and Drayton were clearing tables and remarking about what a successful event it had been when Jory Davis stuck his head in the door.

"Knock, knock," he called.

Theodosia glanced up, a stack of dirty dishes balanced in her arms. "I thought you were going to call." She wasn't exactly thrilled that Jory had just dropped in out of the blue.

"It's starting already," Drayton muttered under his breath.

"No, it isn't," Theodosia hissed back.

Jory touched two fingers to his head. "Sorry, I was supposed to call first, wasn't I? But this might work out better. Since I brought along a few things for you."

"Things," Theodosia repeated. "Like what?"

"Stuff that belonged to Abby," said Jory. "A couple of files and her appointment book. Oh, and I have news. The police released Abby's body late yesterday. She's . . . well, we're having a viewing tonight. At the Rafferty Brothers Funeral Home."

"That was fast," said Theodosia. She set her dishes down on the table, then stepped aside as Drayton leaned in to scoop them up.

Jory gave a sad nod. "The family decided we'll have this one single visitation tonight, rather than drag things out. Then the casket will be sealed and we'll have a proper memorial service on Thursday." He hesitated. "Anyway, I'd really appreciate it if you came by tonight. I could introduce you to a few relatives."

"I think I met most of them when your uncle Jasper died," Theodosia responded.

Jory turned puppy-dog eyes on her. "It'd mean a lot to me if you came."

"Then I'll certainly try," said Theodosia. Somehow, she had the feeling she was being maneuvered. She wasn't thrilled at the prospect, but she wasn't exactly angry, either. This time around with Jory she was more like . . . curious.

8

❧

Jory held up a small leather-bound book. "Abby's address book. Still willing to take a peek? Maybe do some snooping?"

"We'll take a look, then decide," said Theodosia, pulling off her apron. "Why don't we go back to my office?"

They threaded their way past the kitchen and into the cramped confines of her office.

Jory looked around cautiously, then said, "You've still got a photo of my boat on your wall." He sounded pleased. Touched, almost.

Theodosia glanced up from where she'd transferred a messy stack of tea catalogs from her desk to the credenza behind her, and gazed at the wall across from her desk. It was her memory wall, hung with a montage of photos of her parents and Aunt Libby, framed tea labels, opera programs, funny cards, French tea posters, and a lace doily with a tricky bullion stitch she'd always promised herself she'd master someday.

"Haven't had a chance to update that wall lately," she mumbled. Fact was, she hadn't really cleaned her office since moving in. Boxes of teapots and tea strainers were stacked alongside cartons of tea and reams of computer paper. Hats and baskets hung from the ceiling, and four boxes of T-Bath products sat next to her desk with grapevine wreaths teetering on top. "Sit down," she invited Jory.

Jory settled into the plump chintz-covered chair facing her desk. "Here's what I've pulled together so far," he said, placing the address book and a stack of manila files on Theodosia's desk. "Not a lot, but hopefully a place to start."

"The files are from . . . where?" asked Theodosia.

"Abby's home office," said Jory. "We haven't picked up her stuff from Trident Media yet." He thought for a minute. "Actually, I think the police may have done that already."

Theodosia took a quick ten minutes to paw through everything.

The address book contained literally hundreds of names and addresses, phone numbers, and e-mail addresses. This was something, Theodosia decided, that should probably be turned over to the Charleston police. They had the computer capability to input this amount of data and see if it rang any bells in their system. People in the media weren't exactly adverse to associating with crooks and criminals in order to get inside information, so that could be a possible angle into Abby's death.

Abby's files were something else. They were haphazard with lots of jottings, clippings, and xeroxed photos interspersed with handwritten notes on what appeared to be Abby's favorite stationery, white linen paper with raspberry-pink edging and a gold A at the top. Most of the files contained stories she'd been working on, though some looked like they'd dead-ended. One of the files contained Abby's Trident Media contract. Theodosia didn't read it, but thought she might glance at it later.

In another file, Theodosia found copious notes about a man named Truman McBee. "Truman McBee," she murmured, searching her memory bank, coming up empty at first, then shuffling the pages and finding a newspaper article, complete with clipping. She experienced a sudden ping of recognition.

"You know who he is?" asked Jory.

Yes, she actually did. Theodosia tapped an index finger against the file and thought for a couple more moments. "There was a sensational case a year or so ago," she told Jory. "Truman McBee is Charleston's own software king, he started a company called Beeware. Something about firewalls and the next generation in network security. Anyway, his son, Travis, who was twenty-six or twenty-seven at the time, was kidnapped. Carjacked, really. They took Travis and left his Cadillac Escalade idling on Concord Street over by the river. When the ransom call came in from the guys who claimed to be holding Travis, Truman McBee didn't hesitate to shell out five million dollars." She hesitated, staring at the grainy newspaper photo of Truman McBee. "But Truman never got his son back."

"Wow," said Jory.

"Apparently," continued Theodosia, "Truman and his son, Travis, didn't even get along all that well, but the father still anted up the money. Didn't hesitate, though Travis had been your basic, indolent rich kid who'd been in and out of rehab."

"The police never came up with a clue?" asked Jory. "About Travis or his kidnappers?"

"They pursued hundreds of leads," said Theodosia. "But still no Travis. As I recall from the stories that ran back then, the investigators on the case felt enormously frustrated about it going unsolved."

"I can imagine," said Jory.

Theodosia continued. "Even when Truman McBee offered a one-million-dollar reward for information leading to his son's recovery, nothing ever turned up." She gazed at Jory. "That reward is probably *still* hanging out there."

"You think Abby was working on this McBee story?" asked Jory. "Taking a second look?"

"Possibly," said Theodosia. "I know that law enforcement sometimes approaches the media and *requests* they do follow-up pieces on unsolved cases. Those stories often shake new clues or witnesses out of the woodwork."

"What if Abby discovered some new evidence?" asked Jory. "Got a little too close to the truth?" He seemed to be getting his hopes up on determining an angle for his sister's murder.

"Maybe," said Theodosia. "Anyway, you should tell Detective Tidwell about this file, too—if he hasn't already interviewed the staff at Trident and picked up on the McBee thread." She opened the last file, which was filled with letters, greeting cards, and personal notes. Pawing through this jumble, one of the letters jumped out at her. "Okay, this could be considered a little strange."

"What?" asked Jory, leaning forward.

Theodosia turned the file around so they could both read

the letter. It was basically a nasty rant from Webster Hall, accusing Abby of stealing his job.

"I guess Hall was pretty unhappy," said Jory.

"More like enraged," said Theodosia. "Could Webster Hall have worked himself into a cold-blooded frenzy and murdered Abby?" She meant to whisper that thought to herself, but murmured it loud enough for Jory to hear.

Jory looked stunned. "He could if he was crazy out of his head about losing his job!"

"Revenge can be a powerful motivator," added Theodosia. She made a mental note to ask Tidwell to check on Webster Hall's whereabouts this past Sunday.

"So we turn that letter over to the police, too?"

"Yes," said Theodosia, shuffling through the rest of the notes and cards. "Absolutely." The last card in the file was a small beige card rimmed with an embossed gold band. It said, *Loving you more and more each day.*

"What's that?" asked Jory.

"Love note," said Theodosia, a little stiffly. She glanced at the card. It was signed with a single initial. "What is that, a D?"

Jory nodded emphatically. "Drew. Even after four years of marriage he positively adored Abby. Sent flowers to her every week, showered her with jewelry. And boy did she love all the hot designer names. Bulgari, John Hardy, Tiffany, Cartier. Drew paid a pretty penny for that stuff and was extremely generous with his gifts."

"They were lucky to have each other," said Theodosia. "Even if it was for such a short time." She sighed, flipped the file closed. "So that's it."

"And Abby was investigating . . ." began Jory.

"The secret society," said Theodosia. "Yes, I remember."

"But that's all I know," said Jory. He held his hands out in a *that's all there is* gesture. "Obviously none of Abby's secret society notes are among this stuff."

"Someone at the TV station might know more," said Theodosia. She leaned back in her chair, frowned, realized her back was bugging her. At the same time, she noted that she was beyond merely interested in the Abby Davis murder. She was becoming slightly fascinated.

"I'm gonna copy a few pages from these files and then bring you the whole shebang tonight," said Theodosia. "Then you can pass everything on to Detective Tidwell, okay?"

Jory nodded agreeably. "One more little thing. I have something else for you."

"Pardon?" Theodosia peered at him with curiosity.

He handed her a white box tied with a bright purple ribbon. "A gift."

"No," she said, suddenly. "That's really not appropriate. I . . ." she stopped. Words seemed to fail her.

"It's not much," said Jory, gently pushing the package across the desk to her. "Please take it. I'll feel a lot less like an imposing jerk if you do."

That brought a smile to her face. "I still don't see . . ."

"Please," said Jory.

It was a small white mouse. An antique Steiff mouse to be exact, white and fuzzy with tiny, perfectly formed felt ears and tail and beady, bright glass eyes.

Jory saw Theodosia hesitate and quickly said, "It came from an estate sale on Cape Cod." He shrugged. "I saw it and couldn't resist. It reminded me of, you know, the dormouse. From the tea party in *Alice in Wonderland*."

"It's too much," said Theodosia. She wasn't sure whether

she meant the price, the gift, or the sentiment. She just suddenly felt overwhelmed.

"No," said Jory. "It's the least I can do."

"You're getting too involved," said Drayton in a chiding, sing-song voice. He was standing behind the front counter, wiping out a Royal Pansy Chintz teapot. Theodosia had just walked Jory to the door, shown him out, and flipped the latch.

"By 'too involved,' do you mean with this murder investigation or with Jory?" Theodosia asked as she plunked her elbows on the counter and leaned across toward him.

"Well . . . both," said Drayton, a little flustered at being confronted.

"Then I have a favor to ask," said Theodosia.

"Which is?" said Drayton, gazing at her with a mixture of nervous curiosity and deep concern.

Seeing Drayton's lined face at that moment, sensing his obvious worry, Theodosia knew that if she asked him to hitchhike to Alaska with her, he'd probably say yes. The two of them were that much on the same wavelength.

"I was wondering if you'd go with me to the funeral home tonight?"

Drayton's head jerked in surprise. "What?"

"The visitation for Abby Davis," explained Theodosia. "I know it's short notice . . ."

"It is," said Drayton. "We talked about doing the Tradd Street Lamplighter Tour tonight. The Bentley House is open." Every year during the annual Lamplighter Tour, privately owned historic homes and mansions opened their doors for a public tour. Many even served refreshments and tea in their elegant, backyard gardens.

"What if we did the tour tomorrow night?" Theodosia suggested.

"And you *really* want me to accompany you to the funeral home?" asked Drayton

"Yes," said Theodosia. "That way you can chaperone me. Put your concerns to rest and assure that I *don't* get overly involved."

"And if I perceive you are?"

"I don't know," said Theodosia, a smile playing at her mouth. "Smack me upside of the head with a wet teabag or something."

"Hah," snorted Drayton. "A teabag versus fresh tea leaves. That'd be the day."

As Haley rattled dishes in the kitchen, Theodosia and Drayton finished tidying up the tea room and chatted about the upcoming Masked Ball.

"Thandie and Claire mentioned that the Opera Society will have actual props on display," said Theodosia.

Drayton suddenly looked ecstatic. "We most certainly are! We'll have the complete gallows set from Act Two, as well as some spectacular jewels on loan from the Lugori Museum of Venice. The actress who'll play the Amelia character will wear them in the opening performance the following week. Oh, and there'll be strolling musicians and actors in actual costumes, too."

"You're pretty excited about Saturday night's Masked Ball, huh?" asked Haley.

Drayton cleared his throat. "I positively *adore* opera. And the fact that this ball is themed after one of my absolute favorites! Well . . . nothing quite compares to Verdi!"

Theodosia smiled to herself as Drayton rattled on. He and Timothy Neville would be escorting two women from the Opera Society's board of directors. Wealthy women. Generous patrons. It would appear that Drayton didn't exactly mind rubbing elbows with the upper crust.

"You know," Drayton continued in a serious tone, "a masked ball is one of those notable themes that appears time and again throughout music and literature. Might I remind you, the star-crossed lovers, Romeo and Juliet, met and fell head over heels at a masked ball. And Edgar Allan Poe's *Masque of the Red Death* gave us Plague mingling with revelers at his masked ball." He gave a mock shiver. "How is it our dear Mr. Poe phrased it? *He had come like a thief in the night.*"

"He's not exactly *our* Mr. Poe," said Theodosia, amused.

"Of course he is," said Drayton. "Even if it was only for a short while, Edgar Allan Poe lived right here in Charleston!"

Just when Theodosia was about ready to hang up her apron and dash upstairs, the phone rang.

Drayton cast an eye toward the offending technological object. "You or me?" he asked.

But Theodosia was already reaching for it.

"Theodosia?" came a sharp, staccato voice. "This is Constance. Constance Brucato over at Trident Media."

"Of course, Constance," said Theodosia. Constance was the producer for *Windows on Charleston*, a magazine-type morning show. Theodosia had been a past guest, talking about brewing tea and tea etiquette.

"Such a shame about Abby, isn't it?" said Constance as her opening salvo.

Is that why she's calling? wondered Theodosia.

Turns out it wasn't.

After they'd chatted about the strange circumstances of Abby Davis's death and Theodosia's involvement, Constance said, "Trident Media's just signed on a flock of new advertisers. And I'd like to schedule a tea for them. To sort of welcome them into the Trident fold." She hesitated. "It would be a *business* tea. You can do that, can't you?"

"Of course," responded Theodosia, even though, deep in her heart, she felt tea time was reserved for gentle conversation, for unwinding and setting aside the cares of the day.

"Anyway," said Constance, "seven of us this Friday. Noonish. Can do?"

"Absolutely," said Theodosia as she pulled out her appointment book and scribbled *Trident—7.* "I've got you down. Any special requests as far as menu?"

"No, no," said Constance, and now she sounded harried as always. "Just do what you do best."

"While I've got you on the line, Constance, I was wondering if you could help me with a couple of things," said Theodosia.

A sigh. "Like what?"

"I'd be interested to know what Abby was working on," said Theodosia. She stretched across the counter and grabbed a small white notepad.

A few moments of silence spun out, then Constance said, "You realize, I wasn't Abby's producer anymore. She'd been moved up to investigative reporter and, more recently, to news anchor."

"I understand," said Theodosia, trying to inject an encouraging note in her voice.

"That was a huge promotion for Abby," said Constance.

And now a slightly grudging tone had slipped in. "Of course, I'm still stuck here doing daytime TV. Producing *Windows on Charleston* and *Charleston Garden Stories*. Same old, same old."

"I think you do a really terrific job," said Theodosia. And she meant it. Constance might be difficult to deal with, but the production values on her shows were consistently top notch.

"Oh, Theo, do you really think so?" The need in Constance's voice was unmistakable.

"You'll catch a break," said Theodosia. "Move on up, too."

"So you want to know about Abby," said Constance. She sounded like she might be chewing her nails, balancing the question.

"Obviously I have a vested interested in this," said Theodosia, trying to nudge her along. "Since I'm the one who found her."

"Must have been awful," murmured Constance.

"If you have any information at all . . ." Theodosia let her words trail off.

Constance made a slight disapproving sound in her throat. "You'd keep this in complete confidence?"

"Absolutely," said Theodosia.

"You won't tell Mr. Gillette?" Linus Gillette was the general manager of the station. The one who'd changed the station name from Channel Eight to Trident Media. A man who also thought rather highly of himself.

"Of course not," said Theodosia. She'd never really experienced any warm, fuzzy feelings for the cool, imperious Linus Gillette.

"The only thing that comes to mind," said Constance, "was that Abby was still allowed to work on some investigative stuff. An animal cruelty story and something about water pollution that had to do with that, uh, paper mill. Despard Industries."

"That's it?" asked Theodosia, crossing her fingers.

"Well," said Constance, "there's personal stuff that goes on here, too. We're pretty small, so it's never any big secret. It's not like we're CNN or anything."

"So Abby was having personal problems with . . . ?"

"Abby absolutely despised Joe Fanning, our news director. Didn't get along with him from day one. They were constantly at odds. Like oil and water."

"Why was that?"

"Oh, I don't know," said Constance. "Maybe 'cause Abby was a pain in the butt, maybe because Fanning really wanted to go on camera and do investigative stuff himself. Who knows?"

"But since Fanning was news director," said Theodosia, "wouldn't Abby have to work fairly closely with him?"

"Uh . . . *yeah*," said Constance in a mocking tone.

But not anymore, Theodosia thought.

9

The Heritage Society, established in the late 1800s and run these last thirty or so years by the firm, autocratic hand of Timothy Neville, was an archive, a library, and, most of all, a museum. The great limestone building was three sagging floors and two basement storage rooms filled with historic documents, antique furniture, Civil War memorabilia, and oil paintings by regional artists.

Theodosia thought the place marvelous as she padded down a long, carpeted hallway, Earl Grey at her side. She'd been a visitor here many times, coming for poetry readings, art shows, and lectures. She'd even catered a few teas here, in the great hall as well as outdoors on the newly designed patio. But the claret-red walls, pecan wood paneling, carved staircases, and enormous stone fireplaces really got to her.

It was like some sort of magnificent hunting lodge right out of Anthony Hope's *Prisoner of Zenda*. And she'd always harbored a secret fantasy of living here on a grand and luxurious scale. There'd be plump leather sofas in front of roaring fireplaces with acres of books just awaiting her perusal. And lamps made from stag horns and a wonderful wine cellar, too. Quite a cushy, fantastical setting.

"You brought your friend along," said Camilla Hodges. Sixty-something and petite, with a waft of white hair, she was the majordomo receptionist at the Heritage Society as well as membership coordinator, marketing executive, and number one go-to person. Camilla knew all the names of the staff, volunteers, board members, and big-buck donors and treated them accordingly on her sliding scale of Camilla efficiency.

"When I told Earl Grey I was going to pop over and see Timothy, he begged to come along," Theodosia told her.

Camilla giggled as she rummaged through the bottom drawer of her desk. Kleenex, Zone bars, and makeup bags were pushed aside, a dozen miniature perfume bottles knocked over, until she finally unearthed a cellophane package of dog treats.

"You want one?" She held up a single beef jerky stick.

Earl Grey glanced at Theodosia as if to ask, *Okay?*

"Okay," Theodosia told him. "Take the treat."

Stretching his neck out, he gently accepted it.

"Such a good boy," praised Camilla.

"I don't have an appointment," began Theodosia, "but I only need two minutes of Timothy's time."

Camilla snatched up her phone, pressed a series of buttons. "For you he's got time." She murmured into the receiver, then smiled up at Theodosia. "Go ahead." She grabbed a stack of papers from her desk that seemed to carry a faint scent of the perfume she wore. "Here, you can take these to him. Tell him the letters all need to be signed so I can catch the five o'clock mail."

Timothy Neville was hunched over his desk as Theodosia entered his palatial office. He glanced up without raising his head and Theodosia was struck by what a strange little man he was. Thin skin stretched over a skull-like head with high, almost Asiatic cheekbones, thin lips communicating impatience, bright eyes that bored into you like a prosecutor who held all the trump cards. Timothy was a rich octogenarian and looked it.

"She gave you correspondence for me to sign," was all he said.

"Is that a problem?" asked Theodosia. At one time she'd been horribly intimidated by Timothy Neville. She wasn't anymore. Not since she'd done a stint of house-sitting at his wonderful mansion on Archdale Street. Not since she'd been an invited guest at a few of his lavish parties. Not since she'd realized he had a huge soft spot for Earl Grey.

"What's she wearing today?" asked Timothy, pursing his lips. "My Sin or Arpège?"

"I don't think they make My Sin anymore," Theodosia told him. She dropped the leash and Earl Grey immediately headed around the desk to greet Timothy.

"The letters I send out to prospective donors all smell like a French boudoir," groused Timothy.

"Maybe that's a positive," said Theodosia, placing the letters in his already cluttered in-basket. "Sets the Heritage Society apart from every other group asking for money."

Timothy swiveled in his green leather chair and clasped Earl Grey's head between his gnarled hands. "Stir the heartstrings and the purse strings will follow?"

"Nicely put," chuckled Theodosia.

Timothy gave a couple gentle tugs on Earl Grey's ears, then patted his neck and shoulders.

Earl Grey let loose a satisfied woof. After all, Timothy was his big, important buddy taking time out just for him. A fellow whose wealth and power made many people tremble. But not Earl Grey. As a member of the canine persuasion, he was an equal opportunity recipient of pets and ear tugs. Money and power meant nothing to Earl Grey. His only criteria was gentle hands and heart.

"Come take a look at this." Timothy gave a come-hither gesture with his fingers and Theodosia stepped closer to the expanse of oak that was his desk.

"A new acquisition," he told her. "An English looking glass."

"Beautiful," said Theodosia. The looking glass was a framed convex mirror, made popular in the eighteenth and early nineteenth centuries. This one had an elaborate gilt frame and was topped by decorative molding that featured a graceful, winged bird.

"Sometimes called a butler's mirror as well," said Timothy. "On the mistaken notion this type of mirror would aid household servants in providing better service to their employers."

"But the convex glass was . . . what?" asked Theodosia. "A fashion, a fancy?" They both peered into it and their distorted faces, as well as a wide expanse of office, were reflected back.

Timothy nodded. "Exactly that. And when the household burned candles or lamps in the evening, convex mirrors offered the added benefit of reflected illumination."

"Neat," said Theodosia.

Timothy's crooked index finger traced the outline of the embellished frame. "What was it you wanted?"

"I have a question."

"Yes." He eased himself back in his chair. "Ask."

"What can you tell me about the Peninsula Club?"

"And you are inquiring . . . why?" Timothy brushed an invisible speck of lint from his bespoke camel-hair jacket.

"You know about the Abby Davis murder," said Theodosia.

Timothy's head inclined slightly.

"And that I had the unfortunate luck of finding her."

Now Timothy steepled his fingers under his chin. "Very unfortunate."

"The thing is . . ." said Theodosia. "Abby might have been working on a story about the Peninsula Club."

"And you think Miss Davis poked her little TV reporter nose smack dab into business that wasn't hers?"

"Yes," said Theodosia. "Something like that."

"No," said Timothy.

"Pardon?"

"She didn't. I doubt she even got close to them."

"You're telling me there really is an organization couched in such secrecy?" asked Theodosia.

"Let's just say the members are closemouthed," said Timothy. He tapped his fingers on his desk. "Most people think the organization is only a crazy, made-up rumor. That it doesn't really exist."

"There have been stories," mused Theodosia. "I've heard them for years." She paused. "Are you a member?"

"No," said Timothy. "Although my forebears were asked."

"Asked to join?"

"Yes, of course," said Timothy. He leaned forward. "If I

tell you something in confidence, will you promise never to repeat it?"

"Yes. I think so," said Theodosia.

"The Peninsula Club is secret. It started with a dozen or so of the oldest families in Charleston. Membership has been passed down through generations. In a patriarchal line."

"But why the secrecy?" asked Theodosia. "Does it have something to do with what they're involved in? Maybe . . . politics?"

"The Peninsula Club is mostly about business," said Timothy. "You can see the advantages, of course, regarding contracts, deals, club memberships, and so on."

"So it's a good old boys' club," said Theodosia. Which, to her, sounded awfully tacky.

"The Peninsula Club is much more than that," said Timothy. "Realize, please, they probably support seventy percent of the arts and social service organizations in this town."

"Really?"

"Remember when the symphony was feuding? And unable to pay musicians as well as their executive director?"

Theodosia remembered.

"The Peninsula Club quietly stepped in and suddenly funding was available."

"Okay," said Theodosia.

"And when a certain senior center in North Charleston was floundering?"

"They funded that, too?" asked Theodosia.

Timothy nodded.

"So they're really a philanthropic organization."

"Yes and no," said Timothy. "Let me put it this way, as they prosper, so does Charleston."

"Can you give me a name?" Theodosia asked. She still wanted to get a little closer to this mysterious organization.

"That would be highly inappropriate," countered Timothy.

"How about . . ." Theodosia searched the database in her mind. Suddenly thought of Truman McBee, the software king who seemed to be a generous supporter of arts organizations and had lost his son. The one that Abby had started a file on. "How about Truman McBee?"

"Good heavens." Timothy's startled reaction told Theodosia she'd struck a nerve.

"So Truman McBee is in the Peninsula Club," murmured Theodosia. She wondered if there was some sort of connection. A file on McBee, a file on the Peninsula Club.

"Why are you so inquisitive about this?" asked Timothy. Then he answered his own question. "Ah, because Abby Davis is just one step away from Jory Davis."

"Well . . . yes," said Theodosia.

Timothy lifted an eyebrow. He was well aware that Theodosia had dated Jory. "There's no way the club's involved," said Timothy as he reached down and patted Earl Grey again, eager to change the line of questioning. "On a happier, more appropriate note, you're coming to my gala, aren't you?"

"Yes, of course," said Theodosia. Since Timothy was an opera buff of the first magnitude, he was having a pre-ball gala at his house this Friday evening. A couple of weeks ago, even though Drayton had assured her she was on the guest list, Theodosia had been secretly thrilled when her thick, parchment invitation had arrived in the mail. The party would be two hundred or so of Timothy's closest friends, plus a dozen performers from the Charleston Symphony. She wouldn't miss it for the world. "I'm really looking forward to it," she told him.

"As a tasty little extra I'm going to put the jewels on display," he told her. "The ones borrowed from the Lugori Museum of Venice."

"You have the jewels here?" asked Theodosia.

Timothy nodded. "Locked in the vault in our downstairs storage room. The only time we took them out was when the Bravissimo Club came by to photograph them."

"Sure," said Theodosia, "for the newspaper piece that ran last Sunday."

Timothy waved a hand at Earl Grey. "Au revoir, nice dog. See you later."

"Bye," said Theodosia, considering herself dismissed. She moved toward the door, beckoning Earl Grey to join her. Just as she was about to close the heavy office door behind her, she heard Timothy mutter these parting words: "They meet Wednesday nights in the Provost Dungeon."

The day was gorgeous and brimming with hope. Puffy white clouds scudded across an azure-blue sky as treetops plunged to and fro, frisky from the wind that swirled off the Cooper and Ashley rivers. Where those two rivers converged, at the tip of the peninsula that was Charleston, the Atlantic Ocean surged in. Always restless, always sweeping in scope, these were historic tides that had carried clipper ships, invading armies, as well as countless hurricanes.

As Earl Grey stepped smartly beside her, Theodosia decided to turn down Murray Street and stop at the Featherbed House Bed and Breakfast. Angie Congdon, the proprietor, had endured some hard luck over the past year, but that was hopefully all behind her now. Even after fire had ravaged her three-story structure, the B and B had been rebuilt better than ever.

Looping Earl Grey's leash around the front railing, Theodosia skipped up the front steps and into the lobby. And could hardly believe her eyes. The place was even more cozy and adorable since last she'd visited. Angie's trademark geese were scattered everywhere. Quilted patchwork geese, plaster geese, carved wooden geese, ceramic geese, and needlepoint geese decorating fat patchwork pillows that were propped against the backs of overstuffed chintz sofas and matching chairs.

Bottles of wine and sherry stood on a long, rough-hewn wooden side table, along with a wheel of orange cheddar cheese and baskets heaped with sliced French bread and crackers. A few guests milled about, enjoying the warmth and hospitality of the place.

"Theodosia?" Angie's voice tinkled merrily over the soft music that played on the sound system. And then she was running toward Theodosia across the planked wooden floor that had somehow miraculously survived the fire. Angie's hair was curly blond and shorter than ever, her lovely oval face held a wide smile.

"What can I say," said Theodosia, accepting a hug from Angie. "I was in the neighborhood."

"About time," said Angie. "What have you been up to?"

"Working," said Theodosia, suddenly feeling guilty that it had been so long between visits.

Angie grinned and thrust her hands into the front pockets of her denim skirt. "Me, too. I can't believe how many hours I put in here. When I was a commodities trader in Chicago, I thought that was tough duty. But screaming my head off on the floor of the CBOT was a breeze compared to this."

"Welcome to the wonderful world of female entrepreneurship." Theodosia laughed.

"But it does have its rewards," said Angie. "You get out of it exactly what you put in."

"There is that," said Theodosia, looking around. "Gosh, the place looks wonderful."

"Doesn't it?" said Angie, pleased at her new and improved B and B. She lowered her voice. "And guess what. We're booked solid right through the holidays."

"Excellent," said Theodosia. "Always good to make a profit."

"Oh," said Angie, "I've even got Teddy Vickers working for me again."

"Your old manager? He came back?"

"Things didn't quite work out the way he'd hoped at that fancy hotel over in Hilton Head."

"So the grass wasn't necessarily greener," said Theodosia.

"But it is here." Angie laughed. "The garden's been replanted, the pond in the backyard is bigger than ever, and we've even got new goldfish arriving tomorrow."

"Alert the neighborhood cats." Theodosia laughed.

"Hey," said Angie. "Speaking of neighborhood. Did you know there's a house for sale down the block?"

Theodosia shook her head.

"It's not a big house," said Angie. "In fact, it's actually the carriage house that went with the Kingstree Mansion. It was sold off maybe, oh, fifteen years ago. Before we were here, of course. Anyway, it's come up for sale again and I naturally thought of you."

"I'm not house hunting," Theodosia told her.

"I hear you," said Angie. "But it's really cute and just the right size, you know? So just walk by it. Trust me, it's the kind of place that should have your name on the mailbox."

Theodosia checked her watch as she untied Earl Grey. She was running late. The viewing at the Rafferty Brothers Funeral Home was tonight and she still had to run home, feed Earl Grey, and then make herself appropriately presentable to face Jory and his relatives. Oh, and pick up Drayton on the way, too.

She didn't really have time to look at a carriage house that was for sale, didn't really have any interest in the place.

That is, until she saw it.

It was, believe it or not, a storybook English cottage. Sharply pitched thatched roof, gingerbread trim, leaded bow window, plants tumbling down a brick walkway.

She wondered how she could have missed this. Perhaps recent owners had added to the charm of the earlier carriage house. In any case, it was quite amazing. Instead of being set behind the Kingstree Mansion, this cottage was slightly off to the side. So it had a small amount of street frontage.

Peering through a wrought-iron fence that pushed up against a tangle of wild dogwood and crepe myrtle, Theodosia stared at an actual corner turret on the top floor and wondered if it afforded a view to the water. Wondered what kind of cozy bedroom or reading room it might make.

She smiled and drew a breath. It was, quite simply, love at first sight.

"Can I help you?" called a woman's voice.

The question snapped Theodosia out of her reverie. "Just looking."

"It's for sale, you know," said the woman walking toward her on the sidewalk. "My agency just listed it. Cute little place, huh?"

"It's perfect," breathed Theodosia.

"Oh, you're interested?" asked the woman. She had a friendly, open face surrounded by a tumble of gray hair and wore a pair of narrow turquoise glasses on a chain around her neck. Her dark blue suit was sturdy but stylish.

"Not really," said Theodosia. Then hedged. "Well, maybe a little. Now that I see it."

The woman shifted two metal signs and a battered leather briefcase to her left hand. "I'm Maggie Twining." She stuck out her right hand. "Listing agent for Sutter Realty."

"Theodosia Browning."

Maggie looked at her sharply. "The lady with the tea shop?"

"Guilty as charged," said Theodosia.

"My friends rave about your tea and scones," said Maggie. She hefted her briefcase and signs. "Of course, I'm always working so I haven't been by yet. But I plan to." Now she set her briefcase down and dug inside. "Let me give you a brochure for this place. So you get a feeling for the features and square footage, that sort of thing."

"Thank you." Theodosia quickly scanned the one-fold brochure and noted the listing price. "Pricey."

"Location, location, location." Maggie laughed. "And look at the place. Cute as a button, isn't it? Even has a name. Hazelhurst."

Theodosia stared longingly at the renovated carriage house

that had been turned into the pluperfect English cottage. She could imagine the cozy interior, could even picture herself moving her furniture in, hanging oil paintings on the walls, and throwing down the dark green Aubusson carpet she'd purchased two years ago, only to find it was a smidge too large for her little apartment. It would fit here, she decided. She would fit here.

There was only one small, inconvenient problem. She didn't have the money.

10

~❦~

Organ music greeted them, the smell of overly sweet flowers assaulting their senses, as Theodosia and Drayton stepped into the vestibule of the Rafferty Brothers Funeral Home. Drayton wore a black suit, as did Theodosia, although she worried her skirt might be a little too above the knee.

"I hate this," said Drayton as they gazed about tentatively. "Reminds me of how old I'm getting. What I've got to look forward to."

"Don't talk like that," Theodosia hissed. "You're not old."

"Right," said Drayton mildly. "I'm just amazingly well preserved." He peered past a jungle of potted plants and a wooden podium with a white guest book resting on top.

"Where do we go?" Theodosia asked. She moved toward the guest book, then hesitated. Noted that only a few signatures had been entered. Early yet.

"Oh, there's a sign," motioned Drayton. They crossed deep pile carpet that was an appropriately somber shade of gray and peered at a small sign with white plastic letters that stood against matching somber gray draperies. "Love their decorator," whispered Drayton. "Who do you think it was? The Grim Reaper?"

Theodosia choked back a giggle, feeling guilty.

Drayton squinted. "Davis viewing in Parlor A, Bailey viewing in Parlor B. Looks like we have a full house to-night."

Theodosia knew Drayton's macabre sense of humor was covering up his nervousness. Come to think of it, she was feeling a little shaky herself. Funeral directors referred to this ritual as a *viewing*, which was, of course, a nice neutral term. But when you got right down to the hard reality of the situation, viewing really meant gazing at a casket that contained a lifeless body while all around you the deceased's relatives sobbed their eyes out.

"This way," said Drayton, guiding Theodosia by the elbow toward Parlor A. "It's probably best we locate Jory right away."

"Oh no!" Theodosia murmured as they stepped through an arched doorway into a room that felt a little too cool and was hideously decorated in shades of muted green and lilac. A couple dozen people, dressed mostly in black, whispered together in small groups. "It's an open casket! I really wasn't prepared to see her again!"

"Steady as she goes," whispered Drayton. He placed a hand on Theodosia's shoulder and gave a reassuring pat. He wasn't keen on the idea of an open casket, either, but he'd seen enough of them that he wasn't totally unnerved.

"People are staring at us," Theodosia whispered. "We probably look like a couple of deer frozen in the headlights." Indeed, one group of people, no doubt Abby's grieving relatives, had turned their curious, sniffling attention on the two of them.

"We're going directly to Plan B," muttered Drayton, under his breath. "Not to be confused with Parlor B. In other words, we walk up, take a *very* brief peek, look as sorrowful as possible, and then we're *out* of here."

"Really brief peek," agreed Theodosia as they shuffled reluctantly toward the casket that sat against the far wall.

Flickering white candles in tall brass candleholders stood at each end of the coffin. Dozens of white calla lilies were banked behind it. An ivory satin cloth covered the bier. The scene wasn't just surreal, it reminded Theodosia of a scene from a movie. Except this was real life and she and Drayton had somehow scored walk-on rolls.

Lifting her eyes from where they'd been glued on the carpet, Theodosia forced herself to gaze inside the casket.

Fragile and waxy-looking, Abby Davis lay on ruffled layers of ivory silk. Theodosia found it unnerving that a woman who'd always been so animated, so vocal, now lay so utterly still. Abby's makeup was flawless, of course, with rouged cheeks and slightly mauve lipstick that matched her mauve-colored suit. No doubt the mortuary cosmetician had seen to that last detail. Or maybe the TV station had sent over their own makeup artist.

Abby's short, dark hair was coiffed to perfection and artfully arranged to cover the bullet hole in her forehead. And it was lacquered with enough hairspray to last for perpetuity. Abby looked like she was ready to go on air. Except for the fact that she was dead. Her microphone had been unplugged; her show had been cancelled.

"She's wearing that same cameo," said Theodosia, gazing at the brilliantly sparkling piece that lay nestled at Abby's throat.

"So what?" said Drayton.

"Must have really meant something to her."

Drayton shrugged. He'd never really forgiven Abby for treating Theodosia so badly. From his attitude earlier, it was obvious he hadn't forgiven Jory, either.

"Can we leave now?" asked Theodosia.

"I thought you'd never ask," whispered Drayton.

They turned in concert, ready to make their escape, when Jory suddenly stepped in front of them.

"You came," he said, leaning in quickly to deliver a chaste peck on Theodosia's cheek before she could raise a formal objection. "Thank you. And Drayton . . ." Jory extended his hand and Drayton, acting the gentleman now, clasped it. "Nice to have your support."

"Mmm," said Drayton.

"I want you to meet . . ." Jory turned and looked about. "Drew."

At hearing his name, a man with red-rimmed eyes looked up from where he was crouched on a black metal folding chair. His dark, close-cropped hair was a distinct contrast to his pale face. In another situation he might have been handsome. Here he just looked miserable.

Dabbing at his face with a white handkerchief, Drew Donovan croaked, "Yes?" His voice was rough as tree bark, as though he'd been crying or screaming for a couple of days. Which he probably had been.

"Drew," said Jory, "this is Theodosia Browning and Drayton Conneley."

Drew, still holding a hanky to his face, tried to clear his

throat and managed, "Nice to meet you," in a pathetic whisper.

"My condolences," said Theodosia.

"Condolences," repeated Drayton.

Drew bobbed his head wearily. "Abby would have been touched."

Would she really? wondered Theodosia.

Then, as if forming up a rugby scrum, the rest of Jory's relatives suddenly pressed in around Theodosia and Drayton. They continued to move in tightly, virtually capturing them in the middle.

"You remember Aunt Marie and Uncle Otto?" asked Jory.

"Of course," said Theodosia. She had no memory of them.

"And Darnell?" continued Jory. "And Jimmy Joe?"

"Nice to see you both again," said Theodosia. Again, no clue.

"My sympathies," said Drayton.

Jory's uncle Otto put a hand on Theodosia's arm. "Thank you for trying to help Abby. You know, out in the . . . field."

"Sorry, I wasn't able to, uh . . . sorry," said Theodosia.

A few more relatives pressed in and Jory rattled off their names.

"I'm going to get some air," said Drayton, moving off once the myriad of introductions had finally slowed.

Which left Theodosia and Jory staring hesitantly at one another.

"She looks lovely," said Theodosia, glancing back at the open casket. She'd already returned the sheaf of papers to him and didn't know what else to say.

"Doesn't she?" said Jory. "So natural." He almost choked on his own words.

"I take it Drew chose her clothing and jewelry?" Was she really having this conversation?

"No," said Jory, thoughtfully, "I think Sarah did."

"Sarah's your . . ."

"Cousin," said Jory. "Sarah," he waved an arm, "come over here again for a minute."

"No, that's okay," said Theodosia. "She doesn't have to . . ."

A woman in her early thirties joined them. She was slim and petite with dark hair, not unlike Abby Davis.

"You selected Abby's clothing, right?" asked Jory.

Sarah nodded, a sad smile on her angular face. "Her favorite suit. The one she wore the first time she anchored the evening news." Her voice cracked. "Abby was so proud."

"I'll bet she was," said Theodosia. "And the cameo. It's, uh, *interesting* that it's the same one she was wearing when I found her."

Jory looked surprised. "It is?" He gazed at Sarah. "Is that why you chose it?"

Sarah suddenly looked nervous. "Not really. I picked it because Abby seemed to be wearing it constantly these past few weeks. Because it seemed so precious to her. Sometimes, when she wasn't even aware of it, her fingers would reach up and . . . and touch it."

"Must have been a gift from Drew," said Theodosia.

"Sure," said Sarah. "That would explain it." But she didn't look all that confident in her answer.

And still Theodosia couldn't make a clean getaway. Linus Gillette, Abby's boss and the general manager at Trident Media, noticed her, blocked her way, then engaged her in conversation. Maybe because she was the only person who looked familiar to him at the moment; maybe because he was a blowhard who loved to hear himself talk.

"Hello, Linus," said Theodosia in a neutral tone.

"Theodosia," said Linus. "Lovely to see you, even though these are such difficult circumstances." He paused. "When are we going to see you at our station again? I haven't forgotten those tea segments you taped for us. Got a heck of a lot of calls. Our viewers were very impressed."

"That's what it's all about, isn't it?" said Theodosia. "Ratings."

"Exactly right," said Linus. "We live and die on ratings." He suddenly realized his terminology might have hit a little too close to home, then amended his words to, "Ratings are the heartbeat of a TV station."

"When you dismissed Webster Hall," said Theodosia, "you did it because of ratings?"

Linus clenched his jaw tightly and lifted his eyes to stare at a point slightly above Theodosia's head. "Web was never dismissed." His words were clipped and terse.

"His contract just wasn't renewed," Theodosia prompted, giving a friendly, conspiratorial smile.

"What are we talking about?" asked a tall, dark-haired man with a slightly craggy, just-this-side-of-handsome face.

"Theodosia," said Linus, "meet Joe Fanning, our news director."

"We were just talking about Web Hall being let go," said Theodosia, unwilling to change the subject.

Fanning's smile turned to a frown. "That's private business," he growled. "Nothing to be dragged out and discussed here."

Theodosia plunged doggedly ahead. "But Web Hall was very upset when he was let go. Some might say deeply disturbed?"

"It was a difficult time for everyone," said Fanning.

"For Abby, too?" asked Theodosia.

"Doubtful," muttered Fanning. "Now, if you'll excuse me . . ."

"Must go convey our sympathies," echoed Gillette, who edged away from her, too.

"Your friend the station manager didn't exactly look heartbroken," said Drayton, at Theodosia's elbow now.

"Neither did the news director," said Theodosia. "And Linus Gillette really didn't want to talk about Webster Hall's contract not being renewed." She'd filled Drayton in on the contract situation on the way over.

"I'm sure that's still a bone of contention," said Drayton. "And speaking of such things, I overheard another bit of information that might interest you."

"You've been eavesdropping on the relatives," said Theodosia. She could always count on Drayton, no matter what.

"Apparently," said Drayton, dropping his voice, "Abby inherited some sort of plantation house out on Yonges Island. Now it all goes to Drew."

"You see him as a *suspect?*" asked Theodosia. To her, Drew seemed like a sad, gibbering soul, completely lost in grief.

"I thought it an interesting coincidence," said Drayton, a trifle stiffly. "The death and subsequent spousal inheritance."

"Then I'll follow up with Jory," said Theodosia. Something caught her eye in the doorway and she glanced over, only to see a large bulky form suddenly appear. "Tidwell," said Theodosia.

"I'm going to pass on this conversation," said Drayton, slipping away again.

Detective Burt Tidwell glanced around quickly, twitched his nose like a wary predator, then allowed his hard, beady eyes to settle upon Theodosia. He sped across the room like a fox making a run at the henhouse.

"Surprise, surprise," he chirped. "Look who's here."

"Surprise yourself," Theodosia told him in a somewhat sour tone. "I hope you haven't come here just to harass these people in their hour of grief."

Cocking his head sideways, like an inquisitive magpie, Tidwell said, "Hour of grief. How poetic. Anyway, I thought harassing the bereaved was *your* role. Asking one too many questions, snooping around." He raised his bushy eyebrows to punctuate his words.

"I've been asked by the family to help look into things," Theodosia told him. "Lots of people asking for favors these days," she added.

"Indeed," said Tidwell, pretending to look surprised. "And this request came via Jory Davis?" A mischievous gleam shone in his eyes.

He had her there. "Yes, of course from Jory. We're friends, after all."

"Good friends?" he asked, the wild gleam intensifying.

"Just friends," she replied, emphatically.

"We're taking off," Theodosia told Jory. There were so many people packed into the room now, they could hardly move. Theodosia was surprised at the enormous turnout.

Jory clasped both her hands firmly. "Thank you for coming. It meant a lot to me. To all of us."

"Jory," said Theodosia, "I heard something about a family plantation that Abby inherited? Is that something I should be looking into?"

He gazed at her for a few seconds, then a smile played at his lips and erupted into an amused snort. "If you suspect Drew just came into something wonderful, you've got another think coming. It may be called the Mobley Plantation, but that old place is practically falling down—nobody's lived there for forty years. And the land around it is a tangle of swamp. Besides, the place isn't really passing into Drew's hands at all. Abby told me a month ago that they'd both signed papers to donate it to some sort of preservation society. The, uh . . ." He thought for a minute. "Carolina Heartland Trust."

Theodosia relaxed. And suddenly realized she had developed a slightly fonder impression of Abby Davis. The woman's heart was certainly in the right place if she'd donated property to a preservation society. With fewer and fewer old South Carolina plantation homes left standing, it was critical to preserve them. Not just for tourism, but to help future generations get a feeling for the history and culture of the Carolina low country.

"But, hey," said Jory. "If you think that old plantation means something and you want to look around, I'll give you a key. Lots of crazy stories about that place, though."

"Crazy how?" asked Theodosia.

Jory shook his head. "Nothing based on fact. Just . . . what would you call them? Ghost stories."

"Ghost stories," purred a female voice. "Now that sounds interesting."

"Delaine!" said Theodosia. She had no idea Delaine was going to show up.

But dressed in a prim black suit, with her face arranged in an interested pout, Delaine looked properly sedate. "Had to extend my condolences to Jory," she murmured, giving him a hug plus double air kisses.

"Thank you," said Jory. "Now if you'll excuse me?" And he was gone.

"How could I not come?" whispered Delaine, as Jory retreated, "Since you two were once an item. Back in the day."

"Ancient history," said Theodosia. "And how did you know about this visitation anyway?"

"Drayton mentioned it," said Delaine. "I called the tea shop this afternoon but you weren't around."

"Right," said Theodosia. She'd been visiting Timothy.

"So what's the deal with that plantation you and Jory were talking about?" Delaine snuggled in closer. "Tell me about it."

Theodosia filled her in on Abby's donation to the Carolina Heartland Trust.

"And you say the place is really old?" asked Delaine.

"Practically falling down," said Theodosia. "It's supposedly in very tough shape."

Delaine's violet eyes sparkled. "Still . . . you look like you might be planning to do a little exploring."

"I hadn't thought about it," said Theodosia. It didn't sound like an angle worth pursuing. There were too many other aspects to look into. The McBee kidnapping, the Webster Hall thing, a secret society angle, even some of the other stories Abby had been working on.

"Oh, let's take a look anyway," suggested Delaine. "It'll be fun. Like exploring a haunted house."

Oh great, thought Theodosia. Delaine had been so helpful at the wacky séance she'd staged at the Belvedere Theatre a few months ago. Especially when she got scared and started screaming her head off.

"Where is this wreck of a house, anyway?" asked Delaine.

"On Yonges Island. Out near Adams Run."

"What a perfect coincidence," said Delaine. She hooked her arm through Theodosia's, dragging her reluctantly back toward the casket. "There's a lovely antique shop nearby, out by Turner's Crossroad. Last time I stopped in I found the most marvelous carnival glass vase." When they reached Abby's casket, Delaine stared at the flowers, the candles, and the sad figure in the casket. "Poor girl," she said.

"Yes," Theodosia agreed, taking a final glance at Abby. For some reason, her impression of Abby seemed different now. The light was different? Maybe the candles had burned down? Then Delaine was propelling her back through the crowd, looping toward the lobby.

"Ready to leave?" Drayton asked Theodosia. "I've signed the guest book, extended condolences to everyone including the two funeral directors and the janitor, and am probably coming down with a miserable head cold due to this dreadful air-conditioning."

"It's a *funeral* parlor, Drayton," said Delaine sweetly. "Not Caribbean Joe's tanning salon."

"Good-bye, Delaine," said Drayton.

"Bye-bye." She waved, then turned and headed for a cluster of Jory's relatives.

"Ready?" asked Drayton. Fidgeting with his bow tie, it was obvious he couldn't wait to leave.

Theodosia hesitated.

"What?" asked Drayton.

Something niggled in the back of Theodosia's brain. "I need to take another look at Abby," she told Drayton.

He took a step backward. *"What?* Are you *serious?"*

She grabbed his arm. "Just . . . indulge me, okay?"

Drayton let loose a deep sigh, but followed Theodosia over to Abby and her bronze Eternalux coffin. Most of the guests were milling around on the opposite side of the room now, so they had some privacy.

"The cameo," said Theodosia, peering at the piece of jewelry. "Does it look different to you now?"

"Not really," said Drayton.

But it did to Theodosia. For some reason the carving didn't look quite as sharp, the jewels didn't have the same glow and luster.

"Who do you suppose gave it to her?" murmured Theodosia.

Drayton shrugged, clearly uninterested. "Don't know. Her husband?"

Theodosia thought about the *Loving you always* note. Wondered if the initial at the end of the note had been a D. Or had it been signed with an F or a G? What if Drew hadn't been the gift giver? What if it was someone else, a lover perhaps, and the relationship had soured? What if . . . ? Theodosia knew she was projecting a worst-case scenario. But that was what investigators did, right? Develop theories? Look at all the angles?

Angles.

"Stand behind me," Theodosia whispered to Drayton. "Obstruct the view."

Drayton glanced at her sharply. "Just what is it you want me to do?"

"Oh, for goodness sakes," murmured Theodosia. "Pretend you're praying or something."

Shielded by Drayton, Theodosia edged closer to the casket. Overhead, a cool breeze from an air duct ruffled her hair.

The air conditioner was working overtime to keep the room cool, keep everything carefully refrigerated.

Theodosia rested her hands on the edge of the bronze casket, let her fingers play across the pleated satin lining.

"Don't you dare!" Drayton hissed from behind her.

She did dare.

Bending forward for an instant, Theodosia fumbled with the catch, then pulled the cameo from Abby's throat and slid it into her jacket pocket. "Did anyone see me?" she hissed.

Drayton cocked his head and frowned slightly. "There was one fellow standing behind that potted palm. But he's moved off now. I don't see him."

"Good," said Theodosia, giving a relieved sigh. "That means we're outta here."

Hustling out of Parlor A, Theodosia never stopped to sign the guest book, never stopped to bid adieu to the relatives.

Out on the sidewalk, the dark autumn evening wrapped around them like a protective cape. Drayton, unnerved by Theodosia's little theft, whispered his stunned mantra over and over, "I can't believe you did that, I can't believe you did that, I can't believe you did that."

While all Theodosia could think was, *Good grief, now I've gone and robbed the dead!*

11

"Where are you?" demanded Haley. "We've got a really crappy connection. Is something wrong with your cell phone?"

"I'm going to be a little late this morning," Theodosia told her as she accelerated past a slow-moving tour bus, then cut over two lanes. Traffic was starting to build on Royal Street. Tourists who'd arrived early had grabbed all the good parking spots and were now wandering around, taking snapshots of the palm trees that marched single file down the boulevard past redbrick buildings with tall, narrow, whitewashed doorways.

"How late?" asked Haley. "It looks like we're going to be really busy today. Reservations are pouring in."

"Be there in an hour," Theodosia promised. She thumbed the Off button on her phone, caught sight of a single, lone parking space, and zoomed into it, knowing she was extremely lucky to have scored a spot on the street.

This area of Royal Street was the antique capital of

Charleston. It was where a lot of family silver, antique furniture, jewelry, artwork, and trinkets ended up. Charleston was an old city with old families. And those old families had been hoarders for centuries.

But as photos in family albums faded, as silver lost its luster, and subsequent generations lost touch with their ancestors, many of those treasures found their way into King Street antique shops. And, if a few items weren't quite as old as the customers who pounced on them, well, what harm was that, really?

Vianello was the kind of shop Theodosia would have loved to own if she was selling antiques and antiquey-looking things. Housed in a small, renovated warehouse, the wood-planked floors were dark and rich, with a scattering of Oriental carpets. Whitewashed walls and ceilings lent a fresh feel and small white chandeliers, probably French or Italian in origin, sparkled and dangled from the ceiling.

Of course, the place was jammed to the rafters with a tasty array of inventory. There were tiny lamps with feathered shades, wrought-iron garden ornaments, velvet hatboxes, silk gloves, French milled soap, sterling silver cache pots, Murano glass vases, silk flower arrangements, and an array of French cosmetics called La Dame Beauté. Venetian masks, evening bags, and framed etchings of Venetian and Parisian landmarks hung on the walls. Along one wall was a rack jammed with one-of-a-kind couture-looking clothing. On the opposite wall was an enormous glass jewelry case filled with shimmering objects of delight.

"What a lovely shop!" exclaimed Theodosia.

A man looked up from where he was unpacking boxes of jeweled sandals and smiled brightly. "Thank you. And welcome."

"Mr. Bruno?" said Theodosia. Theodosia figured this had to be Julian Bruno, the owner. He was tall, with olive skin, slicked-back dark hair, and a hawk nose. Although he wasn't classically handsome, he projected a certain European charm and worldliness.

Julian Bruno crossed the shop to greet her. "Call me Julian," he said, a wide smile lighting his face.

"Thandie McLean told me I absolutely had to stop by," said Theodosia, putting a little impetus in her voice. "So here I am." She gazed around. "I've been meaning to get a mask for Saturday night, but . . ." Now she let her hands flutter. "I simply didn't get around to it."

"Ah," said Julian Bruno, sizing her up in an instant. "You'll be attending the Masked Ball." He gave a slight frown, as though disapproving of her lateness. But then he said, "I apologize, our selection of masks is rather picked over. Perhaps we can still manage one or two . . ." He scanned the wall, then reached up and selected a gold mask with a spray of colorful feathers. "Perhaps . . . this one?" He held it out to her.

"Lovely," said Theodosia. She hefted the mask, found it rather substantial. "Made in Italy?"

Julian Bruno nodded in deference. "From the noted Mondonovo factory in Venice. Lambskin with a papier-mâché and gesso overlay." He smiled. "You're looking forward to the Masked Ball? You enjoy opera?"

"Very much," said Theodosia.

Julian Bruno touched a hand to his chest. "I've traveled to Italy many times. Had the good fortune to attend operas at La Fenice in Venice as well as Teatro dell'Opera in Rome." He led her to the closest wall where a half dozen framed photos hung. "See? These are my photographs of Venice. The Grand Canal, the Ponto del Sospori."

"Lovely," said Theodosia. She held the mask up to her face. "And this is very comfortable."

"You flatter it." Julian Bruno smiled. He made a slightly theatrical gesture. "With your lovely hair . . . dare I call it Titian? It is very *complimentore*." He cocked his head. "What color is your gown?

My gown, thought Theodosia. *I haven't stopped at Delaine's to pick one out yet!*

"Somewhere between champagne and silver," she lied.

"Perfection then!" enthused Bruno. He gave a sly smile. "Shall I wrap this or does madame prefer to wear it?"

"What I'd really like," said Theodosia, edging over to the jewelry case, "is to try on one of those lovely bracelets." She pointed to a single-strand bracelet set with sparkling yellow and white crystals.

"That piece was created by a jewelry maker in Atlanta," explained Bruno. "She had a real piece of luck when she discovered some eighteenth-century French jewelry molds in a Parisian flea market. Now she's retooled them for modern use." He scurried around to the back of the case, pulled out the bracelet, and handed it to Theodosia. "See? Swarovski crystals impeccably matched and set." His hand reached back inside. "Matching earrings, too. Just like Madame du Barry might have worn." He smiled at his little historical reference.

Theodosia tried the bracelet and earrings on. "You're a jewelry maker, too?"

He shrugged. "I dabble. But my pieces are not of this caliber."

Studying the price tags on the pieces, Theodosia said, "I think . . . just the mask and bracelet today."

Bruno placed the earrings back on their velvet pillow. "Perhaps the earrings another day."

"Perhaps," murmured Theodosia. She slid a hand into her pocket, fingered the cameo she'd taken from Abby Davis's throat last night.

"Anything else?" Julian Bruno's wide smile stretched across his face.

Theodosia set the cameo on top of the glass case. "What can you tell me about this piece?" she asked.

Julian Bruno bounced on the balls of his feet and gave her a slightly inquisitive look. "I believe it's from here," he told her.

"I thought it might be," said Theodosia. "It was owned by Abby Davis. You may have heard about her recent death. Or, should I say, her unfortunate murder."

Bruno looked shocked. "Good heavens, yes. I read about it in the newspaper."

"I'm trying to determine," said Theodosia, "if Abby's husband bought it for her. A man by the name of Drew Donovan. Does that ring a bell?"

Bruno looked puzzled. "Perhaps." He studied the cameo again. "I wish I could help . . ." His voice trailed off. "This means something to you, to her family?"

"I think so, yes," said Theodosia. "Do you remember the price of this piece?"

"It's costume jewelry, so . . . not too expensive." He registered the disappointment on Theodosia's face, then said, "A piece given, no doubt, from the heart."

"The best way," agreed Theodosia.

"A moment while I wrap your treasures," said Bruno. He slid through the doorway into a small back room. Theodosia edged over and watched as he carefully wrapped the mask and then the bracelet in gold tissue paper.

Just as he was about to slide them into a gold paper bag with raffia handles, she asked, "Could you possibly wrap the mask in bubble wrap?"

"Of course."

As Bruno bent down to gather up a piece of bubble wrap, Theodosia moved closer and peered through his doorway. His office was small and almost as jam-packed as hers. Cardboard boxes were stacked floor to ceiling next to a small built-in desk and an adjacent counter for wrapping. Not much room for anything else.

A bell tinkled at the front of the shop and the front door swung open. Theodosia turned and watched the faces of two female customers light up with excitement as they entered. And why not? This place was filled with wondrous treasures.

"On your charge card?" asked Bruno, sliding the newly wrapped mask into the bag with the bracelet.

"Cash," said Theodosia, pulling out bills.

Bruno pointed to a small leather-bound book. "If you'd like to jot down your name and address, I'll put you on our mailing list. We're having a trunk show of beaded silk bags next month."

"Thanks," said Theodosia. "I'd like that."

Haley had been right. The Indigo Tea Shop was getting slammed. Every table was occupied and at least ten people were waiting outside on the sun-dappled sidewalk.

"Thanks goodness, you're here," said Drayton, as Theodosia slipped through the green velvet curtains into the tea room. "Even though Miss Dimple's helping out, we're frightfully busy."

Theodosia scanned the room. They were busy, yes. But she didn't see any guests glancing about with unhappy looks. They were drinking tea, nibbling scones, scooping up jam. It was just past eleven and the lunch crowd had yet to arrive.

"We could seat people outside," said Drayton. "It's nice enough today. Warm enough that I even whipped up some of my green tea granita."

Theodosia was quick to agree. "If you can drag three tables around from the back, I'll bring the chairs." She smiled at Miss Dimple, who was bravely hoisting two chintz-patterned teapots. "You okay?" she asked their bookkeeper, who, for some reason, loved filling in.

"Ready and raring to go," Miss Dimple assured her. Then took off on her squat little legs.

"Better make that four tables," Theodosia told Drayton. "I have to make a quick phone call and then I'll grab those chairs."

"Got it," said Drayton.

After five minutes of sleuthing, Theodosia determined that Web Hall was now selling time for a local radio station, KQSF, the Mouth of the South.

She called KQSF and was routed through to Hall's cell phone.

"Hello?" said Hall.

"Mr. Hall? This is Theodosia Browning at the Indigo Tea Shop. I was wondering if we could get together and talk?"

"I remember you," said Hall, all salesman hearty and jovial. "You're that tea lady who came to Channel Eight. Did the demos."

"That's me," said Theodosia. "Would you have any time today?"

"I'll make time," enthused Web Hall. "You want me to drop by your shop?"

"I've got a few . . . uh . . . questions," said Theodosia. She knew she was sounding a little presumptuous.

"No problem," answered Hall. "I'll bring my rate card, a sharp pencil, and our new Arbitron ratings. Answer every cotton-pickin' question you got. Be there midafternoon." There was a loud click and Webster Hall was gone.

Theodosia stared at the receiver. Somehow they'd gotten their wires crossed. Web Hall thought she wanted to buy time on his radio station. On the other hand, she hadn't been terribly specific about what her questions were. Hmm.

Haley had visited one of Charleston's outdoor produce markets early this morning and taken full advantage of the late-season offerings.

Zucchini squares, cranberry scones, potato-leek soup, poached plum compote, blue crab salad, and cheddar-carrot tea sandwiches were on the luncheon menu today. Theodosia accepted compliments from their guests, poured tea, dashed outside to pour more tea, then packed up leftovers and a half dozen take-home scone orders into indigo-blue cardboard boxes.

By one thirty the rush was over and the Indigo Tea Shop had settled into a more leisurely pace. Daria Shand, from the Antiquarian Map Shop a couple of doors down, dropped in for take-out and stayed for lunch. She was mid-forties with long, reddish-blond hair and a curvaceous figure. She was also smart as a whip.

"This is a real treat for me," Daria told Theodosia as she nibbled her scone and tea sandwiches. "Until I hired an assistant, I was always wolfing down a brown-bag lunch while trying not to smear mayonnaise on antique maps. Oh, by the way . . ." Daria dug into her oversized tote bag. "I brought that book Drayton asked about. The one with the Gilmer Civil War maps? My new assistant picked it up at an auction in Savannah."

"Who is this new person?" asked Theodosia. "Sounds like an absolute whiz."

"His name is Jason Pritchard and he's quite the go-getter." Daria smiled. "Which means I finally have time to eat a civilized lunch."

"Say," said Drayton, hustling over and thumbing through his new book. "Do you think you could get me the Civil War maps of Beaufort Harbor?"

"I'll try," Daria told him.

Theodosia stood in the kitchen doorway, spooning up bites of plum compote. She'd just given Haley a quick rundown on the carriage house she'd seen for sale down from the Featherbed House.

"Ooh, you should buy it," enthused Haley as she smoothed her cheddar cheese—carrot mixture onto slices of whole wheat bread. "Then I can move into your apartment!"

"I thought you loved your garden apartment." Haley lived across the alley in a small but elegant studio apartment with French doors that led out to a tiny green gem of a garden.

"I do," said Haley. "But your place is much bigger. Plus, you've done a fair amount of decorating. That's a major plus." Haley checked the three chickens that were roasting in the oven, chicken for tomorrow's chicken chutney salad, as well as four pans of scones in the lower part of the oven.

"How many scones did Delaine order?" asked Theodosia.

"Twelve dozen," said Haley. Delaine was chairman of the Tradd Street Lamplighter Tour and prided herself on supervising refreshments, too.

"She's stopping by to pick them up?"

"If I don't kill her first," said Haley. "Honestly, she's like the block commissar or whatever those old guys in Moscow were who oversaw forty families in one cramped building. She's already called about a hundred times."

"Just making sure everything's perfect," said Theodosia. Delaine could be a pest, but she sure was organized.

Haley grabbed an oven mitt and slid two pans out of the oven. "So when do you think you'll decide on the house?"

"Not in the near future," said Theodosia as she set her bowl and spoon in a plastic bin and slipped back toward her office. "But if anything changes, I'll let you know."

"Knock, knock." It was Drayton.

Theodosia glanced up, pushing a mass of curly hair from her face. "Please tell me you brought tea."

In response, Drayton set a steaming cup of dark red tea on her desk. Or what passed for Theodosia's desk since it was still a clutter of magazines, tea catalogs, recipes, and to-do notes.

"Assam," he told her. "From the Madoorie Garden."

She tasted it. "Mmm. Lovely body."

"A nice pungent liquor as is fairly typical with teas from northeast India." He let her take another sip, then said, "You look worried."

"Concerned," said Theodosia.

"New wrinkles in the Abby Davis investigation?"

"That's the problem," said Theodosia. "There are wrinkles, but nothing seems to lead anywhere."

Drayton sat down across from her. "Tell me."

"I thought you preferred a strict hands-off policy. That you didn't want to get involved."

"After last night," said Drayton, "I'm hardly uninvolved. In fact, I'm at least complicit, wouldn't you say?"

"Yes, I suppose so." Theodosia leaned forward and quickly filled Drayton in on her visit to Julian Bruno's shop this morning.

"So you bought a couple of trinkets and found out the brooch was only costume jewelry. What did you think it was?"

"Not sure," said Theodosia. "Something more, I guess."

One of Drayton's eyebrows quivered. "Now you're looking for jewel thieves?"

Theodosia sighed. "Now I just feel silly. I suppose I'm going to have to return that brooch to Jory."

"I suppose you are," said Drayton.

"Uncomfortable," said Theodosia.

"Well," said Drayton, stretching his legs out, "that's nothing new, is it?"

"Hey, Theo." Haley stood in the doorway, looking a little languid and a little tired at the same time. "You've got a visitor."

"Web Hall?" asked Theodosia.

"Yeah, the TV guy," nodded Haley. "Well, he *used* to be on TV." She paused. "Whatcha gonna talk to him about? We gonna do a TV commercial? Can I be in it?"

Drayton threw a knowing glance at Haley. "Theo thinks Abby Davis had Webster Hall fired so she could move into his anchor chair."

"Gack," said Haley, making a face. "This whole thing is sounding more and more like a soap opera."

Drayton waved a hand. "I rarely watch TV."

"This isn't about TV, Drayton," said Theodosia. "It's about a motive for murder. Abby Davis went after Web Hall's job with a vengeance and eventually got him canned."

"And you think he hates her for it?" asked Drayton.

"He sent her a very vitriolic letter."

Drayton pursed his lips, thinking. "You have a point."

"So a prime suspect," said Haley, suddenly looking interested.

12

Webster Hall was chubby and affable. A former anchorman who was now too old to play the handsome leading man and had settled for the part of gray-haired, folksy neighbor. But his navy-blue blazer was well tailored and his khaki slacks sported a sharp crease.

"I brought the latest Arbitrons as well as the Nielsens," said Hall, "so you can gauge and compare ratings." He was all business with his charts and papers spread across one of the tables. Smiling at Theodosia, who was seated across from him, he glanced around the Indigo Tea Shop where afternoon guests sipped tea and selected sweets and savories from three-tiered silver trays. "You could definitely benefit from radio advertising. Morning drive time might be a little pricey for your purposes, but we have a couple of afternoon slots with a solid thirty-five-to-fifty-five female audience. Now I also brought our rate card . . ."

"Mr. Hall . . ." began Theodosia.

An eager salesman's smile bloomed on his face. "Web, call me Web."

"Web," said Theodosia, "I think we might have gotten our wires crossed on a few things."

Web Hall gazed at her, a little wary now. "Hah?"

"I called you this morning because I wanted to ask a couple of questions," said Theodosia. "And you . . . well, you assumed I was interested in buying airtime."

Web Hall brightened. "You'd rather do a sponsorship? Because I've got a dandy midmorning show called *Tick Talk*. Pretty good numbers on the female audience."

"Web," said Theodosia, starting to really feel guilty now, "I wanted to ask you about Abby Davis."

Web Hall stiffened in his chair and his cheeks flared pink. His mouth worked furiously, but no words came out. Finally, his voice a low growl, he asked, "What are you talking about?"

"Is it true Abby got you fired?"

Grabbing for his charts and rate cards, Web Hall hastily folded his papers and started jamming them into his briefcase.

"Excuse me," said Theodosia, feeling really awful now. "I didn't mean to upset you."

"Well, I am upset," said Web, his face turning crimson, his mouth a tight line. "Your bringing that up." A small stack of papers slid to the floor.

"I'm sorry," said Theodosia, leaning over to pick them up. If Web Hall was putting on an act, it was a good one. Worthy of an Academy Award. She handed him his papers. "I had the misfortune of actually discovering Abby Davis . . ."

"You were at that jumping race?" asked Hall, glancing at her sharply. "Me, too."

"Really?" said Theodosia. That was interesting.

"The whole thing was a real tragedy," said Hall. And he sounded like he meant it.

"Yes," said Theodosia. "And I know Abby's brother rather well, so I've been . . . um . . . looking into things, so to speak."

"You shoulda told me that," said Hall. "Instead of getting me over here on a false pretext . . ."

"You're right," said Theodosia. "I apologize. It was wrong of me to let you assume I wanted to buy airtime."

"Besides, the police already quizzed me about being at the race and working with Abby. Probably, they talked to everybody at the station. My *former* station."

"Sorry again," said Theodosia.

Web Hall seemed to relax a little at Theodosia's apology.

"When I got let go, that was a bad time for me," he told her.

"I can imagine."

"Contract negotiations are tough."

"So I've heard," said Theodosia, in what she hoped was a soothing, encouraging voice.

"And that Abby Davis . . ." Web Hall shook his head. "She had a way with men, could twist them around her little finger. Particularly Linus Gillette, our general manager." He pulled out a hanky, mopped at his brow. "Abby also had a very tough, demanding agent." Web Hall seemed eager now to set the record straight. "Rumor was, she negotiated a pile of money for Abby."

"That so?" Theodosia murmured.

"That's not the worst of it," said Web Hall, looking slightly woebegone. "Abby Davis spread some pretty nasty rumors about me."

"Like what?" asked Theodosia.

"Told folks I was a drinker. She had a field day dropping little innuendos here and there. That kind of stuff can kill a guy. Then management discovered a booze bottle in my desk drawer and another one stashed under the anchor chair."

"Were they yours?"

Web Hall dropped his shoulders and extended his hands, palms upward. "Please. My momma made sure I had a strict Baptist upbringing. The only time I take a sip of spirits is at weddings and on New Year's Eve."

"I'm sorry," said Theodosia. "Sounds like you had a rough time of it."

Web Hall was still smoldering. "You know who really hated Abby? Joe Fanning, the news director."

"Yes," said Theodosia. "I've heard that."

"She tried to do a number on him, too! Maybe you should be talking to *him*."

"You're right," said Theodosia. "Maybe I should."

"You were playing confessor to that poor fellow," observed Drayton, once Web Hall had left. He was standing behind the front counter, measuring out spiced chai into a tall, red-and-gold-paisley teapot.

"But I didn't extract any sort of confession at all," said Theodosia. "I just got a sense that Web Hall feels extremely devalued. The way I see it, he's either a very sincere man who got the short end of the stick or a terrifically gifted actor."

"He was in television," Drayton said in a droll tone.

"Yes, he was," agreed Theodosia. "For a lot of years." She knew that television personalities were just that—personalities.

They were constructs that actors developed and honed to appeal to a certain type of audience.

"So Web Hall is still a suspect?" Drayton asked, as he slipped a plastic drip catcher over the spout of his teapot.

"Let me get back to you on that," said Theodosia.

In her office, Theodosia dialed Detective Burt Tidwell's direct line. When he came on, she said, "You've already talked to Webster Hall."

"I assume you have, too," was his reply.

"Well . . . yes. Just now, in fact."

"Never let it be said that a single blade of grass grew under your feet," said Tidwell in a clipped voice.

"Did Web Hall tell you that Abby and Joe Fanning were completely at odds?"

"Yes, he did," said Tidwell. "Made a big point of it, in fact."

"So what do you think?" asked Theodosia.

"I think they were probably at odds," responded Tidwell.

"But you don't think Fanning killed her," said Theodosia.

"Nothing points toward the man, nothing points away."

"So you're in limbo, too," said Theodosia.

"No," said Tidwell in a testy voice, "I'm still in the middle of an investigation."

"Listen," said Theodosia, "what I really called about . . . did Jory give you those files?"

"He passed them on to me last evening," said Tidwell. "And I assume your sticky little fingers have been all through them?"

"I took a look, yes," said Theodosia. She paused. "What did you make of the love note?"

"Love note," said Tidwell.

Theodosia sighed. "The one that said something like *Loving you more each day.*"

"I'd say her husband was very much in love with her," replied Tidwell.

"What if . . . what if that note wasn't written by her husband?" asked Theodosia.

"That's a startling accusation," said Tidwell. "Did you just come up with that on the spur of the moment?"

"Kind of," admitted Theodosia. "Just take a look at the note again, will you? It's hard to tell what that initial is. If it's signed with a D or a G or an F."

"Mmm," said Tidwell, being noncommittal.

"Oh, and I also think you should ask Drew if the cameo Abby wore last night was a present from him. I'm wondering why a man who gave his wife gifts of Bulgari and Cartier jewelry would revert back to giving her costume jewelry."

"Now you're asking about a cameo?" said a surprised Tidwell. "You think her *jewelry* is important?"

"It might be," said Theodosia.

"The one that was pinned at her throat," said Tidwell. "The one she'll be buried with."

"Um . . . yes," said Theodosia, feeling a huge twinge of guilt. "I think it was purchased from that shop on King Street. Vianello."

"You think Abby Davis was having an affair?" Tidwell asked, bluntly.

"With the owner of Vianello?" said Theodosia, startled. "I . . . wasn't looking at it from that perspective. And I don't know of any evidence that points to it. No relationship with another man or any other unusual behavior."

"There is unusual behavior . . ." muttered Tidwell.

"What?" asked Theodosia, pouncing on his words.

"Abby Davis's toxicology report just came across my desk and it turns out she had a taste for cocaine."

"Are you serious?" Theodosia was shocked at first. Then, as Tidwell's words set in, she could see it. Abby had seemed to enjoy life on the edge.

"You know anything about that?" asked Tidwell.

"No," said Theodosia. "Of course not." She paused. "Who would have turned her on to drugs? Friends? People at Trident Media?"

"No idea," said Tidwell. "But it's going to be a tough conversation with her husband."

"I can imagine," replied Theodosia. She thought about the cocaine angle, which had just reared its head unexpectedly, as well as the cameo. She wasn't sure how to pursue the drug thing, but she had a good idea how to find out more about the jewelry.

She hung up quickly and dialed the number for Heart's Desire.

Brooke Carter Crockett, the fifty-something dynamo who was the proprietor of Heart's Desire, the premier jewelry store in the historic district, wasn't there. Her answering service rolled the call over to Brooke's cell phone. Turns out she was down in Savannah, doing an appraisal.

"I'm having a very boring afternoon," Brooke told Theodosia. "A dealer, who for now shall remain unnamed, wants a rush-rush appraisal on a mishmash of sterling silver flatware he's putting up for sale."

"That sounds like fun," said Theodosia. "Anything I might like?"

"Maybe a few pieces," said Brooke. "Some Narcissus by Durgin and a couple of spoons by Frank Whiting. But that's about it. No killer pieces. On the bright side, I brought along a small tin of that Keemun tea Drayton gave me. Lovely orchid flavor. It's the only thing that's keeping me sane."

"How long will you be in Savannah?" asked Theodosia. "I was thinking of making a trip down there myself to pick up some YiXing teapots."

"I'm planning to be back Friday," said Brooke.

"I wanted you to take a quick look at something," said Theodosia. "But it can wait."

"Well, I'll be back in time for Timothy's party. Wouldn't miss that for the world."

"Drayton's all keyed up about that, too," said Theodosia.

"How *is* my favorite tea blender?" Brooke laughed.

"The customers can't get enough of him." Theodosia chuckled. "He had a table of women in stitches today, going on about the old English superstition that bubbles floating in your tea predict romance."

"I've never heard that one before," said Brooke.

"Oh yeah," said Theodosia. "And if you get a swirling froth in the middle of your teacup, then it means riches."

"Wait a minute," said Brooke. "I'm looking into my cup now. Hmm. Nothing."

"Oh well," said Theodosia. "You know those old superstitions."

Drayton was pushing a broom across the pegged floor and Theodosia and Haley were stacking white bakery boxes filled with fresh-baked scones when Miss Josette tap-tapped at the front door.

"It's open," called Haley, then ran coltishly over to tug the door open for her.

She was greeted by a stack of sweetgrass baskets. "Gadzooks," said Haley. "More baskets."

Miss Josette's amused face peered around her stack. "You still want 'em, don't you?"

"Of course we do," said Theodosia, hurrying over to greet her. "Can I help carry them in?"

Stepping across the threshold, Miss Josette turned her head and nodded at a young African American man who was following closely behind her. "My nephew Dexter's got the rest. He drove me today," she explained.

Dexter was tall, thin, and athletic-looking. Moving with ease, he deposited the stack of baskets on one of the empty tables. "This okay?" he asked.

"Perfect," declared Theodosia.

Then before complete introductions could be made, Delaine came charging in. She headed for her boxes of scones, swerved, and changed course when she spotted the baskets.

"Good heavens!" she shrilled. "Sweetgrass baskets? I think I've just died and gone to heaven!" She snatched the top basket from Dexter's pile and held it up. "This basket is gorgeous, simply gorgeous."

"Thank you," said Dexter.

"You're the artist?" asked Delaine.

Dexter nodded at Miss Josette. "My aunt Josette made it."

"Miss Josette," said Drayton, helpfully.

Delaine began her immediate appeal. "Miss Josette, I realize these baskets are intended for Theodosia. But I would love . . . no, I would simply *adore* getting a few of your sweetgrass baskets for my shop."

"Delaine owns a clothing store," Haley pointed out as Theodosia and Drayton watched in amusement as Delaine continued to go gaga over the baskets.

"This flat one would be perfect for silk scarves," trilled Delaine. "And this circular one is ideal for long strands of opera pearls." Now Delaine turned toward Theodosia, a look of sublime need on her face. "Theo, dear, you don't have to have every *single* basket, do you? You see, I have a very pressing need since I've taken additional space and am trying to decorate in a very Charleston-inspired spirit." She finally paused to take a breath. "And these sweetgrass baskets would lend such artistry and authenticity."

"I'm sure we can work something out," Theodosia assured her. "And I'm positive Miss Josette won't mind having another customer."

"Don't mind at all," said Miss Josette with a brisk nod.

"Thank you," said Delaine, surprising Miss Josette with a quick hug accompanied by double air kisses.

Then, as if he was afraid of being peppered with air kisses himself, Dexter said, "Want me to carry this bakery stuff out to your car?"

"Would you?" squealed Delaine. "Thank you!" She grinned at Drayton. "Don't you just love a fortuitous turn of events?"

"Kismet," Drayton told her, his eyes dancing with mirth.

"Miss Josette," said Theodosia, changing the subject. "You live out on Yonges Island, don't you?"

"Sure do," replied Miss Josette.

"What can you tell us about the old Mobley Plantation?"

Miss Josette suddenly looked unsettled. "Why do you want to know about that crazy place?"

Theodosia shot a quick glance at Drayton. "It's just that we were acquainted with the woman who inherited it."

"Then she might have inherited a passel of bad luck," said Miss Josette.

"Well," said Delaine, squinting, "she's dead now. That's pretty unlucky."

"What's the deal with that place, anyway?" asked Haley, suddenly looking intrigued. Sometimes Haley was as voracious as Delaine when it came to crazy stories.

Miss Josette looked reluctant, but said, "There's kind of a bad story attached to that place."

"You mean like a legend?" asked Delaine. Her eyes suddenly lit up. She really was an avid fan of local legends and tales, especially the spooky ones.

Miss Josette nodded. "That's right. But not a pretty legend. More like a ghost story."

"That's what Jory Davis called it, too," murmured Theodosia.

"Tell us," urged Delaine.

"Yeah," said Haley.

So, of course, they all settled around a table and Drayton poured a round of tea.

"This ghost story goes back a long way," began Miss Josette. "To about 1910. Almost a hundred years."

They all leaned in, almost as though they were huddling around a crackling campfire, listening to scary stories.

"There was a wedding held on that old plantation," said Miss Josette. "Nothing fancy, just friends and neighbors dressed in their Sunday best come to watch the local preacher read the vows. Back then, weddings, especially country weddings, weren't such elaborate affairs as they are now. Anyway, the happy couple said their 'I do's' and then everyone settled in for a nice picnic lunch. After a while, a couple jugs of 'shine got passed around and everybody started feeling a might frisky.

So the best man proposed a game of hide-and-seek. The new bride was elected as the first person to go and hide. Anyway, off she scampered in her pretty white lace dress while everybody sat around on the lawn and counted to one hundred.

"Then a funny thing happened," said Miss Josette. "Everybody went searching for that bride, but nobody could find her. They looked high and low, inside that house and all through the nearby woods. Still no one could catch a glimpse of her. An hour goes by. Two hours. Four hours. Still nobody could find her."

"Wow," whispered Haley, completely caught up in the tale.

"Did they really, truly look for her?" asked Delaine. "I mean, did they tromp through the woods? Did they send out a real search party?"

Miss Josette nodded sadly. "Oh, honey, those folks looked everywhere. Sent two dozen men and a pack of those bloodhound tracking dogs deep into the woods."

"And they *still* couldn't find the bride?" asked Drayton. Even he was caught up in the story.

"That poor groom combed the woods and swamps for five full days before he finally gave up," said Miss Josette. "They say he was half-crazed with grief. I think his family might have eventually confined him to the state sanitarium he ended up in such a sorry state."

"So what do they think happened?" asked Theodosia. She figured there had to be a logical explanation. All folktales and ghosts stories were rooted in some fact, weren't they?

"In the end," said Miss Josette, "everyone pretty much resigned themselves to the fact that the bride got cold feet and simply ran away. Changed her mind about being married. She wasn't from around here, so they all figured she just some-how made her way back to her own people."

Delaine pursed her lips and frowned. "That's so sad."

"Think she made it home okay?" asked Haley.

"Probably she was just fine," said Drayton. "Just changed her mind."

Delaine glanced sideways at Theodosia and jabbed her sharply with an elbow. "Sounds like someone *we* know," she whispered. "Another case of cold feet."

Theodosia thought about Delaine's words for a few mo-ments. She knew Delaine was making a direct reference to Jory Davis. And the fact that a couple of years ago, he'd moved to New York without her.

No, Theodosia decided. Jory hadn't gotten spooked. He hadn't gotten cold feet and dashed for home like the runaway bride. His actions had been even stranger, even more unex-plainable. He'd simply slipped away from her.

13

Fat, grinning pumpkins squatted on the curving wooden staircase that led to the expansive veranda of the Bentley House on Tradd Street. On that veranda, lit with glowing lamps and flickering candles, a bevy of young women wearing southern belle hoop skirt dresses of pink, blue, and green organza greeted visitors and handed out colorful brochures.

"Thank you," said Drayton, accepting one of the brochures. He squinted at the fine print, then finally relented and pulled his tortoiseshell half-glasses from his jacket pocket. "Built in 1824," he murmured, "by Ebenezer Bentley, who was an indigo merchant by trade. According to the local . . ."

"Drayton." Theodosia touched his arm gently. "What if we went inside and looked around first? Then, if we want to glean any historical facts, we can always refer to the brochure."

"Oh." Drayton's head jerked up. "If that's your preferred

methodology, then fine. We'll step inside." He held the door open for Theodosia and she slipped through.

"Drayton," she said, pausing in a cherry-paneled entry hall, "I didn't mean to turn your world upside down. If you want to stand here and read the brochure . . ."

"No, no," said Drayton, propelling her forward. "Far be it from me to hinder the progress of our tour."

"Now you're humoring me," said Theodosia.

"Not in the least," said Drayton, as they dodged a group of visitors. "I'm indulging you. Here now, let's step this way into the dining room. See what lovely things, if any, are on display."

The dining room featured tall, narrow windows hung with white silk draperies, walls painted a Williamsburg green, and a lovely English mahogany dining table set.

"My goodness," said Theodosia, gazing into a glass-paned china cabinet. "They have a set of Pink Dragon dinnerware."

Drayton stepped closer. "Crafted by Meissen in the 1850s, yes." He scanned the dishes for a few moments. "Fairly rare. Mmm, but not a *complete* set."

"You can count that quickly?" asked Theodosia.

"I'm a detail person," Drayton replied. "Details intrigue me. What say we move along to the main parlor and library?"

The parlor of the Bentley House was glorious. Peach-colored plaster walls with carved cornice moldings in a pale eggshell color. Louis XV chairs and a settee covered with grospoint. A French decoupage screen with capering Chinese figures. The carved marble fireplace featured fanciful colonettes, classic festoons, and a scene that detailed Greek gods and goddesses.

"Love that fireplace," remarked Drayton.

Theodosia murmured in agreement, although, to her eyes, it reminded her a little of the carved figure on Abby Davis's cameo.

"Hello!" came Delaine's chirpy voice.

Theodosia and Drayton turned in unison to find Delaine Dish speeding across the dark-blue-and-cinnamon-colored Chinese carpet toward them. Dressed in a pale peach suit with gold buttons, cream stilettos on her feet, she seemed to coordinate perfectly with the room's interior.

"I didn't think we'd see you here," said Drayton.

"That's a fine greeting," said Delaine, giving a slight pout. "Especially since I'm chairman of the Tradd Street tour."

"Of course," said Drayton. "Silly me."

"It's a lot of work!" protested Delaine. "Especially since we have six homes open over the course of three nights."

"Do you put in appearances at all six homes?" asked Drayton.

"Sometimes," said Delaine. "Depends on how busy I get or if any problems come up. Last night, at the Atkins House, we had some disturbed cats."

"Too much catnip?" inquired Drayton.

Delaine, who was a serious cat lover, hastened to set the record straight. "I didn't mean to imply there was anything *wrong* with the cats. Rather, that a couple of overzealous guests ventured beyond the velvet rope boundary and disturbed the owners' cats. Tabby cats," she added. "Darling creatures."

"We were just going to peek in the library," Theodosia told Delaine, trying to edge forward.

"I'll tag along," said Delaine.

The library was expansive, paneled in native cypress, and filled floor to ceiling with books.

"Heaven." Drayton sighed. Then, a pair of Audubon prints hanging over a massive marble fireplace caught his learned eye and he was off to inspect them.

Delaine gave an inquisitive cock of her head at Theodosia. "I really enjoyed Miss Josette's ghost story today."

"From the . . . what would you call it? . . . conviction in her voice, it almost sounded authentic," Theodosia replied.

"Didn't it just?" said Delaine. She eased a notch closer to Theodosia. "You see, that's why I think it'd be great fun if we paid that place a little visit."

"The Mobley Plantation," said Theodosia.

Delaine nodded, and her diamond earrings glinted as brightly as her violet eyes. "Yup."

"You really want to go out there?" asked Theodosia. For some reason she wasn't all that interested. Figured the answers to Abby's murder lay in the present, not the past.

"Sure," said Delaine. "I think it might be a kick. Besides, where's your sense of adventure?"

"Back home in my sock drawer." Theodosia laughed.

"That's exactly my point, Theo," continued Delaine. "You need to put a little crazy back in your life."

"My life *is* crazy," said Theodosia. She thought about the conversation she was probably going to have with Jory about Abby's cocaine use. Dreaded it.

"Not work crazy," said Delaine. "Experience crazy. You know, like impromptu trips or trying new restaurants or learning to tap dance." She glanced sideways at Theodosia. "Or dating two men at once."

Theodosia held her smile. This was slightly dangerous territory.

"You'll be attending the funeral tomorrow?" Delaine asked.

Theodosia nodded. Abby Davis's funeral was scheduled for nine o'clock at Grace Episcopal Church.

"Why don't we take a run out there afterward?"

"Afterward I have to serve lunch at the Indigo Tea Shop," said Theodosia.

"Then after that," pressed Delaine.

"Let me think about it," said Theodosia.

"Know what your problem is?" asked Delaine. "Sometimes you think too much instead of just *doing*."

"*Do you think* I'm too serious?" Theodosia asked Drayton some twenty minutes later. They'd finished touring the Bentley House and were seated at a wobbly wrought-iron table on the back patio, sipping so-so tea and nibbling sugar cookies. Unfortunately, Haley's scones seemed to have long since disappeared. Or maybe Delaine had dispersed them to one of the other houses on the tour.

"You're asking me?" said Drayton. "I'm the one who's always accused of being solemn verging on somber."

"You do project a certain gravitas," Theodosia told him, but in a friendly way.

Drayton brightened. "I do? That's awfully good to know."

"You're one of a kind, Drayton." Theodosia gazed across the patio at the three-tiered fountain that pattered away merrily in the center of the courtyard garden. Surrounding the fountain was a wide circle of greenery and around that were three curved stone benches. Probably, she decided, when spring came calling, this place was a riot of color, filled with songbirds, butterflies, and thousands of blooms. A hidden Charleston garden, as so many of them were, seen only by the eyes of the family who lived here.

"Can I refresh your tea, sir?" asked a waiter who'd finally circled back to their table.

Drayton frowned. He hadn't really touched his tea. "What kind of tea is this?"

"Not sure," said the waiter. "Maybe . . . Chinese?"

"It does taste a little like the dregs of the Yangtze River," said Drayton.

"Perhaps you'd rather have lemonade?" asked the waiter. "Or a glass of white wine?"

"Is the wine cork finished or did someone truck it down from New Jersey in a large tanker?"

"Sir?" said the waiter.

"Bring him a glass of lemonade," Theodosia said pleasantly. "In fact, make it two lemonades."

"Very good," said the waiter.

"Doubtful," Drayton muttered as the young man beat a hasty retreat. He pulled the crumpled brochure from his jacket pocket. "Are you up for a visit to the Eddington House?" he asked. "It's just down the street and we've still got time." He checked his watch, an ancient Piaget that perpetually ran ten minutes slow. "I *think* we've got time. There are a couple of other homes listed as well." He flipped through the brochure.

"Wasn't the Eddington House on the tour two years ago?" asked Theodosia. "Haven't we already been inside?"

Drayton closed his eyes and tilted his head back. "Front room is a curved bay with Palladian windows?" he asked. "Hideously painted portrait of the owner's great-great-grandmother over the fireplace?"

"That's the place," said Theodosia.

"And every bedroom has a four-poster bed swathed in flounces," said Drayton. He watched silently as the waiter placed two tall glasses of lemonade in front of them, then cleared away their teacups. "I detest flounces."

"You'll get no argument from me," said Theodosia.

Drayton took a sip of lemonade, made a face. "Remember when we catered one of these affairs? Which one was it exactly? The Church Street tour?"

"That was it," said Theodosia. She was finding the lemonade rather tasty.

"People adored our tea selections," said Drayton. "Gave us compliments galore. And, of course, we served far better cookies and madeleines. Made from real butter and eggs, not the prepared mixes so many bakeries rely on these days."

"The world could certainly use your brand of quality control," Theodosia told Drayton. She barely managed to keep a straight face.

"You laugh," said Drayton. "But just wait until someone comes up with take-out tea."

"They already have," said Theodosia. "It's just not very good."

"Wait until there are ten thousand tea franchises nationwide," warned Drayton. "Silly places with insulting names like Teastar or Teabiddies."

"Heaven forbid," said Theodosia.

"*Want me to* play the gentleman and walk you home?" asked Drayton. They were standing on the front veranda of the Bentley House. Candles burned low, the giggling girls had disappeared. Down on the front sidewalk, visitors strolled slowly through the dark warmth of the night, their voices soft drawls upon a gentle breeze.

Theodosia turned and put a hand on Drayton's arm. "Drayton . . ."

"Yes?"

"I have a favor to ask." Theodosia waited a few seconds, then said, "Would you go by the Old Exchange and Provost Dungeon with me?"

Even in the darkness, Theodosia could see that her request surprised Drayton.

"Why on earth would you want to go there?" he asked. "Don't tell me that place is open for tours at night?"

How much to tell him? Theodosia wondered. Then decided she had to spill the whole thing. It was only fair. "When I visited Timothy yesterday, he kind of let slip that the Peninsula Club met in the Provost Dungeon on Wednesday nights."

"They do? Down *there?*" The Provost Dungeon was a dark, damp dungeon located beneath the historic Old Exchange Building. It dated back to the late 1700s when local citizens were held by the British and questioned about their politics and loyalty to the crown. Over the years, visitors who'd descended into the depths of the Provost Dungeon often emerged with tales of ghostly specters and strange noises. Of course, the dungeon's barrel-vaulted ceiling, arched columns still hung with chains and manacles, spooky hidey-holes, seeping groundwater, and tales of torture just added to the growing myth of that rather loathsome, oppressive place. The Provost Dungeon had even been featured on the Travel Channel's *America's Most Haunted Places.*

"Apparently the Peninsula Club has scored a special pass to hold meetings there," said Theodosia. "I imagine one of the club members is on the board of directors or happens to be a big-buck donor."

"Hmm," said Drayton.

"That's not an answer," said Theodosia. "It's commentary."

"Hmm," Drayton repeated.

"Is that a yes or a no?" asked Theodosia.

Drayton exhaled loudly. "Consider it a cautious yes."

"Excellent," said Theodosia.

But when they got there, all was dark. The three-story Old Exchange with its classical Palladian architecture showed no sign of any meeting going on.

"You see," said Drayton. "Nothing. Sorry to disappoint you, but there's no secret society convening in spooky darkness." He spun on his heels, ready to leave. "No sense hanging around here when I could be home reading Milton or Shelley."

"Not so fast," said Theodosia. "We didn't even try the door."

"It's locked," said Drayton impassively. "Trust me."

"I meant the back door," said Theodosia. She struck off around the side of the building, slipping down a brick path that was shadowed and hidden by a dense tangle of magnolias.

"What?" said Drayton, following reluctantly. "You have a vibe? Some sort of inkling?"

"Not really," said Theodosia, as she made her way cautiously through the darkness. "It's just that we're here."

"No lights back here, either," Drayton grunted.

Theodosia paused when she reached a large wooden door hidden in shadows. "Shh," she told him. She pressed her hand against the rough boards, then slid it down to the wrought-iron handle. Grasping the handle, she gave a pull. Nothing. The door didn't budge.

"See?" whispered Drayton. "Now can we please . . . ?"

Theodosia hesitated, then turned the handle to the right. Was rewarded with a soft click. Now she pulled down on the tricky door handle and, wonder of wonders, the wooden door yawned open with a low creak.

"Rats," said Drayton as Theodosia slipped inside.

She hesitated, poked her head back out. "You coming?"

"Yes, yes," muttered Drayton.

"Be careful," said Theodosia, still whispering. "There are steps here and they're very steep." They tiptoed down a curving stairway as damp stone walls closed in ominously. "And dark."

"I don't like this at all," said Drayton.

"I think it's kind of exciting," Theodosia whispered back as they continued their descent.

"Please," said Drayton.

Rounding the final turn, they emerged into a dimly lit corridor.

"A few lights, thankfully," said Drayton. There were lights, but they were of the five-watt variety and set at ankle level. Not particularly helpful.

"What's that?" asked Theodosia. She had taken a few steps forward and was pointing at a pit of shimmering water just off to their right. It looked nasty and deep, reflecting an eerie blue.

"Groundwater seeping in," said Drayton. "And notice that weird blue cast? It's from when indigo was stored down here."

"Creepy," said Theodosia.

"You know," said Drayton, "people have been known to see orbs in this place."

Theodosia lifted an eyebrow. "Orbs?"

Drayton seemed suddenly exasperated. "Yes, you know, orbs. Small, dancing circles of light."

"Drayton," said Theodosia, "you of all people do not believe in the spirit world."

"But I believe my eyes. And I've seen actual photos."

Theodosia let her eyes rove around the dungeon. She took in the low arches, dangling chains and manacles, small coves cut into bricks. And something else . . .

"What the . . . ?" sputtered Theodosia. Could it be? Grasping Drayton's arm, she whispered in a hoarse voice, "Drayton, I think there's someone standing over there!"

14

❧

Drayton jerked nervously. "What? Where?"

"Straight ahead of us," said Theodosia. "Maybe . . . twenty feet?" She could just barely make out a shadowy figure.

"Oh my," said Drayton, a note of panic rising in his voice. "And I see another person just beyond him."

Theodosia clutched Drayton's arm. "Peninsula Club members? They heard us coming?" They stood there whispering for a few seconds, staring at the two figures, trying to figure out what to do. How to handle the situation.

"They're not moving," Drayton said finally.

"What are they waiting for?" whispered Theodosia. She could feel her heart pounding wildly inside her chest, figured that any minute the two figures would lurch toward them, intent on chasing them away.

"I don't know what's going on," Drayton whispered back.

They gave it another minute, then Theodosia tiptoed slowly forward.

"Wait!" called Drayton. But, of course, she didn't.

Stepping quietly, mustering all her courage, Theodosia approached the first figure. She stared at it for a few seconds, then reached a hand out tentatively, let her fingertips brush across rough cotton. Finally she called, "Drayton!"

"What?" He seemed rooted to the spot where he stood.

"They're mannequins. It's a display."

That broke his trance. "What?" His voice rose in a high-pitched squawk. There was a rustle of footsteps, then suddenly he was standing beside her.

"It's some sort of historical display," Theodosia repeated. "Look. This one's in manacles. And this other poor fellow . . ." She gestured toward the other figure, clad in rags. "He's chained to the wall and his feet are . . . well, never mind."

"Depicting the horrors of dungeon life in Colonial times," said Drayton, peering at the re-creation. "We should have guessed there was some sort of exhibit down here."

"Disappointing," said Theodosia.

"You were expecting . . . ?" began Drayton. Then he stopped abruptly as a low noise suddenly resonated within the room.

"What's that?" asked Theodosia, still jumpy.

"I don't think it's supposed to be part of the display," whispered Drayton. "This isn't exactly Disneyland and these poor devils in chains are not animatronic."

"You think the Peninsula Club?" asked Theodosia, a hopeful note rising in her voice.

They crept forward, soundlessly, toward a low arched doorway.

"They *are* here," whispered Theodosia.

"The question is," said Drayton, "what are they doing?"

Theodosia motioned to Drayton and crept forward a few more feet. When she reached the doorway, she placed a hand on the damp stone, and slowly, ever so slowly, like a soldier peering out from a foxhole, eased her head a few inches forward. Just to get a glimpse.

A glimpse was all she needed. She sprang back, grabbed Drayton's sleeve, and tugged him backward.

He mouthed, *What?* She shook her head.

Slowly, trying to be as quiet as possible, they eased their way back to the stone staircase and ascended it quickly.

"What did you see?" asked Drayton, once they were safely outside. He sounded both fearful and curious.

"I don't know if they were talking or chanting," said Theodosia, "but they were wearing robes."

"Robes?" said Drayton.

"Red robes," said Theodosia. "With hoods." She looked up at the sky for reassurance. Was rewarded with a view of blue-black sky and a sprinkle of bright stars.

"How bizarre," murmured Drayton.

"They really *did* look like a secret society," said Theodosia, still feeling a little shaken by their adventure. "And why do you suppose they were wearing robes? That part kind of creeped me out."

Drayton shrugged. "Tradition? Suits at the dry cleaners? I don't know. You'd have to ask them."

They trod, single file, around to the front of the building and crossed the street to where a number of nicer cars were parked. Theodosia realized now that these BMW, Mercedes, and Lexus vehicles probably belonged to the red-robed members inside. The Peninsula Club.

"What did you just say before?" Theodosia asked Drayton.

He glanced upward, scratched his head. "I said, uh, you'd have to ask them."

"Then that's what we're going to do."

"Oh, I don't think so," said Drayton, frowning. "Sounds like a very bad idea."

"C'mon, Drayton, we gotta stick around," coaxed Theodosia. "In for a penny, in for a pound, right?"

Drayton's only answer was a deep sigh.

They didn't have to wait long. Ten minutes later, men began to emerge from the back of the building. As they eased their way furtively toward their vehicles, Theodosia and Drayton crouched in a thicket of dogwood.

When a man with a thatch of white hair headed directly for them, Theodosia gave a start of recognition. She knew this person. Or thought she did. Or at least *recognized* him. Wait a minute, she thought, could that be . . .

Truman McBee?

Theodosia studied him carefully. Yes, he looked pretty much the same as the man she'd just seen in Abby Davis's file of newspaper clippings.

Theodosia nudged Drayton. "Truman McBee," she whispered.

Drayton caught on right away. "The one Abby was writing about? The man whose son was kidnapped?"

Theodosia bobbed her head.

As Truman McBee headed for a large, dark car, maybe a Cadillac or Lincoln Continental, Theodosia stepped directly out in front of him. A deliberate ambush. Drayton followed.

Truman McBee threw up his hands as if to shield himself,

as if he feared he was being mugged. "Who are you?" he cried in a painfully shrill voice. "What do you want?"

"Mr. McBee," said Theodosia, extending a hand, hoping to reassure him, "I mean no harm. I only want to ask a few questions."

He peered at her. "You're a reporter?" He sounded only slightly less fearful.

"No," she said. "I'm Theodosia Browning and this is my associate, Drayton Conneley."

"Hello," said Drayton. He seemed bemused by their bizarrely staged encounter.

"What do you want?" asked McBee.

"We're helping investigate the death of Abby Davis," explained Theodosia.

Now Truman McBee just looked confused. "The reporter who was shot?"

"Exactly," said Theodosia. "We know Abby had been working on a story about you and the, uh, the abduction of your son, Travis."

"You're working with the police?" A hint of pain flickered in Truman McBee's eyes.

"In a manner of speaking," Theodosia replied.

"Let me see your identification," he demanded.

"Show him your ID," Theodosia instructed Drayton.

Drayton blinked. "What?"

"Your ID," snapped Theodosia. "Mr. McBee is quite correct. We should properly identify ourselves."

"By all means," said Drayton as he fumbled in his jacket pocket. He pulled out a brown leather wallet and sifted through a half dozen cards that were stashed in a hidden pocket. Plucking out a single plastic-coated card, Drayton flashed it in front of Truman McBee's frightened eyes, then, just as quickly, slid it back in his wallet.

Theodosia jumped in immediately to begin her line of questioning. "I understand Abby Davis did several stories concerning your son's disappearance. First, when she was a reporter in Savannah. And also as an investigative reporter at Channel Eight here in Charleston. At Trident Media."

"Please," said McBee, taking a step back. "That woman made my life a living hell when my son was kidnapped."

"I'm sure she was just trying to cover all sides of the story," said Theodosia briskly. "Oftentimes, when you get enough of a press furor going, cases such as yours are more easily solved. The public takes a special interest and pitches in to help."

"We tried to get the public to help," said McBee. "I even offered a million-dollar reward for any information leading to my son's return."

"You must have received *some* leads," pressed Theodosia.

"You *are* a reporter," said McBee, as his face dissolved into a look of unrelenting sadness. "Please, can't you people just leave me alone?" He turned, almost stumbled, then fled down the dark street.

"Mr. McBee . . ." Theodosia called after him. But he had already jumped into his car and locked the doors.

"That went well," said Drayton, as McBee's car roared to life.

"Boy, he's jumpy," said Theodosia.

"Maybe he's afraid the kidnappers will come after *him*," said Drayton.

Theodosia turned to meet Drayton's solemn gaze. "Oh my gosh! That never occurred to me. Now I feel guilty. No wonder the poor man was terrified."

As Drayton stared after Truman McBee's disappearing

taillights, he seemed to be turning something over in his head. "You know what?" he said slowly. "I think Truman Mc-Bee's house is on the Lamplighter Tour tomorrow night."

"Are you serious?"

Drayton pulled out his brochure, scanned it under the wavering, yellow glow of an old-fashioned gas lamp. He tapped the brochure with an index finger. "Yes, here it is."

"Then maybe we should pay him a visit," suggested Theodosia.

"Maybe we should leave him alone," said Drayton. "Poor man, I felt terrible accosting him like that. For a millisecond there, he actually thought we were with the police."

"What card did you show him?" asked Theodosia.

Drayton managed a semi-sheepish grin. "My membership card for the Southern States Tea Society."

At two a.m. Theodosia came awake hard. "What?" she said in a strangled voice, sitting up in bed.

The phone on her bedside table was jangling loudly.

She snatched the receiver off the hook. "Hello?"

"Theo." It was Haley, whispering and sounding breathless. "There's somebody creeping around outside in the alley."

"Huh?" Theodosia swung her legs over the side of the bed, stumbled a couple of steps to her window, and stared down. "I don't see anybody." She pressed her forehead against the cool of the glass.

"I didn't see anybody, either," said Haley, "but I heard them. Heard gravel crunching."

"Somebody walking by," said Theodosia.

"I'm pretty sure they stopped right outside your back door," said Haley.

"Uh . . . really?" said Theodosia. This might be something after all.

"Anyway," said Haley, "you've got a better vantage point up on the second floor."

"I'm looking," said Theodosia, peering down into the alley. "But I don't see . . . wait a minute!" She stared, blinked, stared harder. "There *is* somebody down there. Kind of creeping and shuffling around."

"Should I call 9-1-1?" asked Haley.

"They haven't done anything yet," said Theodosia.

"Loitering?" asked Haley.

"This is Charleston," said Theodosia. "Everybody moves slow."

"What if they crawl through the hedge into my garden?" asked Haley. "Throw a brick through my glass doors?"

"No," said Theodosia, keeping her eyes on the shadowy figure. "They're moving away now."

"Think they'll be back?"

"Probably not," said Theodosia. "But I could call the precinct station and ask them to send a squad car through the alley if it would make you feel any better."

"Please," said Haley, still sounding frightened. "Do that, would you?"

So of course Theodosia couldn't fall back asleep. Sighing deeply, she slipped into her robe, padded into her living room, and glanced around. Her eyes fell upon the stack of papers that sat on her dining room table. Copies she'd made of some of the pages in Abby's file. She walked over and touched them with her fingertips for a few seconds as if she could glean some answers from those pages. Finally, she turned on a small lamp and sat down at the table.

She reread the *Loving you forever* note that was signed D. For Drew. Or was it? She squinted at the initial again. Could it be a P? A D and a P scrawled in loopy script could look very similar. Of course, so did a J and a G.

Was Drew saying *Loving you forever* or was it someone else? Good question.

Pushing that note aside, Theodosia looked at the copies she'd made of Abby's contract. Well, not really a contract per se, because that was probably twenty pages. What she'd photocopied was more a letter of agreement from Trident Media.

As she scanned that letter, Theodosia let loose a low whistle. It would appear Abby's New York agent, a woman by the name of Mildred Sharp, had negotiated a whopper of a deal for Abby. Two and a half million dollars over three years. With one million dollars paid up front.

Theodosia looked up and stared out her small dormer into the dark night. Turned her head from side to side, trying to get the kinks out of her neck. That was a lot of serious money on the table. Someone at Trident Media could have been jealous, changed their mind about Abby, or just been seriously enraged.

Or maybe the money and the murder were just a coincidence. But somehow, Theodosia didn't think so. In her experience, money and murder usually went hand in hand.

15

✦

The Gothic steeple of Grace Episcopal Church thrust high above Charleston, joining the dozens of churches, synagogues, and temples that dominated Charleston's skyline, earning it the moniker of Holy City.

Abby Davis's funeral had drawn an impressively large crowd this Thursday morning. There was her family, of course. The same group of sad-eyed relatives she'd met the other night. And pretty much everyone from Trident Media. And a few curiosity seekers. People who'd watched Abby on their television screens, been a small part of her life, and now wanted to be part of her death, too.

The first thing Theodosia did when she arrived at Grace Episcopal was check the guest book set up on a wooden podium at the back of the church. She was curious if someone had signed it with a flowery D or a G or a J.

They hadn't.

Tiptoeing down the center aisle, she took a seat midway down.

The minute Theodosia sat down, the organist launched into the haunting strains of Grieg's *Album Leaf*. There was a quick whisper of footsteps, then a tall man in a black three-piece suit strode down the aisle. Theodosia recognized him as a funeral director, one of the Rafferty brothers from the visitation the other night.

People stood, shuffled, and craned their necks as Abby's casket was wheeled down the center aisle. A young woman walked ahead of it, strewing white flower petals from a basket.

Strange, thought Theodosia, she'd never seen that before. Although, more and more, people were integrating new rituals into their funeral services. Releasing butterflies, blowing bubbles, videotaping the service.

When the casket reached the front of the church, it was turned and placed crosswise. Then the minister, dressed in his black suit with a white notched collar, emerged from the back.

He spoke eloquently and gave heartfelt praise to Abby. Talked about how she'd been a prominent media personality, how she'd brought her bright personality as well as her balanced interpretation of the news into the homes of viewers. Mentioned that Abby had served as a board member for South Carolina Women in Media.

Then it was Linus Gillette's turn. He gave a five-minute eulogy about Abby, acknowledging the fact she'd been a key player in their TV station's success.

Kind words, thought Theodosia. Even though Abby hadn't been at Trident Media all that long.

But the truly heartbreaking testimonial was the one Jory

gave. Tears glistening on his cheeks, he spoke about what a wonderful sister Abby had been. Recalled their youth together, sailing Hobie Cats and spending summers on Kiawah Island.

Jory's words were sad and touching. And almost made Theodosia forget how hateful Abby Davis had been to her on the few occasions they'd met.

That was then and this was now, she decided. Time to abandon old resentments. Nothing was ever gained by holding a grudge.

The strains of a Chopin prelude echoed in the church as everyone bowed their heads in silent prayer. Then Drew Donovan rose from his seat at the front of the church. Filled with grief, his shoulders shaking with emotion, he placed a wreath of white calla lilies on his dead wife's bronze coffin.

And then the service was over, the funeral director wheeling her back down the aisle. Mourners stood, stretched surreptitiously, glanced about. A low hum of conversation filled the church.

Theodosia looked around, searching for familiar faces. And saw a few more than she'd bargained for.

Joe Fanning, Abby's news director was there, looking very matter-of-fact, talking to a young woman who'd been seated next to him.

In back of them, Julian Bruno was just slipping out of his pew. Frowning slightly, he avoided meeting Theodosia's gaze. *What's he doing here?* Theodosia wondered. *Had Abby been a good customer? A really good customer?*

Burt Tidwell sat in the far recess of the church. Arms crossed, head up, watching the mourners exit. When he noticed Theodosia noticing him, he waggled his fingers at her. She chose to ignore him for the time being.

Out on the sidewalk family mingled with guests. Jory saw her and immediately pulled her into the circle of family. "I'm so glad you came," he told her.

"Of course," Theodosia replied. "And my condolences, once again."

Jory took her hand, as if in greeting, then pressed a large brass key into it.

"What's this?" she asked.

Jory shrugged. "A couple of days ago you mentioned taking a look at the Mobley Plantation?" He shrugged again. "I doubt you'll find anything . . ." His smile seemed to fade on his face.

Then Drew was gripping her hand, thanking her profusely for being there today.

Blinking back tears, for everyone around her was highly emotional and the whole thing seemed contagious, Theodosia wished him well.

"And thank you for looking into things," Drew told her in a hoarse whisper.

Theodosia held up a hand in protest. "I haven't really."

Drew put a hand on her shoulder and peered at her earnestly. "You've given the police more than a few things to think about. For that I am eternally grateful." He cleared his throat. "And please believe this. Jory says only good things about you."

Theodosia smiled through her tears. "I believe you," she whispered.

Pulling away from the throng of family, Theodosia ran into Constance Brucato.

"Hello, Constance," said Theodosia. "I thought I might see you here today."

Constance gave a quick smile. "Had to be a good corporate foot soldier," she replied in an even voice. "Show the flag."

"I'm sure Abby's family appreciates it," said Theodosia. Of course they did. This large turnout of mourners had to offer some consolation. As the two of them fell into step alongside each other, Theodosia decided to feel Constance out about Abby's contract.

"I understand Abby had a very tough agent, a woman in New York by the name of Mildred Sharp."

Constance's sharp laugh sounded like a bark. "You mean 'The Shark'?"

Theodosia nodded. "Apparently this agent nailed a two-and-a-half-million-dollar contract for Abby? And that a million dollars was paid up front?"

"That's true," said Constance, "but if Abby didn't work out during her six-month probationary period as anchor, or left for any other reason, Linus would get his money back."

Theodosia's ears perked up. "Was Abby working out?"

Constance thought before she opened her mouth. "I *suppose* she was. There were a few snags. Some rough spots."

"And now that Abby's dead, Linus Gillette gets his money back," said Theodosia. "Or Trident Media's money anyway. Because Abby wasn't there the full six months."

"That's right," said Constance. "He gets every penny back."

Theodosia definitely wanted to hear more. But how to pull it out of Constance?

"You were Abby's producer for *Windows on Charleston*," said Theodosia, "before she became an evening anchor. I'm sure she didn't make your job all that easy."

Now Constance's eyes blazed and her voice fairly crackled. "Are you serious? Abby Davis was egotistical and demanding!

Never gave a person a semblance of a break! Even when you worked hard, tried to do a good job. Tried to book interesting guests!"

"And Abby had lots of extracurricular activities going on," said Theodosia. "Besides the show."

Constance frowned. "You mean the investigative reporting?"

"That," said Theodosia, "as well as Abby's . . . what would you call them? *Friendships?*" She took a stab in the dark.

Constance snorted in disdain. "Abby was plenty friendly with lots of men. Even some of the guests. Like that jewelry guy we had on a few months ago." Constance frowned again and craned her head around. "In fact, I just saw him here."

"You mean Julian Bruno?" asked Theodosia. *Had Abby been having an affair with Bruno? Had the love note been written by him?*

"Yeah," said Constance. "He was always calling her. Like four, five times a day."

"I guess they were really good friends," said Theodosia.

"Thick as thieves, if you ask me," said Constance.

When Theodosia saw Tidwell giving her the evil eye, she wandered over to him.

"Lovely service," said Tidwell. The edge of his lip curled slightly, as if belying his statement.

Theodosia looked askance at him. "You don't really mean that. You're only here to hunt for suspects."

"Isn't that why you're here?" asked Tidwell.

Theodosia chose to ignore his question. "Tell me about the kidnapping of Travis McBee."

Tidwell pursed his lips. "What's your interest in that?"

"Abby Davis was working the story. She'd been bugging Truman McBee, the father."

"From what I hear, she'd been bugging lots of people," said Tidwell.

"Were you on the case?" Theodosia asked. "I mean, when it first happened, a year ago?"

"Initially, yes," said Tidwell. "But by the second day the FBI had been called in." He rolled his eyes. "Not a lot of information shared once that happened. Not much brotherly love."

"Even though you're an ex-agent," said Theodosia.

He shrugged. "When I opted out, I was branded a traitor to their great gray mediocrity."

"But you kept up with the McBee case," Theodosia prodded.

"Somewhat," said Tidwell, and now his beady eyes took on a slightly distant look. "There were sightings of Travis McBee all over the place. Columbia, Beaufort, a plethora of sightings in Savannah. In fact, the investigation centered there for quite some time. Unfortunately, no conclusive evidence was ever found. In the end we chalked it all up to rumors. Started by people who were desperate to collect that reward money."

"So where do you think Travis McBee really is?" asked Theodosia.

Tidwell stared at her. "You want my honest opinion?"

Theodosia narrowed her eyes. "Please. I'm hanging on your every word."

"Probably in a shallow grave somewhere," said Tidwell. "Or dumped in a swamp where his bones have been picked clean by crawfish or blue crabs."

Theodosia grimaced. The crawfish image was downright nasty.

Tidwell noticed her expression and chuckled to himself. "You asked."

"I wish I hadn't," said Theodosia. Then, out of the corner of her eye, she suddenly noticed Julian Bruno again. She nudged Tidwell. "You see that fellow over there? Julian Bruno? He's the one I told you about. Abby's cameo probably came from his shop."

Tidwell gave a nod. "I'm way ahead of you. Per your suggestion, I spoke to him about the jewelry. Also, someone at the station mentioned him. Apparently he was a guest on one of Abby's shows and they hit it off immediately."

Theodosia nodded, asked the question she was suddenly noodling around. "Do you think the two of them might have been romantically involved?"

Tidwell shrugged. "When I talked to him yesterday afternoon, I broached the subject lightly. Bruno said no. A few people at Trident Media said . . . maybe."

"But he's not a suspect," said Theodosia.

"Julian Bruno was delivering a lecture on Edwardian jewelry at the Gibbes Museum when Abby Davis was murdered," said Tidwell. "Over fifty people attended; coffee and lemon bars were served afterward by zealous docents."

"Sounds like an airtight alibi," murmured Theodosia.

"It is," said Tidwell. "But you can grill him yourself if you'd like." Tidwell flapped a pudgy hand at Bruno. "In fact, be my guest."

Theodosia decided she would talk to Bruno. She dashed across the sidewalk, out into the street, and planted herself in front of him.

Julian Bruno lifted an eyebrow. "Something you wanted?" His voice carried a steely edge, a far cry from the friendliness he'd shown her yesterday morning. "Do I have you to thank for sending that lout of a detective to sniff around my shop like a dutiful bloodhound?"

"Detective Tidwell is a fine investigator." Theodosia hadn't been expecting this kind of hostility.

"Then he should investigate," said Bruno. "Instead of meddling."

Theodosia stared at Julian Bruno and decided there was something off about him. But, she couldn't quite put a finger on what it was. Bruno may possess an ironclad alibi for the day of Abby Davis's murder, but still, she felt a tingle of *something* going on.

Theodosia decided to make a bold move.

"Were you having an affair with Abby?" she asked. It wasn't like her to be so terribly blunt. But she wanted to see his reaction when cornered.

"I'm going to ignore that question," Bruno said, indignity seeping from every pore. "I'm going to pretend you didn't just try to poke your nose into my very private business."

"You seem awfully angry about something," Theodosia said softly. "Or, more likely, upset. I'm curious why that is."

"None of your business," he snapped.

"Oh, here you are!" cried a woman's voice.

Bruno's cool eyes gazed past Theodosia's shoulder. "Hello there," he said, his voice suddenly carrying an oily warmth. "We meet again."

Theodosia turned to find Delaine favoring Julian Bruno with a wide smile.

"You two know each other?" Theodosia asked.

"We're acquainted," said Delaine, eyeing Bruno coquett-ishly. "And I intend to pay a visit to Vianello and get even more acquainted."

"No," said Theodosia, physically pulling Delaine away from Bruno. "I don't think that's such a good idea."

"Whaaaa?" protested Delaine as she was tugged across the street against her will.

When they were a good twenty feet away, Theodosia hissed, "I don't think you want to be friendly with that man."

"Why ever not?" asked Delaine, all wide-eyed and pretend-innocent.

"Because he's hiding something," was all Theodosia could manage.

"I don't know about that," said Delaine, glancing back at him, "he seems rather up front to me."

"I mean it, Delaine . . ."

Delaine waved a hand. "Okay, okay, don't go all weird on me, Theo. If I want to date someone, I'm going to . . ." She suddenly caught the glint of key in Theodosia's hand. "What's that?"

Theodosia stared down at it. She'd almost forgot she had it. "Key to the Mobley Plantation. Jory gave it to me."

Delaine grinned. "Excellent. Our plans are falling into place. Now we can take that drive out there."

"I don't recall making any plans," said Theodosia.

"Come on, Theo," chided Delaine. "Shouldn't that old place be part of your investigation?" She gave a mock guilty look, then covered her mouth with a gloved hand. "You *are* still investigating, aren't you?"

Theodosia thought for a minute. She wasn't about to let Delaine goad her into something she didn't want to do. On the other hand, her snooping hadn't been particularly productive thus far. Maybe it *was* worth taking a look at the old Mobley Plantation.

"Okay," said Theodosia, "you can come back with me to the tea shop and have lunch. Then we'll drive out."

But as she put her hand on the driver's side door, Theodosia noticed a piece of paper stuck on her windshield.

"What's that?" asked Delaine.

"Looks like a business flyer," said Theodosia, ripping the paper from beneath the windshield wipers. "Maybe for gardening or lawn care or . . ." Her voice trailed off.

"What?" asked Delaine.

Theodosia crumpled the small beige card in her hand and tossed it in the back of her Jeep. "Nothing." She climbed in, started the ignition, double-clutched into second, and hurriedly pulled away from the curb.

"Hey!" cried a petulant Delaine. "Kindly slow down. I'm getting *jounced*."

But Theodosia didn't hear her. She was thinking of the note she'd just tossed away. The note that said, *Back Off.*

She fervently wondered who'd stuck it on her windshield. Web Hall? Travis McBee? Joe Fanning? Or could it have been Julian Bruno? And, was it her imagination, or had it been written on the same kind of note card she'd seen among Abby's things?

Whoever wrote it must think she was on to something.

But was she really? That *was* the killer question, wasn't it?

16

"*How was the* funeral?" asked Drayton. The Indigo Tea Shop was almost filled to capacity for this Thursday's luncheon crowd. Miss Dimple was helping out again, dashing from table to table, efficiently taking orders, then dispatching them to Haley in the kitchen. Drayton was doing what he did best: charming customers and brewing fragrant pots of tea.

"It was a lovely service," said Delaine.

"Sad," replied Theodosia.

"But so many people showed up," said Delaine, plunking herself down at one of the smaller tables near the door. "A full house, really."

"High ratings then," said Drayton in an acerbic tone.

"Exactly!" replied Delaine. "Just what a TV personality would hope to get for her final send-off."

Drayton shook his head. "Delaine, my dear, you have such an obtuse way of looking at things."

Delaine smiled prettily. "Well, thank you, Drayton."

"May I bring you a honey-mustard egg salad tea sandwich and a ginger scone?" he asked.

Delaine beamed at his attention. "Thank you, Drayton. That sounds perfectly lovely. As long as the carb count isn't astronomical."

"Of course." Drayton smiled.

"What's Delaine doing here?" asked Haley, when Theodosia stepped into the kitchen. "Did she superglue herself to you at the funeral?"

"We're probably going to drive out to the Mobley Plantation," said Theodosia.

Haley was suddenly interested. "And hunt for the ghost of that missing bride?" She deftly spread butter on two rows of sliced challah bread, then added generous mounds of her famous honey-mustard egg salad. "Cool."

"No," said Theodosia. "We're really just going to check things out. From what Jory said, nobody's been out there in years."

"That doesn't sound like much fun," said Haley. "Hey," she said as the wall phone shrilled, "maybe you should wait until it gets dark and I'll go with you. We'll take some candles and have ourselves a dandy little séance." She grinned, then grabbed the receiver and held it to her ear. "Indigo Tea Shop." She listened for a couple seconds, then handed the phone to Theodosia. "It's for you."

"Yes?" said Theodosia, fully expecting the caller to be one of her regulars, trying to cajole a last-minute reservation.

"Theodosia?" came an eager female voice. "It's Maggie Twining. From Sutter Realty?"

"Oh sure," said Theodosia. She figured she'd hear from Maggie again.

"I wanted you to know there's been an offer made on that carriage house. And I know you're interested . . . I mean, it's such a charming little place . . . anyway, I wondered if you wanted to make a counteroffer?"

"What's the offer as it stands?" asked Theodosia.

Maggie told her.

"Gulp," said Theodosia. "Awful lot of zeros in that number."

"Real estate just keeps going up and up." Maggie chortled brightly. "Especially here in the historic district. Obviously it's one of the best investments a person can make. Especially a single gal like you. Give you lots of security and build real equity to boot."

"I haven't even been inside," said Theodosia.

"Easily remedied," chirped Maggie. "I'm thumbing through my appointment book and see that I'm good late this afternoon or first thing tomorrow. What works best for you, dear?"

"Um . . . probably later today," said Theodosia, knowing in her heart of hearts she couldn't afford the little carriage house. But she just had to peek inside.

"Five o'clock," said Maggie. "Bring your checkbook."

It was a glorious autumn day and the drive out to Mobley Plantation took them through woods, abandoned rice fields, and finally, bayous.

"Seems awfully lonely out here," said Delaine, staring out the window at dark water that stretched into misty woods on either side of the road and, as they drove deeper, towering bald cypress trees with bulbous root structures. "Primordial, really." Her fingers clutched the box she held on her lap. They'd stopped at Dugan's Antique Shop back at Turner's Crossroad and Delaine had debated mightily between a sterling silver sugar bowl and a footed glass candy dish. Finally, she'd purchased both of them.

"I must be a real swamp person," Theodosia responded with a laugh. "Because I love it out here." She smiled to herself, remembering the little flat-bottomed pirogue she'd piloted through swamps as a kid in her quest for crawfish and crabs. Thought about the ring-necked ducks, egrets, herons, river otters, and white-tailed deer that lived out here in almost perfect seclusion.

Delaine gave a little shiver.

Theodosia checked the directions she'd hastily written down earlier when Jory had given her the key and eased off the accelerator. "I think we're getting close," she told Delaine.

"It doesn't look like there's *anything* left standing out here . . ." began Delaine.

And then Theodosia suddenly said, "There it is!" She jerked the steering wheel hard to the left and coasted down a slight hill that was really a weedy, overgrown driveway.

"Oh my," said Delaine as Theodosia's Jeep rolled to a stop and they both peered expectantly at the house. "It's a wreck." Her nose wrinkled with disappointment.

The old plantation house *was* a wreck. Though it had once been a formidable-looking home with a broad front and two squared-off second-story tower rooms, the wood was now silvered with age. The roof sagged, the front porch had an alarming list to it, and the side porch was so overgrown with kudzu that the whole place seemed to melt into the swamp. What few windows remained were a myriad of cracks.

The two women stepped out of the car to further appraise the old place.

"Well," said Delaine, in what had to be a massive understatement, "I guess they don't have a gardener on staff anymore." Indeed, weeds obliterated the entire yard and the front walk was barely a trail. "But I suppose we should take a look." She sighed. "After all, we drove all the way out here."

"You're so dressed up," Theodosia said to Delaine, who was wearing a black bouclé suit with a wraparound belt and a jaunty black hat that sported a pheasant feather.

"And you're always so dressed down," said Delaine, a slight edge to her voice.

"What I meant," said Theodosia, "was that this is probably going to be a dusty, dirty place. I'd hate to see your lovely suit get all smudged."

"I'm always careful," said Delaine as they pushed through knee-high weeds, heading for the front door. "Oh, look." She pointed toward a new wooden sign off to one side. Green letters against a cream-colored background proclaimed PROPERTY OF CAROLINA HEARTLAND TRUST. "That's what you were telling me about. Abby and Drew's donation of the property."

"It was a very generous thing for them to do," said Theodosia.

Delaine paused. "I wish more folks were concerned with historic preservation. Do you know that lovely Branford Building over on Bay Street was actually scheduled to be demolished?"

"I didn't know that," said Theodosia.

"Luckily, the Heritage Society stepped in," continued Delaine. "Sometimes the only way to save historic properties is to just buy them outright." She nodded to herself. "Yep, it's the good old American way."

Theodosia pulled the key from her pocket and continued toward the old house. Five feet from the tilting, weathered steps she stopped so suddenly Delaine bumped into her.

"What's wrong now?" asked Delaine, stumbling slightly, then adjusting her hat.

Theodosia stared at the bizarre object that blocked their path. At first glance it looked like an amalgam of chicken feathers and twigs bound together with some kind of leather twist. A totem of sorts.

"Yipes," said Delaine, peering over her shoulder at the strange object. "What an awful-looking thing. What do you think it's supposed to be?"

Theodosia frowned. "Looks like some kind of sign."

"Sign for what?" sniffed Delaine. "The local barbequed chicken shack?"

"Maybe it's meant to be some sort of charm," Theodosia murmured.

"Charm?" scoffed Delaine. "That nasty, gross thing? I'd say it's some kid's idea of a crappy joke."

Theodosia stepped carefully over the bundle of chicken feathers. It didn't *feel* like a joke to her. In fact, the little totem seemed slightly ominous. "Maybe you're right," she said to Delaine. "Let's hope so anyway."

Delaine kicked the little totem off to one side as she passed by, then followed Theodosia up six creaking, wooden steps onto the tilting, rough veranda. Theodosia stuck her key into the rusty lock and fought to make it turn.

"What's wrong now?" asked Delaine.

"Stuck," said Theodosia. She continued jiggling the key, working at the lock.

"Keep trying."

"Needs a shot of WD-40," said Theodosia. But her persistence prevailed. Finally, there was a soft click and the key turned in the lock.

"Success," breathed Delaine.

But when they pushed the door open, both women were shocked at the scene that met their eyes. The entry hall was dank and dirty, the walls covered with a kind of green scum. The sagging wood floor literally had an inch of dust covering it. And a network of filmy white cobwebs flowed down from an old chandelier that was partially ripped from the ceiling and hanging by shreds of bare wire.

"Ugh," said Delaine. "This place is in terrible shape. And so gloomy, too. Are there lights?" As if to answer her own question, she flipped a switch near the door. Nothing. "No lights." Delaine didn't sound as excited about exploring as she had earlier. "Did you happen to bring a flashlight, Theo?"

Theodosia shook her head. For some reason she hadn't planned very well. Probably because she hadn't really planned to come out here at all.

"Great," said Delaine, studying her manicured nails. "Well, let's get this over with."

If there had been any furniture in the old house, it was gone now. Just empty room after empty room that Theodosia and Delaine crept through, leaving in their wake ragged trails of footprints in the dust.

"This is *killing* my allergies," complained Delaine. "Maybe we should cut this visit short." She sniffled loudly as if to add emphasis to her words.

But Theodosia was just warming up. Maybe because she'd come here under duress, maybe because the old, tumbled-down house intrigued her. Exerted a sort of pull on her. Whatever the reason, she didn't intend to leave until she'd explored every nook and cranny.

They made their way through an old parlor, veered off into a sitting room and then another small room, and finally entered a rustic kitchen at the back of the house. Here they found the most furnishings, a wall of cupboards and a rough-hewn counter with an old copper sink, pitted with age.

"It's creepy to think nobody's lived here for decades," said Delaine. She shook her head and the pheasant feather in her hat whispered silently above her head.

"Let's go upstairs," said Theodosia.

"Bad idea," said Delaine. "It's just going to be more of the same. Dirt, dust, and cobwebs."

Delaine was quite correct. Plus, the upstairs was considerably smaller, due to the sharp angle of the roofline.

"Did you just hear something?" asked Delaine. They were standing in the tiny front bedroom. "It sounded, like . . . oh, I don't know . . . a crunching noise. Like gravel?"

"A car?" said Theodosia, stepping quickly to a small, triangular window. She peered out through decades of grim, but saw nothing.

"Jumpy," said Delaine, frowning and making a small sound in the back of her throat.

"Just three bedrooms," said Theodosia as they trooped back downstairs. "And small ones at that." She gazed around at peeling wallpaper that revealed crumbling plaster and rotting strips of wood. "The Heartland Trust is going to have to spend a ton of money to get this place back in shape. Make it suitable for tourists or school groups to come through here."

"I'm not all that familiar with the Heartland Trust," said Delaine, "but I'm sure they're a highly dedicated group. They'll do a fine job." She spun on her heels, headed for the front door.

But Theodosia had her hand on the basement door. "Let's check downstairs, too," she told Delaine.

Delaine spun around. "Are you serious? It's going to be pitch black down there. And there'll be spiders. Lots of spiders." She let loose another of her trademark shudders.

"Then we'll just creep down the stairs, take a quick peek, and zip right back up," said Theodosia.

"Promise?" said Delaine. But Theodosia had already started down.

"Damp down here," called Theodosia. She was already at the bottom of the stairs.

"And dark," said Delaine. She descended gingerly, then looked around. There were two small windows ten feet beyond them, but those were crusted over with dirt and cobwebs. "Listen. Do you hear, like, running water?"

Theodosia cocked her head and listened. She *did* detect the faint sound of water. "Maybe there's an underground spring," she theorized, "that served as a water source."

"Maybe . . ." began Delaine, just as the door at the top of the stairs slammed shut with a loud bang. "Hey!" she yelped. "What's going on?"

"Probably the wind caught it," said Theodosia, fumbling past Delaine and rushing back upstairs. "We left the front door standing wide open, remember?" She grabbed the doorknob, pushed hard.

It didn't budge.

"Stuck," she told Delaine, suddenly feeling a nasty flutter in the pit of her stomach. *Did that door close on its own? Or did somebody give it a little help?*

"Pull harder!" shrilled Delaine, struggling up the stairs and tugging at the doorknob.

"No," said Theodosia, "we have to *push*!"

"Okay, okay," gibbered Delaine.

But shoulders to the door, pushing with their combined strength, the door still wouldn't budge.

"Why won't this open?" moaned Delaine. Her voice had risen to a shrill pitch and her teeth were beginning to chatter.

Theodosia set her jaw firmly. "I think somebody's playing a nasty trick on us." She sincerely hoped it wasn't Jory's idea of a joke. Or maybe, she decided, it would be better if it was.

"We have to get out of here!" cried Delaine, in full-blown panic.

"We will," said Theodosia. She descended the stairs again and Delaine followed, waving her arms helplessly.

"Maybe if we . . ." began Theodosia. Her eyes searched the dim basement, then caught sight of a pile of junk against the far wall.

"What?" asked Delaine.

"There's some junk over there," said Theodosia. "So maybe there's also another way out. A root cellar or a coal chute we can scramble up."

"And if there isn't?"

Theodosia glanced around. "Then we knock out one of those little windows and either climb out or call for help on our cell phone. Okay?"

Delaine gave a nervous, eager nod. "Okay, okay, sounds like a plan."

They made their way tentatively across the basement floor.

"This floor is so squishy," complained Delaine. "Must be some kind of rotted old carpet."

"More like moss or slime," said Theodosia. "Stuff that grew over the packed-earth floor."

"Dear Lord," murmured Delaine. She put a hand on Theodosia's shoulder, following closely on her heels, taking shuffling baby steps. "Don't go so fast," she hissed.

They were halfway across the basement.

"See over there," said Theodosia, trying to put a note of encouragement in her voice. "An old spinning wheel. Probably didn't truck that down those narrow stairs."

"So you think there's a coal chute or a . . . ?" Delaine closed her mouth with an audible snap.

"What?" asked Theodosia. "What's wrong now?"

"My left foot," said Delaine. "It's stuck in the mud."

"That's 'cause you're wearing those high heel . . . oh, my heavens!" exclaimed Theodosia. "It *is* a little spongy. In fact, I . . ."

Creak!

"What was that?" screamed Delaine.

"Sounded like . . . wood cracking?" said a puzzled Theodosia. "Something beneath us?" They stood together, arms akimbo, as if in suspended animation.

"But you said this was *earth*," Delaine cried.

Creeeeeak! This time the noise was louder and seemed to vibrate under them.

"Oh, I don't like this at all!" shrieked Delaine. "I feel like I'm being sucked down!"

Strangely, Theodosia was experiencing the very same feeling. And when she glanced down at her feet, a shock wave coursed through her. They *were* sinking. Through several inches of mud! Or . . . quicksand?

"What's happening?" screamed Delaine, clutching Theodosia as they continued to be pulled down.

"I don't know!" Theodosia screamed back, up to her knees now, batting with her arms. And then, as if the earth dropped out from beneath their feet, they were falling. Foul-smelling mud filled their nostrils, pressed against their eyes; tiny stones seemed to rattle inside their ears!

"Aiiiiiiii!" came Delaine's muffled scream as they continued to fall.

17

A few long seconds, and then . . . Thunk!

They were both silent, shocked by their bone-rattling landing. But, thank goodness, there was no more mud threatening to cut off their breathing, save for the few pieces that plopped down wetly upon their heads.

"Are we dead?" whispered Delaine.

"Pttuu," said Theodosia, tasting foul mud and spitting it out. She wiped her sleeve across her face and eyes. Then she peered around in very dim light, extended a hand out, and touched a damp wall. Tilting her head back, she looked upward. There was a gaping hole in the ceiling above them—a rotted wood ceiling they'd thought had been the basement floor. "Oh wow," she finally croaked.

"Where are we?" moaned Delaine. She was doing a fair amount of spitting and rubbing herself.

"Maybe a subbasement?" ventured Theodosia. She wasn't

entirely sure. Stretching a hand out to touch Delaine, she asked, "Are you hurt?"

Delaine, who'd landed on her side, moved slowly to a sitting position. "I don't *think* so. You?"

Theodosia hunched her shoulders, felt a ripple of pain. She was pretty sure she didn't have any broken bones, but two hard falls in one week couldn't be good for the old musculoskeletal system. "I'll live," she told Delaine.

Delaine eased herself up to a standing position. "This is like . . . a secret room," she whispered. She held out a hand, helped Theodosia to her feet. "What do you suppose . . . ?"

In the dim light, Theodosia studied the small room they'd fallen into. She'd heard about subbasements like this. "Maybe," she said to Delaine, "this was built for the Underground Railroad." The Underground Railroad had been a network of safe houses that smuggled African American slaves to safety in the North.

"Whoa," said Delaine. "You think?" She picked up her hat, which was caked with mud and let loose a little cry of dismay.

"Has to be," said Theodosia.

"How did they get down here?" asked Delaine. "Better yet, how did they get *out* of here?"

Theodosia glanced around. Delaine made a good point. How to get out indeed? She took a step forward, hit something with her toe. Leaning down to investigate, she groped around and found a rustic, wooden farm ladder with most of the steps rotted away. It lay lengthwise across the room. One end was propped atop the frame of an old bed whose mattress had long since moldered into nothing. All that was left was a network of ropes. The other end of the ladder, the heavier end, lay atop a round-topped trunk. "Here's your answer," said Theodosia. "A ladder."

"If we can prop that up," said Delaine, "we can climb out of here."

Grappling with the ladder, they pulled and tugged for several minutes.

"Heavy," grunted Delaine.

"And nasty," said Theodosia. The ladder was damp and covered with slime.

Finally they muscled the ladder upright.

"I'll hold it stable while you climb up," said Theodosia, bracing a foot against a wall and grasping one of the knots on the ladder's side.

Delaine placed one foot on the first crossbar, really just a knotted hunk of wood. "Here I go." But as she shifted her weight to the lower bar, the rotted wood collapsed under her.

"Try the next step," said Theodosia.

Delaine hiked up her skirt, lifted her leg, placed it on the second bar. That one collapsed as well.

"No way," said Delaine. "The wood's completely wet and rotted through."

Theodosia reached higher and tugged on the cross sections. "These next bars feel a little more stable."

"Yeah," said Delaine in a glum tone, "but I can't reach 'em. I'm too short. *You're* too short."

"Maybe if we had some sort of . . . hey, how about that old trunk in the corner?" said Theodosia. "You can hop on top and use it as a kind of stepping stool."

"What?" sniffed Delaine, never good at facing adversity.

Theodosia crossed the little room, bent over, and began tugging. "Sure, this'll work. C'mon, help me slide this trunk over a couple of feet."

Delaine bent down and tugged alongside Theodosia. Pulling together, they gradually inched the trunk across the floor.

"Cobwebs," said Delaine, batting at a sheen of white. "This is disgusting!"

"Got to do it anyway," said Theodosia. They tugged and pulled and maneuvered for a good five minutes, and finally got the trunk positioned directly beneath the hole they'd fallen through.

"Maybe . . . stand it on end?" suggested Delaine.

Theodosia nodded. "Good idea."

"Have to get my fingers under it," said Delaine, leaning down. "Ohhh!"

"What's wrong?" asked Theodosia. "You get pinched?"

"There's mold," said Delaine. "Stinky, wet mold."

"I know," agreed Theodosia. "It's awful down here."

"Feels like the gateway to hell," added Delaine as she shoved and lifted and grunted.

"Almost there," said Theodosia.

They gave the trunk one final shove and the momentum carried it over onto its end.

"What a team," said Theodosia, proud of their work. She slapped a hand on the trunk, was surprised when it gave a little creak and the rounded top swung out.

"What the . . . ?" said Delaine.

"Leather hinges must have rotted," said Theodosia. "That's okay, this will still work. The trunk still feels fairly sturdy."

"Think there's something inside?" asked Delaine.

Both women stared at each other for a moment, then bent down to look. Theodosia grasped the lid that had swung out and pulled it open a little farther. Delaine peered in.

"*Eeeeyowwww!*" Delaine threw her head back and let go another earsplitting, bloodcurdling scream. Then, hopping up and down, she pointed at the thing that had haphazardly half-spilled out.

Theodosia bent closer to see what had sparked Delaine's hissy fit. And was dumbfounded at what she saw! Bleached white bones, finger bones and knuckle bones from a human hand, lay scattered on the floor.

She let loose a pretty good scream herself.

"I don't believe it!" Delaine gibbered for about the twentieth time. "It's her. It's *her*! The missing bride!"

They'd finally gotten their courage up and really looked inside the old trunk. Found what appeared to be a complete skeleton. With bits of moldering lace stuck to its bones.

"I think you're right," Theodosia admitted. She'd never completely bought into Miss Josette's story, but here was living proof. Well, not actually living anymore, but proof.

"How did she get in there?" asked Delaine.

"I suppose she was hiding," said Theodosia, giving her own version of a slow shiver.

"Down here?" squealed Delaine. "In a trunk?"

Theodosia grimaced. "I'm guessing she climbed down here to hide in the trunk. And then the trapdoor, or whatever it was, accidentally slammed shut and then the ladder toppled on top of the trunk."

"So she was trapped down here for all eternity?" said Delaine in a hushed voice.

"For long enough anyway," said Theodosia, thinking of the horror the young bride must have endured. The agonizing death.

"Until today," said Delaine in a breathless rush. "When we finally released her spirit."

Theodosia gazed at the small white bones and moldering wedding dress, and figured the poor woman's spirit had long since fled.

Delaine was still wringing her hands. "Now what do we do?"

"We climb out of here," said Theodosia, "just like we planned."

With more than a few misgivings, Delaine clambered on top of the trunk, then eased herself up the ladder. Theodosia stood on her tiptoes and pressed her fists against the bottom of Delaine's shoes, trying to boost her.

"Almost there," said Delaine, "just one more step."

"Careful," cautioned Theodosia.

Delaine leaned forward, then did a kind of scrambling flop onto the basement floor. "Oh, my goodness," she cried. "I did it, I did it! I'm finally out of that terrible *pit*!"

"Now hold the ladder for me," pleaded Theodosia.

"I'll do better than that," said Delaine, unwrapping her leather obi belt. "I'm going to tie one end around the post here and dangle my belt down. Then if the ladder gives out, you can still pull yourself up."

"I'll certainly give it a try," said Theodosia. She watched as Delaine secured the belt, then dangled it into the hole. Finally, she stepped on top of the trunk and clambered up the ladder as fast as she could. There was no sense hanging around in *that* awful place any longer than necessary.

Working together now, they hoisted the ladder up from the hole, carried it over to the wall, and rammed it hard against one of the windows. They broke glass, but were unable to wiggle out through the narrow opening.

No matter; Theodosia called Parker Scully on her cell phone. Above his sputtering and shrill questions, she gave him driving directions, then asked him to call Sheriff Newton Clay and get him out to Mobley Plantation as soon as possible.

Forty-five minutes later they were all standing around in sunlight, Theodosia, Parker, Sheriff Clay, and his deputy, Walter Bagan. Parker remained closemouthed while Theodosia related her story to the sheriff.

"Sorry," Theodosia told Sheriff Clay. "Every time you see me it seems something's gone terribly wrong."

Sheriff Clay waved a hand. "You'd be surprised to hear about the trouble I've seen."

"Sounds like the title of a song," muttered Delaine. She was sitting on the front steps, her makeup mirror propped on her knees, trying to scrub grime from her face while applying a fresh coat of makeup. It wasn't working very well.

Theodosia stuck a toe in the sand. "Your crime scene team is going to want to take a look at that skeleton," she told the sheriff.

Sheriff Clay narrowed his eyes. "But it's old, you say?"

"Maybe a hundred years," said Theodosia. "Nothing left but bones."

"Not much for me to do then," he said and didn't seem unhappy about the situation. "You were out at this old place . . . why?"

Theodosia went through her explanation about snooping for Jory and gave a quick recap of Miss Josette's story.

"Huh," said Sheriff Clay. "Weird."

"You mean Abby's murder, the missing bride story, or finding the old skeleton?" asked Theodosia.

"All of it," said the sheriff. "Does Detective Tidwell know about this place? You know he's been working with us as a sort of consultant. He's got more experience in homicides than most of our guys."

"He doesn't know about the missing bride episode," said Theodosia. "But he's certainly been looking into the Abby Davis murder like you asked."

"And so have you, it sounds like," said the sheriff.

Theodosia snuck a quick glance at Parker. He didn't look happy.

"Detective Tidwell has been kind enough to keep me somewhat in the loop," said Theodosia. "I'm wondering . . . have you been able to uncover anything . . . uh . . . at all?"

Sheriff Clay hitched his belt and rocked back on his heels. "I talked to the Savannah TV station where Miss Davis had worked. Apparently they were pretty upset when she left."

"I guess she had a better offer," said Theodosia.

"Something like that," said the sheriff.

"You mind telling me who you talked with over there?" asked Theodosia.

The sheriff looked like he did mind. But after a few moments of staring at her, of once again doing a quick assessment of Theodosia's actual involvement in the murder, he muttered, "Woman by the name of Kay Lorillard."

Parker Scully was a whole 'nother problem.

"Tell me again why you were out here?" he asked, once the sheriff and his deputy has disappeared inside the house.

Delaine raised her perfectly waxed brows and gaped openly at Parker. "You mean she didn't tell you?"

"Delaine . . ." Theodosia said in a cautioning tone.

"Tell me what?" asked Parker.

Delaine's lips formed a perfect O as she murmured, "Oh boy."

"Will *somebody* please tell me what's going on?" demanded Parker. "What were you two doing out here, anyway?"

So of course Theodosia had to tell Parker the whole story. About Jory coming from New York to attend Abby's funeral and how he'd sought her out. And then she told him how Jory had asked her to conduct her own brand of investigation. Which didn't exactly make Parker a happy camper.

First Parker looked stunned and then he just looked hopping mad. "I didn't know Abby Davis was that guy's *sister*!" he exclaimed. "Besides, I thought that guy Jory was out of your life! You told me he moved north or something."

"He did," Theodosia said, patiently. "Like I just explained, he came back because Abby was murdered."

"And you've been snooping around . . . for *him*?"

"Him? You mean Jory?" asked Theodosia, starting to get a little perturbed herself. "Because he does have a name."

Parker threw his arms up. "This is crazy. Bizarre, really. Running around the countryside, finding old skeletons, all because of your ex-boyfriend!" He turned an angry gaze on her. "Which makes me think he might not be your ex after all!"

"Of course he is," said Theodosia.

But Parker had already turned his back on her and was walking back to his car. "Sure, right," he mumbled. "Whatever."

Theodosia and Delaine watched him climb into his car, slam the door, and peel out of the driveway with a vengeance.

"He's really upset," said Delaine.

"Gee," said Theodosia, who was more than a little upset herself. "You think?"

Delaine just shrugged. "So what now?"

"For one thing," said Theodosia, "I've got to get in touch

with Jory and tell him we just found his great-great aunt by marriage."

"I wonder what the relatives are gonna think of that?" asked Delaine, trying to dab blusher over a smudge of dirt. "I mean, do you think they'll be grateful or really upset?"

"Who knows?" said Theodosia, feeling disheartened. She walked a few paces, shaking her head at the ridiculousness of it all. Spotted something in the weeds. Then bent down and gathered up the little pile of feathers and leather.

18

❧

Maggie Twining was pacing the sidewalk nervously when Theodosia finally showed up. "Here you are," she said frowning, "I was beginning to think you were a no-show."

"Apologies," said Theodosia. "I dropped in on someone and had trouble getting away." She smiled inwardly at her little white lie that veered dangerously close to the awful truth. Of course, she'd also had to stop at home to shower off all the slime and mud.

"Well, you're here now and that's what counts," said Maggie. She readjusted her attitude and smiled brightly at Theodosia. "Shall we?" Extending an arm, she indicated for Theodosia to proceed through the wrought-iron gate and up the narrow sidewalk.

"This is so exciting," said Theodosia, unable to hold back a grin. Now that she was here, she was falling under the spell of this storybook English cottage with its sloping, thatched roof, asymmetrical design, cross gables, and lovely turret.

"What architecture style would you call this, besides maybe a Hansel and Gretel cottage?"

"Probably Cotswold style," said Maggie. And I've heard cottages like this referred to as a Tudor cottage or Anne Hathaway–style cottage. Anyway, this one is really quite adorable."

"A brick exterior," said Theodosia, pausing to study the outside of the little house.

"With nice, steep cross gables," Maggie pointed out. "Plus a stone chimney, upstairs dormer windows, and arched doors. All remarkable features."

"Is the roof really thatched?" asked Theodosia, gazing up.

"No, just cleverly done," said Maggie. "With cedar tiles that mimic thatch. They're much more durable and really quite imaginative."

"And so adorable," said Theodosia, stepping aside so Maggie could unlock the wooden front door that was actually rounded at the top. Like a hobbit door that would lead to Middle-earth.

"Okay, this is it." Maggie laughed. "The moment of truth. Let's see if the interior captures your heart as well."

Theodosia stepped into a small brick-floored foyer, then into the cottage proper. Gazing about, she took in the high beamed ceiling, polished wood floor, cozy living room with its brick fireplace set into a wall of beveled cypress panels. And knew exactly where she'd place her chintz sofa, her damask chair, and her Aubusson carpet. Her heart literally felt like warm, melted butter as the little house exerted its charm on her.

"You look like you're ready to cry," said Maggie.

"Because I love it," said Theodosia, her eyes sparkling.

"Well, that's a good thing," said Maggie.

"And I don't think I can afford it," Theodosia added as a sad note.

"Let's not worry about that right now," said Maggie, assuming an all-business, real estate broker manner. "Let's not let that thought intrude until you've seen the rest of the place and chatted with your banker."

"All right," Theodosia agreed. A girl could dream, couldn't she?

The kitchen was adorable, but could use updated appliances. Okay, Theodosia decided, she could deal with that. Then she pulled open the kitchen door and walked out into the backyard. The *fenced* backyard that was a perfect little Charleston garden with dogwood trees, magnolias, and a tangle of vines crawling up the back wall.

As the pièce de résistance, a tiny fountain tumbled into a tiny pond filled with wriggling goldfish. All this, she decided, would definitely appeal to a certain creature of the canine persuasion.

Upstairs were three rooms. A nice-sized bedroom with a cozy turret corner that could be turned into the perfect reading nook, as well as two smaller rooms. Theodosia figured one of the small rooms could be converted to a walk-in closet. The other would make a lovely guest room—cum-study.

Yes, she decided, a serious chat with her banker was definitely in order.

"So what do you think?" asked Maggie. Her question was pro forma. She was well aware she had a very interested prospect.

"Perfect," said Theodosia.

Maggie held up a finger. "Realize, an offer's already been made on this place."

"So what do I do now?" asked Theodosia.

"Put in your own offer and hope for the best," said Maggie.

"And I'm hoping for . . . what?" asked Theodosia.

"That the seller accepts your particular offer and the bank green-lights your loan application," said Maggie.

"Right," said Theodosia, with a twinge. That was the hard part. Why did there always have to be a hard part?

Ninety minutes later, Theodosia pulled up in front of Drayton's house and tooted her horn. Two minutes later he popped out of his front door, looking dapper in a dark gray jacket, light gray slacks, and assertive red plaid bow tie.

"You're like a bad date," Drayton joked as he clambered into the passenger seat. "Pull up in front of the house, honk your horn, don't come in to meet the folks."

"Ha," said Theodosia. "Good one."

"Something wrong?" asked Drayton, peering at Theodosia in the glow of the dashboard, suddenly detecting a slight wrinkle in the fabric of her greeting.

And so, on the drive to Truman McBee's house, Theodosia filled Drayton in on her afternoon's misadventure.

"How dreadfully bizarre!" exclaimed Drayton, when the telling was done. "A skeleton? The missing bride? Falling into that horrible underground subcellar?" Fidgeting with his bow tie, he exhaled loudly and said, "You must have been *terrified.*"

"Believe me," said Theodosia, swerving at the last minute

to avoid a red-and-yellow horse-drawn jitney filled with tourists, "it was no picnic."

"What did you tell Parker?" Drayton asked in a low voice.

"The truth," said Theodosia.

"And how did that go over?" Drayton sounded guarded.

"Like a lead balloon," said Theodosia, her fingers gripping the steering wheel tighter.

"Mmm. I can imagine."

"No, no, you can't," said Theodosia. "Parker was absolutely *furious* with me. It was like he'd been jabbed between the eyes with a white-hot poker. I can't imagine he'll ever want to speak to me again."

"Don't say that," said Drayton, as Theodosia slowed the Jeep, looking for a parking space. She pulled nose first into a space, seesawed back and forth, then ended up with her right front wheel up on the curb.

Crap.

Theodosia sat hunched behind the wheel, staring at Truman McBee's house down the block, all lit up like a jewel box and sparkling in the dark blue night. "No," she told Drayton. "I think it might be . . . I think it's over between us."

Truman McBee's house was Classical Revival style. A large stone house fronted with four massive ionic columns, an ample front veranda, and a promenade deck on the second level.

"Have you ever been inside?" asked Theodosia as they stood in front of an elaborately carved six-panel door. Above the door, light beamed through an elegant fanlight.

"No," said Drayton, as the door opened and a guide in a

long white Grecian tunic handed them each a program. "But I've always wanted to, the place looks so intriguing."

"Lovely," exclaimed Theodosia as she studied the crystal chandelier that dangled overhead, the polished marble floor beneath her feet. Quite a change from the old plantation house she'd explored this afternoon.

"All we need to do," said Drayton, under his breath, "is keep out of Truman McBee's watchful gaze. We don't want him to recognize us from last night."

"And flip out again," said Theodosia, as they wandered down the center hallway, rubbing elbows with dozens of other guests.

They turned into the library, which was curiously devoid of books, but offered stunning Pompeian red walls and buff woodwork.

"Tell me again why we're here," said Drayton.

"Not sure," said Theodosia. She let her fingers trail across one of a pair of large, antique globes. "Just sort of reconnoitering, I guess. The fact that Abby Davis was pursuing the story of Truman McBee's kidnapped son seems . . . I don't know . . . like a tenuous link to her murder?"

"Maybe," shrugged Drayton, turning his attention to the antique globes. "Look at this, a terrestrial globe and a celestial globe. Quite a pair of curiosities."

"Lots of that going around," said Theodosia.

They explored the rest of the downstairs, fell in love with the living room that was painted a lovely Williamsburg blue and boasted cove ceilings and some fanciful settees, then climbed one of the double staircases that led upstairs.

Only one bedroom was open to the public on the second floor. But when they wandered in and saw what it contained, they were momentarily stunned. Sitting beside a four-poster

bed was a large bow-shaped English commode. On top of
that were displayed a dozen photographs of Travis McBee, the
kidnapped son. Flanking the photos were two gilt Egyptian
candleholders with tall white tapers burning in them.

"Good heavens," murmured Drayton. "Looks like some
sort of shrine."

"Strange they never found the son," said Theodosia.

They stood, studying the photos of a full-faced young man
in his late twenties who looked like he'd enjoyed every privi-
lege afforded him. Except, perhaps, a long life.

Theodosia stepped off to one side as two women came in
behind them. One wore a lilac suit, the other a black-and-white
herringbone jacket and black skirt.

"Travis," murmured the woman in the lilac suit.

The second woman nodded. "Such a sad story."

"I heard he was in and out of Challenge House most of his
adult life," said lilac suit, a harder edge tingeing her cultured
voice.

"Hmph," snipped the second woman. "What do you ex-
pect from nouveau riche?"

"What on earth is Challenge House?" asked Drayton. They
had come back downstairs and wandered out the back door
into the garden.

"It's a spin-dry place down near Seabrook," said Theodosia.

"Spin dry?" said Drayton, giving her a crooked glance.

"Rehab," Theodosia quickly explained.

Drayton tipped back his head and widened his eyes.
"Ohhh." They followed a brick path that wound around a
clump of palm trees, then sat down at a small glass-topped

table. "You think Travis McBee was there because of drinking?" he asked. "Or drug use?"

"Don't know," said Theodosia. "We could probably find out easily enough, but I'm not sure it matters."

A waiter came by to take their order and they both requested tea.

"May I offer you a small plate of benne wafers, too?" the waiter asked. Benne wafers were Charleston's unique brand of brown sugar and sesame seed cookies.

Drayton nodded. "Please."

"This is a terrific garden," said Theodosia, looking around. An enormous live oak draped in Spanish moss was set back against a tall redbrick wall. A free-form brick pathway meandered its way from the back of the house to the old oak. Magnolias, dwarf bamboo, and palm trees formed tall curtains of green, making the backyard very private and secluded.

When their tea and cookies arrived, Drayton managed a quick sip before the waiter scampered off. "Yunnan?" he asked.

The waiter nodded.

"Decent," said Drayton. He took another sip. "Actually, acceptable verging on good."

"Thank you, sir," said the waiter, a confused look on his face.

"Theodosia!" called a woman's lilting voice.

Theodosia looked around and found Thandie McLean making a beeline for her. And surprise, surprise, Thandie had Julian Bruno with her.

"How are you, Theo!" exclaimed Thandie. "And Drayton, too!" She grasped Bruno by the wrist and pulled him front and center. "You folks know Julian Bruno? He owns Vianello."

"Nice to make your acquaintance," said Drayton, shaking Bruno's hand.

"Hello again," said Theodosia. "We keep meeting." She fixed Bruno with a level gaze, which he pointedly ignored.

"Isn't this a *gorgeous* house?" trilled Thandie. "Wouldn't you just *kill* to live here?"

"Kill's a strong word," said Theodosia, still staring at Bruno.

"Oh, you know what I mean." Thandie giggled. She waved a hand. "Well, great to see you. Sorry to run off, but I'm supposed to rendezvous with some friends. See you later!"

"See you," waved Drayton.

When Thandie and Bruno had moved off, Theodosia leaned forward and said, "What do you think?"

Drayton's brows shot up. "About Julian Bruno? Hard to tell a man's character just by shaking his hand."

"You know what I mean," hissed Theodosia. "Your first impressions are generally spot-on."

"Okay," said Drayton, leaning back in his chair and nibbling a cookie. "He seemed a trifle hostile. And shifty, too."

"Exactly," said Theodosia. "Which leads me to believe there's more to him than meets the eye."

"Since Thandie McLean seemed to be wearing Bruno on her charm bracelet," said Drayton, "I assume she'll be dragging him to Timothy's party tomorrow night."

"Maybe," said Theodosia. "Although Delaine was trying her darndest to get her hooks into him, too. She was very friendly to him at the funeral."

"Delaine's friendly with a *lot* of men," said Drayton.

"Good point," said Theodosia.

"So tell me more about this carriage house you mentioned earlier," said Drayton, changing the subject.

"It's spectacular," said Theodosia. "In fact, we'll swing by on the way home. I'd like you to see it."

"I have a somewhat hazy memory of the place," said Drayton, "although it's been . . ." He stopped in midsentence, glanced up to find a woman beaming down at him. "Hello," he said, curiosity coloring his voice.

The woman, who was probably in her late fifties, extended a chubby arm loaded with jangling gold bangles. "Welcome," she told Drayton with a broad smile. Then she turned her megawatt smile on Theodosia. "Glad you could drop by. I'm Zizi McBee."

Drayton popped up from his chair. "The mistress of the house, of course," he said courteously. "Pleased to make your acquaintance."

"Nice to meet you," said Theodosia, shaking hands with Zizi McBee and deciding that Zizi was probably the perfect mate for Truman McBee. The woman was ample-framed and apple-cheeked with curly reddish-blond hair. Dressed in a powder-blue suit, Zizi teetered on matching blue pumps, although her unsteadiness might be attributed to the empty champagne glass she had clutched in her hand.

"I hope y'all are enjoying the tour," Zizi gushed.

"You have a very lovely home," said Theodosia.

"Wonderful," echoed Drayton. "And so generous of you to open it to the public. That certainly must present more than a few challenges."

Zizi blinked and smiled, obviously wanting her guests to feel welcome. "Did y'all happen to make it upstairs?"

"Yes, we did," said Drayton, who had remained standing.

"I hope you don't think what I did was too over the top," responded Zizi. "But I want everyone to understand that Travis is still a big part of our life."

"A fine tribute," said Drayton, exuding concern and remaining every inch the gentleman.

"It must be very difficult for you," said Theodosia. "I mean, with sightings still being reported." She hesitated. "They are still being reported, aren't they?"

"Oh yes!" said Zizi, biting down on her lower lip. "Which is why I've never given up hope."

"Must never give up hope," murmured Drayton.

"You know," said Zizi, dropping her voice to a confidential tone, "a few months ago I received a phone call that I *swear* was from Travis. Nothing was said, but I could tell somebody was right there, on the other end of the line."

"Really," said Theodosia.

"Anyway," said Zizi. "I had the strangest feeling it was Travis."

"It could have been some sort of prank," said Drayton, kindness in his voice.

Zizi gave an animated nod. "Could have been, but I don't think so." Her eyes took on a glazed, slightly faraway look. "I prefer to think it was Travis, trying to let me know in his own little way that he was all right." She blinked rapidly, eyes filling with tears. "Mothers intuitively *know* things like that."

"They certainly do," murmured Drayton, as Zizi smiled, fluttered her fingers, and eased herself toward the next table.

"Interesting woman," said Theodosia. "She's certainly a . . ."

"Tragic figure?" put in Drayton.

"I was going to say free spirit," said Theodosia.

"Ah," said Drayton. "Yours is a far more charitable characterization."

They stayed for another twenty minutes, enjoying the warm

night, and gazing at stars that sparkled overhead like so
many diamonds.

"What do you think?" asked Drayton as they paused on the
front veranda, staring out at the street. "Learn anything tonight that could be linked to your Abby Davis case?"

"Not really," said Theodosia. "Then again, I didn't exactly
have high expectations."

A piercing scream suddenly broke the gentle calm of the
evening. Then, a woman's shrill words. "No, no, no! Help!
Somebody help!"

"What on earth . . . ?" said Drayton, jerking his head
toward the dark across the street where the screams were
coming from. There was a heavy scuffle of feet and then a
loud thud. Like someone being hurled against the hood of a
car!

"Sounds like a fight!" said Theodosia. She was already
down the front steps and headed for the street.

"Theo!" called Drayton. "Don't! Please don't!"

As she sprinted, Theodosia pulled her cell phone from her
handbag and quickly punched in 9-1-1. But she didn't hit
Send. She was going to make sure help was really needed.

Cutting between a parked BMW and a Volvo, Theodosia
was stunned to see Julian Bruno scuffling with two men.
One had Bruno in a choke hold while he kicked furiously,
the other man was struggling to land punches. Thandie, as
terrified onlooker, stood in the middle of the sidewalk, screaming her head off and waving her arms.

Help!" she cried when she saw Theodosia and then Drayton appear. "Please help! They're beating him up! They're
killing him!"

"What's the trouble here?" yelled Drayton in his authoritative, Heritage Society call-to-order voice. "Take your hands off that man!"

The two men who held Bruno stopped their tussling and stared belligerently at Drayton, who stood on the curb, hands on hips, projecting an air of utter disapproval. But the men kept their tight grip on Julian Bruno, as though he were the pawn in an aggressive tug-of-war.

"The police are on their way!" said Theodosia, who still hadn't hit Send. She was aware of people coming up behind her, knew that Thandie's screams must have attracted attention.

"Stay out of this!" snarled one thug, but he looked unsure of himself.

"This is a private matter," said the other man. But he, too, seemed to have lost his impetus to fight as more onlookers began to gather.

Thandie, who was squatting now, leaned forward and gave a final, ghastly shriek. *"Stop it!"*

That was enough. The two thugs exchanged glances, then reluctantly released Julian Bruno. Free now, seemingly out of danger, he scooted toward Drayton, leaving Thandie in the throes of complete hysteria.

The two thugs melted into the darkness, but they still weren't finished. "This isn't over," one snarled at Bruno. "Next time won't go so easy."

"What's going on?" Theodosia demanded of Bruno, who looked slightly dazed and confused.

"Personal business," snapped Bruno, straightening his jacket and tie.

"In that case," said Drayton in a biting tone, "your *business* associates seem rather loutish."

"A thank-you to Drayton might be in order," said Theodosia. "And you'd better see to Thandie as well." The poor woman was still bent over, crying.

"Do you need a ride home, Thandie?" called Drayton.

But Thandie just shook her head. Then she straightened up and tottered over to Julian Bruno. He put his arm around her and together they shuffled off toward his car.

Drayton shook his head, then turned to Theodosia. "You summoned the police?"

"No. I figured you could handle this."

Drayton put a hand to his chest as if trying to still his rapidly beating heart. "Good Lord, girl. Don't ever assume that again!"

"Who do you think those guys were?" asked Theodosia, as they cruised down Murray Street.

"No idea," said Drayton.

"Looks like Julian Bruno's up to his armpits in trouble," said Theodosia.

"Probably the best thing to do is stay away from him," replied Drayton.

"Mmm," said Theodosia. She turned a corner, then slowed her Jeep. Finally pulled over to the curb. "There's the house. See?" For some reason, just looking at the little cottage, imagining the possibilities, made her feel better. Almost made her forget the nasty scene she'd just witnessed.

"Charming," breathed Drayton as he gazed at the little house. "And to think we'd be neighbors."

"We're already neighbors." Theodosia laughed. Drayton only lived six blocks from the Indigo Tea Shop in a small house that had once belonged to a well-known Civil War doctor. "Plus we work together every day."

"Good point," said Drayton.

"The real point," said Theodosia, gazing at the little cottage, "is can I afford it?"

Drayton shifted in his seat to look at her. "Can you?"

Theodosia stared through the darkness at the house. At the pitched roof, the gingerbread trim, the side portico, the tangle of shrubbery. The place was adorable. And would look even better with warm, welcoming lights burning in the front windows.

"Probably not," she said. "More than anything, I wish I could buy it. But I don't think I can."

"Pity," said Drayton. "Because that little cottage really does become you."

19

❧

Friday morning at the Indigo Tea Shop dawned with a flurry of excitement. Maybe it was the slew of customers, most of them tourists in town for the weekend, that had descended upon them out of the blue. Maybe it was because the Trident Media people were coming for lunch. Or maybe it was just the craziness of the week coupled with anticipation for Timothy's big party tonight and the Masked Ball tomorrow night.

"I've got requests for a Grand Pouchong as well as an autumn Darjeeling," said Drayton, who was measuring tea, checking water temperature, setting out teapots, and trying to pack take-out orders at the same time. "Customers hardly ever request those teas."

"I can't tell if you're pleased or shocked," said Theodosia.

"Probably a little of both," said Drayton, reaching up high to grab a silver tea tin. He pulled it down, checked the label.

"This is it," he told her. "Grand Pouchong. One of the family of Chinese oolongs. Fine gold color, delicate aroma. Do you know, has Haley pulled her cinnamon muffins out of the oven yet? They're the perfect accompaniment to this tea."

"I'll go check," offered Theodosia. But she'd barely taken two steps when the front door swung open and Miss Josette appeared. "Miss Josette!" exclaimed Theodosia. "I almost forgot you were coming today."

Miss Josette edged into the tea shop and peered around. "You look awfully busy. Did I come at a bad time?"

"Not at all," said Theodosia.

"You brought another batch of baskets?" asked Drayton, glancing up and looking more than a little interested.

"They're packed in my car, which is parked out back," said Miss Josette. "But I wanted to talk to you first." She stared straight at Theodosia.

"About . . . ?" said Theodosia.

"I heard about your finding that skeleton," said Miss Josette. "Out at the Mobley Plantation. It was on the news."

This made Drayton's ears perk up. "Theodosia's skeleton was on the news?" He gazed at Theodosia. "I wonder how they found out?"

"I'm guessing," said Theodosia, "that Sheriff Clay contacted Jory and Drew and then Jory called the TV station."

"Why on earth would he do that?" asked Drayton.

"Probably," said Theodosia, trying to gather her thoughts, "probably because it was the kind of story Abby Davis would have delighted in covering. Finding a mysterious old skeleton is a kind of human interest story with a little history and mystery thrown in for good measure."

"I see," said Drayton, even though he really didn't.

Theodosia led Miss Josette through the tea room and into

her office. Then she cracked open the back door and they carried in the dozen or so baskets from Miss Josette's car.

"Miss Josette," said Theodosia. "You know a little bit about the Gullah tradition. I'd like to show you something I found yesterday at that old plantation . . . see what you think."

She opened a desk drawer and pulled out the bit of feathers and twigs wrapped with leather.

Miss Josette stared at it, then shook her head. "You don't want to fool around with that, honey. That's Blue Root. Gullah folk magic."

Drayton chose that exact moment to stick his head in Theodosia's office.

"Magic?" he said, sounding more than a little skeptical. "Are you serious?"

"Very," said Miss Josette. And with her lips pursed and her brow furrowed, she certainly looked like she was.

"Can you think of any reason why a little totem like this might have been out there?' asked Theodosia. "I mean, at that particular house?"

Miss Josette shook her head slowly. "Not really."

"What do you suppose it was meant to do?" asked Drayton, getting interested now. "I mean, if it's magic, what's something like that supposed to conjure?"

Miss Josette was hesitant to answer. "It could be a warning of some kind," she said slowly. "Or, for all I know, maybe it was placed there for good luck. Realize, please, it's mostly previous generations of Gullah folk who knew about Blue Root. Who put stock in it."

"So not kids," said Theodosia. Yesterday Delaine had been sure that kids had planted it as a joke.

"Kids these days are busy with school, friends, listening to their iPods, and text messaging," said Miss Josette. "Most don't bother to learn about old customs and such."

"Still," said Theodosia. "Is there any way you could ask around? See if you can find someone who might know what this is supposed to represent?"

"I could make a few inquiries," said Miss Josette. "But I'm not promising anything."

Theodosia held out the strange bit of chicken feathers and leather lacing to Miss Josette. "You want to take this with you then?"

Miss Josette took a step backward. "No."

"That's a lovely arrangement," said Drayton, as he hurried back to the front counter. Theodosia had taken a square glass vase, filled it with water, and floated apple slices up against each side of the glass. Then she'd added stems of yellow mums and dark red zinnias.

"Thank you," said Theodosia. "Just trying to put together a fun centerpiece for the Trident Media luncheon."

"It's so lovely and autumnal I wish you'd make one for every table."

"Mmm," said Theodosia, popping in a final stem, "maybe I will." She looked up, smiled at Drayton, then looked past him as Jory Davis and Drew Donovan came rushing into the tea shop.

"Theodosia," said Jory, slightly out of breath.

"Hello there," Theodosia responded. She smiled cautiously at both Jory and Drew. Both men were staring at her.

"What a scare you must have had!" burst out Jory. "I mean yesterday, when you went out to Mobley Plantation." He touched a hand to the side of his head. "Believe me, I had no *idea* something like that would happen."

"Must have been a terrible ordeal," said Drew, shaking his head and looking equally concerned.

Drayton surveyed both men. "The question is, how did you find out?"

"Sheriff Clay called me," said Drew. "And then, of course, I got hold of Jory."

Jory nodded anxiously. "I tried to call you last night, but I kept getting your answering machine. Guess you were out, huh?"

"And forgot to check messages when I came in," said Theodosia. "So . . . you called Trident Media and gave them the story?"

Jory and Drew both nodded vigorously.

"We did it for Abby," said Jory.

"It was her kind of story, don't you think?" added Drew.

"Probably was," admitted Theodosia.

Drayton cleared his throat. "Ah, I was sorry to hear about your relative being found in such a state. A sad story indeed."

Jory nodded. "All along I always thought that's exactly what it was. A *story*. A weird old urban myth about a runaway bride. But it's a strange thing to know she really did exist."

"And died such a grizzly death," added Drew.

"So . . . she was a relative?" asked Drayton.

"Relative by marriage," said Drew, still looking a little sad. "Something like a great-great-great aunt. But we don't even know her name."

"Probably because we never thought the legend was true," added Jory.

"But now we're going to acknowledge her," said Drew. "Check out whatever historical records we can find. Then probably hold a memorial service."

"I think that would be quite fitting," said Drayton. He glanced across the tea room, saw a table opening up. "Could I interest you gentlemen in some tea and muffins?"

"Love some," said Jory, smiling at Theodosia.

"That sounds very soothing," added Drew.

"I think," *Jory* was telling Drayton, "that the subbasement was probably part of the Underground Railroad. But our ancestors didn't build the house, so we don't know that for sure."

"That was my first thought, too," said Theodosia, setting a plate of steaming cinnamon muffins on the table.

"That's 'cause you're so smart," said Jory, beaming at her yet again.

"From what we can determine," said Drew, "the plantation was sold in a sheriff's auction back in 1932 and then repurchased by a cousin sometime in the forties."

"So it came back into your family," said Theodosia.

"And was eventually passed down to Abby," said Drew.

"Except now it's been given to the Carolina Heartland Trust," said Jory.

Theodosia smiled at Drew. "I think your donation is just fabulous."

Slightly embarrassed, he nodded and ducked his head. But he looked pleased at the same time. "Thank you. That means a lot to me."

"Historical preservation is critical," said Drayton, sounding like an advertisement for the Heritage Society. "Helps keep our past alive."

"I don't know," said Jory, "that old place is going to need lots of work."

"Believe me," said Drew, "the Carolina Heartland Trust was thrilled to get it."

"I believe you," said Drayton.

"Theodosia," said Jory, while Drew was up at the counter trying to pay and Drayton wasn't having it, "why don't you take the rest of the day off? It's gorgeous outside. The mercury's climbed to almost eighty degrees. We'll go out on the water."

"No rest for the wicked," Theodosia told him. "Besides our regular Friday lunch, we're doing a special luncheon tea for Trident Media."

"Then I'll pick you up afterward. Say two o'clock?"

Theodosia hesitated. "I really shouldn't."

"Of course, you should," said Jory. "For old times' sake."

For old times' sake. Theodosia shifted from one foot to the other and couldn't help but remember all the good times they'd enjoyed together on Jory's sailboat. The races to Sullivan's Island. The Parade of Boats at Christmas. She knew if she went with him, just this one time, they'd probably have a wonderful time. And besides, a little voice in her head was whispering to her that Parker Scully was probably a thing of the past. After all, he hadn't called yet. Probably wasn't going to.

"Well . . . maybe," she told Jory.

Jory pounced eagerly on her words. "That's a yes?"

Theodosia hesitated again. She knew she was treading dangerous ground. Or, rather, dangerous waters.

"Uh . . . I suppose Drayton and Haley could handle the afternoon tea," she told him.

"Excellent," said Jory, jumping to his feet. "I'll be back here around two o'clock and request that you kindly pack a lunch and your swimsuit."

When lunch was finished, when half of the customers had departed, Theodosia and Drayton pushed three tables together and began to set up for the Trident Media lunch. They spread out a cream-colored linen tablecloth, placed Theodosia's floral centerpiece in the middle, and set out the cream-colored Lenox Solitaire china with the silver rims.

"And silver flatware, too," said Drayton. "Make it thematic."

"Then the small silver salt and pepper shakers," added Theodosia.

"Certainly," said Drayton. Then he snickered. "We could do this in our sleep."

"Sometimes we have," she said wryly, thinking of a few Monday mornings when she'd opened the tea room on autopilot.

Drayton gave a quick glance at the customers and determined they were contentedly sipping tea and munching dessert scones. "Let's pop in on Haley and get a final check of the menu."

"Sure," said Theodosia.

As usual, Haley was one step ahead of them. "Key lime scones," she told them, "then we'll segue into my golden beet and smoked trout salad on lettuce *frisse.*"

"With buttermilk dressing?" asked Drayton.

"Of course," said Haley. "It's the best kind."

"And you made extra?" inquired Drayton. He was a buttermilk dressing fiend.

"For you, Drayton, yes," said Haley. "I have an extra pint you will be allowed to take home with you."

"What else is up for today?" asked Theodosia. "Constance specifically asked for a lighter lunch."

"Chilled asparagus soup," said Haley, "accompanied by a tea sandwich of proscuitto, bacon, and sliced avocado."

"And dessert?" asked Drayton.

"Same as what we've been serving," said Haley. "Griddle scones with sliced strawberries and Devonshire cream. Oh, and we've got white chocolate truffles and southern chocolate chess pie."

"Your menu doesn't sound all that light." Theodosia laughed.

"Trust me." Haley said. "Compared to what I usually do, that's light!"

At precisely twelve o'clock, Joe Fanning, Trident Media's news director, came bustling into the tea shop followed by Webster Hall.

Theodosia was so surprised to see Web Hall again, she almost dropped her favorite Shelley Wild Flowers teapot.

"Hello again," she told Web, as the rest of Trident's guests rumbled in and, amidst much hand-shaking and chair-scraping, began seating themselves at the table. She followed Web to his chair, waited until he was seated, then leaned in slightly and let a steaming stream of chamomile tea trickle into his teacup. "I never expected to see you with this group again," she said in a low voice.

Web Hall flashed her a smile so wide she could count the number of caps on his front teeth. "I've been rehired!" he told her. "Starting next Friday I'm gonna anchor the six o'clock news."

20

"You've been rehired?" Theodosia said in a shocked whisper. Just a couple of days ago Web Hall had been an angry, dejected ex-employee of Trident Media. Now he was sitting down to lunch with them—and sitting at their anchor desk, too! "How did this happen?" she asked.

Web Hall suddenly looked slightly uncomfortable. "It's all because of Abby Davis," he said in a low voice. "The station is nervous about any adverse publicity, so Mr. Gillette felt that by bringing back a familiar face, viewers would remain in their comfort zone." He smiled quickly. "Help shore up flagging ratings, too."

"Ratings," Theodosia spat out. She knew the vast corporate greed that drove the television industry lived and died on ratings. Big ratings translated into big prices for airtime.

"Mr. Gillette says it's a six-month temporary position,"

Web continued. "But I know if ratings blip I'll have a home for life."

"And you don't have any hard feelings about this?" Theodosia asked, a little incredulous at the abrupt about-face the man had made.

"Not anymore," said Hall, reaching for a scone.

Theodosia continued her way around the table, pouring tea. Unfortunately for Web Hall, she didn't share his rosy outlook. The way television news was trending these days, she knew that the minute Trident found a suitable, younger replacement, Web would be bounced on his butt.

"Big changes," Theodosia said, when she got to Constance.

Constance regarded her with hooded eyes. "But not so surprising," she murmured. "Since Linus Gillette usually puts his own needs, or should I say the needs of the station, first."

"Is that the only change?" asked Theodosia.

"Actually, no," said Constance. She glanced down the table. "In addition to his role as news director, Joe Fanning is also going to be doing some investigative reporting. In fact, he'll be following up on a couple of Abby's projects—except for the Despard Industries pollution story. That one was dropped."

"Any reason why?" asked Theodosia.

Constance lowered her voice. "Other than the fact that he's sitting at the other end of the table?"

"He is?" said Theodosia. She glanced sharply at an older gentleman with a florid face, thick cap of white hair, and finely tailored suit. He caught her looking at him and held her gaze for a few seconds. Then he went back to chatting with Linus Gillette.

"Donald Despard," muttered Constance.

"He's what?" asked Theodosia. "One of your new advertisers?"

Constance rolled her eyes. "Probably end up on our board of directors."

"So he put pressure on dropping the pollution story," said Theodosia.

"Pressure came from somewhere," Constance replied. "In fact, you'd be shocked if you knew how outside influences from business and government affected the content of TV news."

No, I wouldn't, thought Theodosia. *I'd be angry, but I wouldn't be shocked.*

When Theodosia delivered a beet and smoked trout salad to Linus Gillette, she smiled sweetly and said, "Aren't you the lucky one. Getting all your money back on the Abby Davis contract."

But Gillette wasn't having it. "That happens all the time in our business," he told her in a dismissive tone. "When we wooed Abby away from the Savannah station, she was required to pay money back to them."

"And then some," said Joe Fanning, who occupied the chair next to Linus.

"What do you mean?" asked Theodosia.

"Oh, Abby got herself in a little hot water," said Gillette, reaching for another scone.

Joe Fanning gave Theodosia a long look, then said, "Abby was working on a kidnapping story . . ."

"The Travis McBee investigation?" filled in Theodosia.

Fanning nodded. "Yeah. And Abby apparently became privy to some critical information that she chose not to share with the Savannah police."

"Didn't play ball," said Gillette, his mouth full.

"You mean she withheld a clue?" asked Theodosia.

Still chewing, Gillette inclined his head toward her. "Something like that. Anyway, the station leveled a hefty fine on Abby. She was darned lucky we were already in negotiations. If she hadn't been ready to give notice in Savannah she probably would have been fired."

"I can see why," said Theodosia. In the larger picture, she could also see why Truman McBee might have been hostile toward Abby. If Abby had possessed some sort of clue that might have helped locate his son . . .

Theodosia headed into the kitchen to grab the plates of tea sandwiches while turning her thoughts over in her head. *But what clue?* she wondered. And how could she find out?

The rest of the luncheon went by in a blur for Theodosia. The proscuitto, bacon, and sliced avocado tea sandwiches were an enormous hit, and two guests even asked for seconds. Drayton brewed two pots of Kenilworth Ceylon to go with the dessert course, and when Theodosia brought out the griddle scones with sliced strawberries and Devonshire cream there were words of praise as well as a few groans.

"Got to watch my waistline," Web Hall told her, even though he was spooning extra Devonshire cream onto his dessert. "A TV anchor's gotta look dapper and debonair."

"I think you look very dapper," purred the woman sitting beside him. Theodosia recognized her as Betina Buckner, the owner of a string of seafood restaurants. Betina was obviously one of the new clients being feted and wooed today.

"Thank you!" Web beamed, patting his stomach. "Going back on air has made a new man of me. Given me a new lease on life, so to speak."

"Do you still have that lovely home in the country?" Betina asked. "The one you used to show pictures of?"

"Oh sure," said Web. "But I'm thinking of getting a place here in town, too. In fact, I just made an offer on a carriage house over on Murray Street."

Theodosia jerked her arm at the mention of the carriage house. Could it be *her* carriage house Web Hall was talking so casually about? Sure, it was. It had to be. There was only one property for sale on Murray Street that she knew of. Gritting her teeth, Theodosia felt a sharp pang of disappointment. If Web Hall had scored a new reprieve from Trident Media, and if he could parlay it into a contract, then she didn't stand a snowball's chance of getting that house.

She shook her head. Things just never worked out the way you hoped they would.

Much to Theodosia and Drayton's surprise, their guests mingled in the tea room after lunch, admiring the sweetgrass baskets and selecting tins of tea, jars of honey, and even a few T-Bath products to take home.

"They're *shopping*," murmured Drayton. "Who'd have imagined we'd get a lucky strike extra from these folks?"

"Sell 'em whatever they want," replied Theodosia. "As long as it's not nailed down."

Ducking into her office, Theodosia grabbed the phone and called information. Once she had the number for KSAV-TV in Savannah, she dialed hastily. After all, she had a million things to do and Jory was picking her up in less than fifteen minutes.

"KSAV," said the station's receptionist. "How may I direct your call?"

"Um . . . news director," said Theodosia.

"That would be Kay Lorillard," said the operator. "Hold, please."

There was a hum and a click and then a pleasant female voice said, "Kay Lorillard."

"Ms. Lorillard? This is Theodosia Browning in Charleston. I'm a friend of Abby Davis's family, and I've been—"

"Oh!" Kay Lorillard broke in. "Such a terrible tragedy! We were all so sad to hear of Abby's death."

"I have a few quick questions I'd like to—" began Theodosia. But she was cut off again.

"I apologize," said Kay, "but I'm just on my way out the door."

"I see," said Theodosia. "Would you possibly have a few minutes tomorrow for us to chat? I have a couple of questions about Abby."

"Sorry," said Kay, "but I'm chairing a charity event. The annual Romp and Run to benefit the Lonsdale Animal Shelter."

Theodosia thought for a moment. "What if I happened to drop by?" She'd been planning to make a run to Savannah anyway to pick up a tea order. After all, you couldn't order *everything* out of a catalog.

"Then I'd probably try to sell you a raffle ticket," Kay said in a jesting manner.

"Seriously," said Theodosia, "I really need to talk to you."

"Forsyth Park," said Kay Lorillard. "And that must be some burning question."

When Theodosia pushed her way past the swag of green velvet draperies into the tea shop proper, she was dismayed to see Burt Tidwell sitting at one of the tables. He was just popping a last bite of scone into his mouth. Then, as if by instinct, as if he knew she was there, he swiveled his huge head toward her and watched as she crossed the floor.

Great, she thought. *Now I have to contend with Tidwell.*

Theodosia took the seat across from him. "Sheriff Clay called you," she said as her opening salvo.

"Yes, he did," said Tidwell. "And once again you are pulled into strange circumstances."

"Not my doing," she said. "That basement floor giving way was purely accidental."

"But you went to Mobley Plantation with an intent to snoop." He followed his statement with a not-very-warm smile.

"I wouldn't characterize our visit as snooping," said Theodosia. "It was by invitation from the family."

Tidwell leaned back in his chair and studied her. "Of course it was."

"To change the subject," said Theodosia, "have you spoken any more with Julian Bruno?"

"As a matter of fact," said Tidwell, "I dropped by his shop again this morning. Unannounced."

I'm sure he loved that," said Theodosia. "And Bruno was . . . ?"

"Hostile, uncooperative," said Tidwell.

"Probably still claiming he and Abby were merely friends," said Theodosia.

"Actually," said Tidwell, "he's downgraded her to acquaintance."

"In your eyes, is Bruno a suspect?" asked Theodosia.

Tidwell's jowls sloshed as he shook his head. "He has an impeccable alibi."

"The lecture," said Theodosia.

Tidwell nodded.

"Then who's leading the pack as far as suspects?"

Tidwell stared at her, then reached for a second scone. "No one at the moment."

Theodosia watched Tidwell scoop up an entire pat of butter and slather it on his scone. The butter was followed by a generous dollop of Devonshire cream. She glanced at his expanding waistline, wondered about the health of his heart. Maybe, she decided, she'd ask Haley to concoct some reduced-calorie scones. Feed them to Tidwell on the Q.T. Do her own small part to prolong his life span.

"I was chatting with some folks from Trident Media," Theodosia told him. "They were just here for a luncheon."

Tidwell nodded. "So Drayton told me."

"Anyway," said Theodosia, "I think it was Linus Gillette who mentioned something about Abby Davis withholding a clue in the Travis McBee kidnapping case."

"Withholding a clue," Tidwell repeated.

"From the police."

Tidwell frowned. "First I've heard. Then again, I wasn't fully involved in the McBee investigation." One corner of his mouth twitched slightly. "Pity."

"If there was a clue withheld from the police," said Theodosia, "I imagine Truman McBee would be furious."

"Which in your eyes makes McBee a suspect in Abby's death," said Tidwell.

"Sure," said Theodosia. "Maybe."

"Theo," said Haley, suddenly standing at her elbow. "This just came for you by messenger." She held up a metallic gold box tied with gauzy mauve ribbon.

"Something for the shop?" asked Theodosia. "Did you open it?"

Haley shook her head. "Nope, tag has your name on it."

Theodosia took the package from Haley and set it on the table in front of her. She wondered if perhaps Parker had sent her a "please, can we make up" gift. Heartened by that thought, Theodosia began pulling at the ribbon, then stopped. Remembered she was in the middle of a conversation with Tidwell.

Tidwell's mouth formed a quick, tight smile. "Don't mind me," he told her. "Open your gift if you want."

Excitement building now, Theodosia ripped off the ribbon and pulled the top from the box. Pretty gold tissue paper met her eyes. She unfolded paper, expecting to see a silk scarf or maybe even a fancy blouse. Instead, a cheap black knit ski mask and rusty hunting knife lay rudely nestled in the tissue paper.

"What!" exclaimed Theodosia, jerking backward and tilting the box for Tidwell to see. At the same time she noticed a small, cream-colored card laying next to the knife. The message read, *See you at the Masked Ball.*

Tidwell snorted, then opened and closed his mouth like a gasping fish. "Do you know who sent this?" he demanded in a loud voice.

"No!" Theodosia wailed as Drayton and Haley came running over to see what was wrong.

"Let me see that!" said Drayton, grabbing one side of the box and pulling it toward him.

"No," said Tidwell, tugging back, "*I'll* take that."

"What on earth?" said Haley, sputtering with outrage.

"I think it's somebody's idea of a bad joke," said Theodosia.

"No," said Burt Tidwell, looking grim. "More like someone's idea of a *warning.*"

21

Theodosia met Jory at the back door.

"Hi," he said, peeking into her office. He was dressed in khaki Bermuda shorts and a navy-blue polo shirt. She hadn't seen him looking this casual in a long time and had to admit he looked good. Real good.

"Hi," Theodosia replied. She was his preppy twin in white Bermudas and a dark green polo shirt. Pausing for a beat, she said, "What do you know about Abby's contract at KSAV in Savannah?"

Jory threw her a quizzical look. "Huh?"

"She broke her contract there, right?"

Jory shifted from one sneaker-clad foot to the other. "Yeah, I guess so."

"No," said Theodosia, "she did."

He smiled again. "If you say so."

"So how much do you really know about it?"

"You mean the contractual nits and nats?" asked Jory.

"Yes."

"Not much," replied Jory. "I know Abby supposedly paid some money back . . . that was the deal, of course. For leaving early."

"Okay," said Theodosia, obviously wanting more.

"I offered to look over her contract, but Abby had some hotshot entertainment lawyer from Atlanta who was handling things. And she had her agent in New York, too."

"Do you know her agent?" asked Theodosia. She picked up an oversized canvas bag and slung it across her shoulder.

"Never met her." He gave a quick laugh. "Abby always referred to her as 'The Shark.'"

"And Abby had the money to pay back the Savannah TV station?"

Jory squinted, as if trying to remember. "No," he said, drawing out the syllables. "She came up short, actually. At first she thought about selling the Mobley Plantation to raise capital, but Drew had already talked her into the program with the Carolina Heartland Trust. So she didn't want to go back on her promise to them. In the end Abby just went to her bank and got some sort of bridge loan. And then, of course, after she signed her new contract with Trident she was just fine." He flashed a hopeful, crooked grin at Theodosia. "Hey, you're on to something, huh?"

"Not sure," said Theodosia, pulling the door closed behind them and locking it. She turned around, suddenly noticing the dark green Lexus SUV parked in the alley. Behind it was a black trailer that held two shiny yellow-and-black Sea-Doos.

"Whoa," Theodosia said, holding up a hand. "What's going on here?"

Jory grinned. "These are called personal watercraft."

Theodosia lifted a single, quivering eyebrow. "Personal as in you and me?"

"That's right," said Jory. He obviously enjoyed catching her off guard. "I changed the program a little."

"No kidding," said Theodosia. "You're expecting me to actually ride one of these?"

"You're gonna love it!" enthused Jory.

"No," protested Theodosia. "I'll probably break my neck. Or worse yet, fall off and drown." She contemplated the strange-looking machines for a few moments. "What if we're out on the water—and we *are* talking the Atlantic Ocean here—and the engine craps out. We run out of gas. There are no sails on those things. No radio for an SOS call, no life raft to inflate."

"You like to see the worst in things, don't you?" said Jory.

"No," said Theodosia. "I'm an ex–Girl Scout. I like to be prepared."

"Tell you what," said Jory, guiding her around the front of the Lexus. "We won't go out onto the ocean. We'll head down to Seabrook Island and ride some of the inlets and smaller channels." He grinned. "See? Crisis averted." He opened the passenger side door and gave Theodosia a hand as she climbed in. "Besides, where's that off-road girl I used to know? The one who ran her Jeep deep into the woods, scouring around for wild ginseng and dandelion greens?"

"I still do that," said Theodosia, a tiny grin creeping onto her face.

"Same principle then," said Jory. "Only this is more fun. Like flying across the water." He saw the look on her face, then added, "But perfectly safe. Trust me, you're gonna love this."

"You keep saying that," said Theodosia.

"Because I *mean* it," said Jory.

"Where's your sailboat?" she asked. Theodosia was still hoping she could wheedle him into a sail instead.

"In dry dock," said Jory. "Being repaired." He closed the passenger door, came around the front of the Lexus, and hopped into the driver's seat.

"Who owns those sea dogs back there?"

Jory laughed. "Sea-Doos. This whole rig belongs to Drew."

"And you swear you've done this before? This isn't your maiden voyage?"

Jory turned the key in the ignition, hit the accelerator, and roared out of the alley. "Trust me, Theo, we're gonna have a ball."

They cut across James Island, drove the length of Johns Island, and finally crossed over the bridge to Seabrook Island. Just outside the Seabrook Island gate, they crunched down a road covered with tiny shells and rocked to a stop at Bohicket Marina.

Jory backed the trailer into the water and unloaded the Sea-Doos. While he fussed with them, Theodosia dashed into the ladies' bathhouse and changed into a black maillot.

"Here," said Jory, when she finally ambled over to where the Sea-Doos bobbed in the water. He handed her a pair of black mesh surf shoes and a black rubber neoprene vest. "I think these will fit."

"Okay." She put them on and decided she looked like a member of the Cousteau underwater team. "So what now?" she asked, spritzing sunscreen on her arms and legs, rubbing it in, then slipping on a pair of large oval sunglasses. "We do our biker-surfer-dude thing?"

Jory grinned. "I was afraid you'd never ask."

She stuck her sunscreen and a bottle of cold water into the flip-top compartment on the side of the Sea-Doo, and then Jory gave her a five-minute lesson. Starting the ignition, using the choke, changing gears, cornering, and stopping. Theodosia listened diligently, nodded, stored the information away. Navigating a Sea-Doo, she decided, was much easier than a motorcycle. And she'd ridden one of those when she was in college. Well, a 125cc scooter, anyway.

Twenty minutes later Theodosia felt like an old hand, as she and Jory chased back and forth, taking turns at following each other and jumping over each other's wakes.

They followed the curve of small streams and inlets through the tangle of salt marshes. Here, salt-tolerant grasses and plants grew in brackish, soggy soil known as "pluff mud" that was flooded and drained each day by the ocean's shifting tides. These salt marshes were the provenance of shellfish, crabs, snails, and insects. Hungry wildlife such as raccoons, grackles, egrets, and ibis were often drawn to this feast.

Pushing farther inland, Theodosia and Jory zoomed down streams that led to more turgid, blackwater swamps. Here, in the lush, humid, semitropical atmosphere, tupelo rose like towering spires and palmetto trees thrived. Of course, more dangerous wildlife thrived here, too. Rattlesnakes, alligators, even the occasional coral snake.

But dangerous creatures were the farthest thing from Theodosia's mind as she skimmed across the water. It was a glorious day and she caught slivers and snatches of sunshine and bright blue sky through the leafy canopy that spread overhead.

Pulling ahead of Jory now, Theodosia bent low to her Sea-Doo and kicked it into high gear. She pulled ahead with a jolt, leaving a huge rooster tail of spray in her wake.

Grinning, deciding to have a little fun with him, Theodosia peeled off down a narrow inlet, then quickly zoomed around a corner. Looking back over her shoulder, she fully expected to see Jory coming hard after her. But he wasn't.

"Hah," she said aloud, then throttled back a little. Probably, she decided, if she followed this small stream, it would curve back around to the main channel they'd been chasing down. For the last forty minutes they'd been doing exactly that. Weaving and dodging their way through the swamp, always returning to the main channel. Besides, the sun was high overhead in the southwestern sky, a fine beacon to guide her and serve as directional compass.

She kicked her Sea-Doo into high gear again and nosed it down the stream. Sleepy turtles sunning on half-sunken logs didn't seem at all surprised to see her flash by. Overhead, a pileated woodpecker drilled noisily into a tree and she could just imagine miniature wood chips flying like crazy.

She flew through one curve, bent low, and took another. But this stream was leading her on a twisting path. Now the sun was over her left shoulder, so she should . . . what? Maybe head toward the right?

Seeing another small inlet, Theodosia headed into it. But as she rode along, the water seemed to get more and more shallow. Not only that, the terrain was shifting somewhat, too. On her left was a slight hill. Was she running out of swamp? Should she just turn around and go back the way she came?

Theodosia slowed to a crawl. She'd spotted a sign ahead. Wondering what on earth it could be, she eased over toward the fern-covered bank.

She was almost on top of the rough, wooden sign before she could read it. PRIVATE PROPERTY. KEEP AWAY. And un-

derneath the carved letters were the words DESPARD INDUS-
TRIES.

Theodosia took off her sunglasses and squinted up the hill.
Sure enough, she could see a corner of a dark green building
through the trees.

*This is Despard Industries? The paper plant? The same one
Abby had been doing an investigative report on? And then was told
to stop?*

Theodosia idled the Sea-Doo for a few moments and
watched as a bright, metallic-green tiger beetle buzzed about
her head. Then she negotiated a slow, tight turn. Okay, this
was an interesting side trip. An interesting turn of events
that had once again jogged her memory about Despard Industries. But now she had to get back to where she'd started.
Since she'd obviously veered off course, she needed to make a
correction.

Theodosia hit the throttle and roared out. Found her
stream, chased her way down it, found another stream, hooked
a left.

But wait, this didn't seem like the way she'd come.

Theodosia kicked it harder and decided she'd keep going
anyway. Even though these streams were a tangle, she'd eventually come out near the salt marsh. And then it would be
easy to find the boat launch, right?

She was suddenly aware of a buzzing in her ears. Another
Sea-Doo? Had to be. Jory?

Theodosia glanced back over her shoulder and was momentarily stunned. Another personal watercraft was closing in behind her. But it wasn't Jory. This rider was chubby and wore
black wraparound sunglasses and a black bandana pulled low
over his forehead.

Unnerved, Theodosia skimmed through a turn and headed

down a different stream. Surely he wouldn't follow her, would he?

But he did!

She chanced another glance. Bent low over his machine, the mysterious man seemed intent on catching up to her!

But why? Theodosia wondered. Then decided, it didn't matter. She was being chased and it scared her to death.

Pouring on more speed, she twisted and turned her way down the stream, coming perilously close to hidden logs, practically jumping over the occasional sandbar. Still her pursuer kept coming!

Not only that, he was gaining on her!

Theodosia's mind was racing as fast as her overtaxed Sea-Doo. She needed a plan, a diversion. Most of all, she needed to *stop* him. But how?

He was practically on her tail now, so Theodosia knew she had to think fast. Up ahead, where the stream narrowed somewhat, where the banks seemed steeper, Theodosia spotted another sandbar. If she could somehow navigate toward the deeper side and cause her pursuer to stop on the sandbar, maybe he'd get stuck! Buy her some time!

She headed to the far left of the sandbar, throttled back hard, and yelled back at him. "Hey, I've got somethin' for you!"

She sluiced to a stop, let her left hand drift back, and waited.

Five seconds later he was almost upon her. Black bandana, mirrored sunglasses, dirty bare feet, skin diver's knife in a black rubber sheath strapped to his thigh. He was beefy with red hair. At least the hair on his arms looked red. As he drifted toward her, his body language told her he was wary. He was watching out for a trick.

"Come closer," she yelled over the drone of almost-idling engines.

The man edged closer, as water slapped the banks.

When he was almost alongside her, his mouth a tight rictus of intensity, Theodosia whipped out her bottle of sunscreen, aimed for his nose and mouth, and let loose a thick stream of white, perfumed goop. The result was immediate. The man yelped like a stuck pig, then let loose a gut-wrenching cough followed by a series of violent sneezes.

Too bad he was wearing sunglasses, of course, but his nose and mouth still made dandy targets. Keeping her finger on the aerosol spray, Theodosia continued to pour it on.

"How do you like that!" she yelled. "How does that taste!"

Gasping for breath, the man's bellow turned into a high-pitched wheeze. He coughed, spit, wheezed again, then leaned over and dipped his hand in the water, trying to cup enough liquid to rinse out his mouth.

Throwing the empty can at him, bonking him on the side of the head as a final insult, Theodosia yelled, "Take that!" then took off in a burst of speed. She opened the throttle wide, running at almost blinding speed. Tupelos whipped by, sunken logs threatened, vines clawed at her. Theodosia didn't care. She raced down the inlet, twisting and turning, rounding corners, running as fast as she could.

The landscape was beginning to change now, the darker swamp receding, the land beginning to sprout more waving green grasses.

Yes!

She was finally heading back toward the saltwater marsh.

Her heart lifted as the inlet widened out. Then she was

racing around a corner, suddenly seeing another Sea-Doo coming directly at her.

Jory? This time, yes.

But now she was on a collision course with him!

Throttling back and using her brake, Theodosia made a hard three-sixty-degree spin in front of him and promptly spilled off her Sea-Doo.

As she foundered in water, her feet sinking into bottom-less muck, Jory reached down, grabbed her hand, and lifted her. His eyes bulged, the cords on his arms and shoulders stood out, but he pulled her up, up, up, until she was able to get one foot on the base of her watercraft. Then she was able to hoist herself to safety.

"Somebody was chasing me!" she yelled, her words spill-ing out.

Jory looked surprised and a little skeptical. "What?"

"Back there!" She pointed in the direction she'd just come. "Some . . . weird guy."

"Seriously?" Jory throttled back his engine. It putt-putt-putted, then killed. "I don't hear anything."

Theodosia listened carefully. She was positive they'd hear the roar of another Sea-Doo zooming toward them, but Jory was right. There was only the gentle lap of waves and trill of warblers. Her pursuer must have gone some other way.

"Probably that jealous boyfriend of yours," joked Jory. "Coming after me."

Still puzzled, still feeling jittery, Theodosia said, "Be seri-ous. There *was* someone."

"I believe you," said Jory, but he still didn't sound con-vinced.

They rode back slowly and didn't speak again until Jory

was turning a crank on the trailer, pulling the Sea-Doos out of the water.

"Do you have a date for the Masked Ball tomorrow night?" Jory asked.

"Yes, of course," said Theodosia, although her heart told her that Parker probably wasn't going to call to confirm. Probably wasn't going to call at all.

"Because if you don't," said Jory, "I'd love to be your escort."

"No," said Theodosia, her mind still a jumble of thoughts. "I don't think that's a very good idea." Probably, she decided, this whole afternoon hadn't been such a good idea. She was feeling stupid and more than a little guilty.

Jory eyed her as he coiled a length of plastic line. "And I suppose the boyfriend is taking you to Timothy's party tonight?"

"Why are you so suddenly hung up on my social calendar?" Theodosia asked. She meant her words to be light, but they came out sounding sharp and shrewish.

"Probably because I care about you," murmured Jory.

"Well, that's . . ." Theodosia cast about for the right word. "That's really inconvenient," she finally told him.

Her phone was ringing as she came flying up the stairs into her kitchen.

"Can you get that?" she called to Earl Grey.

He lifted his sleek head and looked at her calmly as if to say, *I'm not a secretary and, besides, as a canine I have no thumbs.*

She managed to grab the receiver off the hook just before it rolled over to the answering service. "Hullo?" she said breathlessly.

It was Parker Scully. Sounding sweet as pie and launching into a rapid-fire apology for being so mistrustful and possessive. "I was out of line," he told her. "Acting like a total dufus. But when you phoned from that old plantation, I didn't know what to think."

"Sure, you did," said Theodosia. "You thought I was hooking up with Jory again."

"Yeah," Parker said slowly, "I sorta did."

"Even though I wasn't," said Theodosia.

Well, not at that exact moment, she thought to herself and felt guilty all over again.

"I realize that," said Parker. "And I realize you're your own person."

Theodosia felt another twinge of guilt about her afternoon outing with Jory. Still, Parker had hit the nail on the head. She *was* her own person. Sort of.

"Please," said Parker, and now he really sounded worried. "I still want to escort you to that Masked Ball tomorrow night, even though I have to honcho the appetizers. And, of course, to Timothy's party tonight. I want to be with you. Truly." There was a brief hesitation. "If that's okay with you."

A wire seemed to loosen in her chest. She really didn't want to break it off with Parker. She really cared about him. "I was hoping everything was still on," Theodosia told him.

"Whew," said Parker. "I'm glad that's settled. I'm glad we're still okay."

"We're okay," said Theodosia.

"Then I'll even bring you a corsage, just like a dutiful prom date."

"You don't have to do that," said Theodosia, though she was tickled by the thoughtfulness of his offer.

"I know I don't *have* to," said Parker, "but I *want* to. Tell me what you're wearing tonight. So I can color-coordinate with your dress."

"Uh . . . dress?" said Theodosia. She hadn't given any thought to her dress for tonight. Decided she'd probably just dig something out of her closet. But thinking about getting all dressed up also sparked the realization that she hadn't picked out her gown for the Masked Ball tomorrow night! Theodosia glanced at her watch. Maybe, just maybe, if she hopped in her Jeep and drove like a madwoman, she could get to Cotton Duck before it closed.

"I'll probably just wear a black dress tonight," Theodosia told Parker.

"And what about tomorrow?" he asked.

"I'm still kind of . . . um . . . undecided," murmured Theodosia. And that, she thought to herself, was the understatement of the decade!

22

Delaine glanced up from behind her sales counter. When she saw it was Theodosia slipping into her store at such a late hour, her smile morphed into a concerned frown. "Well, you certainly took your own sweet time about getting here. I'm closing in ten minutes."

"Sorry," said Theodosia. "It's been crazy."

Delaine sauntered out from behind the counter. "And don't you look all sun-kissed and healthy. You must have been serving tea all afternoon at your outdoor tables."

"Something like that," said Theodosia. If she told Delaine she'd been out riding Sea-Doos with Jory, the news would be all over town in a heartbeat. And if she told Delaine she'd been chased by a crazed stalker she'd probably post it on the Internet. Theodosia shook her head as if to chase away that thought. "Delaine," she said, in a slightly contrite tone, "I am in dire need of some fashion assistance."

"You have a fashion *emergency*," said Delaine, almost reveling in Theodosia's dilemma.

Theodosia glanced around the interior of Cotton Duck. Racks of long gowns hung next to circular racks of silky tops with matching pajama pants. Elegant peekaboo camisoles nestled in silk-lined boxes that sat on antique highboys. Strands of opera pearls hung down and mingled with an array of charm bracelets, initial necklaces, and diaphanous scarves. Glass shelves displayed handbags of supple leather, gleaming reptile, and whisper-soft suede. A display of shoes offered teetering high heels by Louboutin, Christian Lacroix, and Jimmy Choo.

"There must be *something* here," said Theodosia. Among all this glitter and glam there had to be something that would let her put her best foot forward tomorrow night.

"The problem is," said Delaine with a sigh, "we're down to the absolute *dregs* when it comes to ball gowns. I suggested you make your choice early, but once again you chose to wait until the last possible moment."

"Do you still have the green silk gown?" asked Theodosia. "Or the peachy-gold one?"

Delaine shook her head sadly. "Not anymore. Now I only have a silk-chiffon degradé left."

"And that is . . . ?"

"An Alberta Ferretti in gradated colors. A rather striking dress. Midnight blue at the top fading down to a pale, almost washed-out blue at the hem. Similar principle as the old tie-dye, but far more sophisticated."

"Then I should try that one," said Theodosia.

"Gee," said Delaine, "do you think?"

"Delaine . . . please," said Theodosia. "It hasn't been my best week."

"Oh, I don't know. Looks to me like you've been having a pretty sweet time of it." Delaine wrinkled her nose in a catty gesture. "Parker *and* Jory."

But Theodosia had already made up her mind not to argue this subject with Delaine. Instead, she turned and began perusing a rack of clothes. "Are these vintage?"

"Yes, they are," said Delaine, all business again.

"A lot of them are really neat."

"Vintage is one of the hottest things going," confided Delaine. "Kind of an insider's fashion secret. I'm sure you've noticed lots of big-name Hollywood stars wearing vintage gowns on the red carpet? Marvelous eighties Halstons, flouncy Diors, even Lagerfeld's early Chanels. Since I expanded my shop, I've made a conscious effort to increase my vintage collection."

"Where on earth do you find it?" asked Theodosia.

"Here and there," shrugged Delaine, trying to look mysterious. "I have a couple of contacts in Palm Springs, a pair of ladies in Beverly Hills, and this perfectly delightful fellow who runs a consignment shop down in West Palm Beach. Once in a while you even get stuff that's NWT!"

"What's NWT?" asked Theodosia.

"New with tags," replied Delaine. "It's amazing how many wealthy women go on shopping binges, then let their fabulous finds just *languish* in their closet. So frivolous!"

"Oh," said Theodosia. She wasn't much interested in the shopping habits of wealthy women. What she needed, what she was here for, was something she could wear right away. Pawing through the racks, however, was more than a little confusing. There were dresses and gowns as well as tunic and pants sets that were practically art statements. But . . . which one to choose? "What are you wearing to Timothy's party tonight?" Theodosia asked.

Delaine arched her back and stretched languidly. "Nothing special. I have a Marc Jacobs in a sample size four I'm going to squeeze into."

"Fancy?" asked Theodosia.

"Mmm, very," said Delaine. "Georgette silk in carmine red, but a red without too much blue. I'm contemplating pairing my silver Manolos with it. Should be very glam."

"Wow," said Theodosia. "I was just going to wear my black cocktail dress."

"The same one you wore to the last three cocktail parties you attended?" Delaine inquired in a flat tone.

"Yes," said Theodosia.

"Your black dress always looks nice," allowed Delaine. "But when one wishes to stand out in a sea of conservative taste, one opts for a color with lots of va-va-voom."

Va-va-voom, thought Theodosia. *I might need a little va-va-voom to jump-start things with Parker again.*

"Any recommendations?" asked Theodosia.

"I was hoping you'd ask," said Delaine, moving in deftly for the kill. "For one thing, I've got this truly spectacular Claude Montana dress. Very red carpet."

"Sounds a little over the top," said Theodosia.

"Slip it on, dear," urged Delaine. "Let's just see what we're working with."

So, of course, Theodosia slipped it on. And wasn't at all displeased by the cocoa-brown number that was draped and bias cut.

"Now that's promising," cooed Delaine, when Theodosia walked out of the dressing room. "A little Joan Collins crossed with rock and roll."

Theodosia scrutinized herself in the three-way mirror. "You don't think the shoulders are a little prominent?"

Delaine studied Theodosia's image in the mirror. "It might be a little *Dynasty* at that. Why don't you try . . . hmm . . ." Her red fingernails picked through the rack, then grasped a plum-colored Halston. "This one!"

Theodosia headed back into the dressing room, slipped into the Halston, and once again presented herself for approval.

"I like it," Delaine said with enthusiasm.

Theodosia had to agree. It was practically perfect. No, it really was perfect. A simple sheath dress that hit slightly above the knee. Just the right amount of beading at the neckline.

"Good," said Delaine. "One down, one to go."

"I can't just wear this dress again on Saturday night?" asked Theodosia, making another small pirouette.

Delaine exploded with high-pitched laughter. "Oh, my dear. You mustn't engage in such pedestrian thinking. Besides, you need a *ball gown.* Something long and distinctly formal."

"So maybe the . . . what did you call it? The degradé dress," said Theodosia. "If it fits."

"If it fits," agreed Delaine, not sounding all that hopeful.

But when Theodosia emerged from the fitting room, looking rather radiant in her long blue dress, Delaine changed her tune. "Why, that one's perfect, too," she exclaimed. "Very slinky and dramatic." Fidgeting with Theodosia's neckline, Delaine pulled it down to reveal a hint of cleavage. "Mark my words, you're going to turn heads in that dress." Now Delaine sounded a little jealous.

Theodosia gazed at herself in the mirror. The midnight blue around her shoulders set off the auburn in her hair, the long column dress made her look at least two inches taller than she really was. And, of course, the silk moved with an airy swoosh.

"You like?" asked Delaine.

"I like," said Theodosia, tugging up the neckline Delaine had pulled down. Deciding the dress would match the gold mask she'd picked up at Julian Bruno's shop.

"A real glam-o-rama dress," chortled Delaine. "Parker's going to take one look and think he died and went to heaven."

Theodosia grimaced. "Parker. Yeah. Looks like I'm going to have to tread a little more lightly with this Abby Davis investigation. If he knew how involved I was, I don't think we'd still be dating."

"I don't see that as a problem, honey," Delaine purred. "These days it seems to me you have your *choice* of dates."

Theodosia felt like Cinderella arriving at the ball when she and Parker entered Timothy Neville's house. Candles blazed, champagne corks popped, and strains of classical music wafted from the conservatory where a twelve-piece orchestra played.

"Holy smokes," said Parker. He was suddenly rooted in his tracks on an antique Chinese silk rug.

Theodosia smiled, adjusting her camellia wrist corsage. People often had that reaction when they first entered Timothy's Archdale Street mansion. "Yes, it's a lot to take in, isn't it?" she asked.

"Timothy lives here *alone?*" Parker's eyes darted crazily from the dramatic curved staircase to the huge crystal chandelier that hung overhead to the enormous parlor filled with a mélange of Chippendale, Sheraton, and antique French furniture.

"He has a butler," said Theodosia, trying to ease Parker along. "A lovely man by the name of Henry."

"This place is *huge*," marveled Parker. He was having trouble adjusting to this type of grandeur.

"Yes, well, Timothy is rather wealthy," said Theodosia.

"The Heritage Society pays this kind of money?" asked Parker.

"No, no," said Theodosia, smiling. "Timothy's wealth is the best kind of wealth. Inherited."

"You're telling me his ancestors are old Charleston society," said Parker.

"Something like that," replied Theodosia.

They pushed their way through the crush of people and into one of the parlors, where a sleek wooden bar was set up. Three uniformed bartenders manned the station, turning out standards like martinis and bourbon and water, as well as more trendy Cosmopolitans and Mojitos.

"Your friend Timothy's got more bartenders working tonight than we do during out busiest weekends at Solstice," said Parker, still impressed.

"It's a big party," said Theodosia, patting his arm. Glancing around, she spotted Drayton, elegant in his tuxedo with a red-and-green tartan bow tie, lounging in a corner with two other board members from the Heritage Society. From out of the corner of her eye she saw Delaine waft by in a spectacularly bright red dress. She was on the arm of someone, but Theodosia couldn't quite see who it was. Her boyfriend du jour, she supposed. Herbert or Hubert or maybe it was Hobart. You never knew with Delaine.

Parker held up two crystal flutes of pale gold liquid. "I got us champagne. Scharffenberger Brut." Theodosia accepted the glass and they both took a tiny sip. "Ahh," said Parker, "Timothy's not afraid to serve the good stuff."

"Probably because Timothy lives the good life," said Theodosia, enjoying the tickle of bubbles against her tongue.

Still in a slight daze, Parker sidled over to a marble fireplace and gazed at the half dozen ceramic figures displayed on the mantel. "Toy soldiers," he said with an almost nostalgic smile.

Theodosia nodded. "Officers from Napoleon's army done in bone china. Timothy collects them. Those figures are antiques by the way, made by the old French firm Sevres."

"Expensive?" asked Parker.

"You don't even want to know."

Theodosia and Parker meandered through Timothy's home, admiring the solarium and then the dining room, and finally met up with Drayton again in the library.

"Delighted to see you," said Drayton, shaking Parker's hand.

"It's great to be here," said Parker, gazing at floor-to-ceiling shelves of leather-bound books as well as Timothy's collection of antique pistols, which were mounted in shadow boxes against dark green felt. "This is quite a place, huh?"

"Timothy does live in what I like to refer to as baronial splendor," murmured Drayton.

"The good life," said Parker.

Drayton threw Theodosia an approving glance. "You're still coming to the Masked Ball tomorrow night?"

"Wouldn't miss it," said Theodosia, squeezing Parker's hand. "Now that I've found the perfect dress."

"And I know *you* are," said Drayton, nodding at Parker. "I hear your chefs have a lovely Italian menu planned. Should be the perfect complement to the Verdi theme, as well as the strolling musicians and actors and special props on display."

"It promises to be a memorable evening," enthused Parker.

"Well," said Drayton, in a giddy, conspiratorial tone. "If you want a sneak peak, Timothy's put the Lugori jewels on display in a small parlor. He thinks they're so stunning everyone should get a preview." Then he struck off through the crowd.

"Want to check out the food?" asked Parker. "I'm absolutely starved."

"You go grab yourself a plate," Theodosia urged. "I see my friend Brooke over there. I want to have a quick gab."

"Done," said Parker, moving away.

Brooke Carter Crockett was mid-fifties and petite with a sleek mane of white hair. Besides handling a spectacular array of estate jewelry at Heart's Desire, Brooke also crafted her own line of jewelry. Her Charleston-themed charm bracelets included miniature palm trees, churches, magnolia blossoms, pineapples, and wrought-iron gates. Her sterling silver oyster-shell pendants featured real pearls tucked inside them. And her "teacup" bracelets and pendants incorporated authentic pieces of colorful, broken antique china outlined in both gold and sterling silver. For this last line of jewelry, Theodosia had contributed more than her fair share of broken cups.

"You're back," said Theodosia. "How did the appraisal go?"

"Nobody's ever happy with the number you give them," said Brooke, brushing an imaginary speck off her pink St. John knit jacket. "Everybody thinks their jewelry or silver or loose gemstones should command top dollar."

"Speaking of which," said Theodosia, "Timothy has some rather rare jewels on display here tonight."

"That's what I've heard," said Brooke as they linked arms, then wandered down the hallway into Timothy's small parlor. In the center of the room a glass museum case stood under a series of pinpoint spotlights. Three shelves of jewelry sparkled from within the locked case.

"Imported all the way from Venice," said Theodosia. "To be featured in *Un Ballo in Maschera*."

"Mmm," said Brooke, pulling a pair of red half-glasses from her handbag as they peered at the jewels.

"That's strange," said Theodosia, staring at the pieces and suddenly looking quite stunned. "The cameo that's on display here? It's almost identical to the one Abby Davis was wearing!"

"Abby . . ." said Brooke. Then recognition dawned on her face. "Oh, you mean the murdered woman?" She grimaced slightly. "The one that you found?"

Theodosia nodded as she stared, entranced, at the collection of jewelry nestled on thick cushions of lustrous black velvet.

"I certainly hope her cameo was better than this one," said Brooke, out of the corner of her mouth.

Theodosia gave her friend a sharp glance. "What do you mean? What are you talking about?"

Brooke gazed speculatively at the jeweled cameo that was showcased in front of them. "Because I doubt this particular cameo is real. It's a very skillfully done piece, but I don't believe those are antique gemstones."

"But . . . but all these pieces came from the Lugori Museum in Venice. They're supposed to be almost priceless!"

"Then the Lugori must have made some sort of switch," said Brooke, standing firm, trusting her instinct and especially what she saw before her eyes. "Because that cameo is not the real deal."

"What you're telling me is . . . exceedingly strange," murmured Theodosia. "Are you . . . are you quite sure?"

Brooke nodded. "I'd stake my reputation on it."

"Then we have to find Timothy immediately," said Theodosia, glancing about, trying to fight a rising tide of panic.

23

Timothy Neville *was* not amused. In fact, he was outraged. "What do you mean the piece isn't real?" he shrilled. Though he wore a sedate black tuxedo, his simian face was beginning to turn as red as a chili pepper. Not a good look for him.

"Tell him, Brooke," urged Theodosia. The three of them stood huddled in front of the glass case, which was blessedly free of onlookers for the moment.

"That cameo is an imitation," said Brooke.

"Can't be," said Timothy. He gritted his teeth and pressed his forehead against the glass case. "Can it?"

"Happens all the time," explained Brooke. "I'm constantly getting people in my shop who are trying to sell gemstones that are really crystals, or diamonds that turn out to be CZs or Moissanite. Most folks aren't trying to con me, they just genuinely don't know."

"What's wrong?" asked Drayton, coming up behind the

trio. He'd seen Timothy and Theodosia in tense conversation together and wanted to know what was brewing.

They quickly filled him in.

"Fake?" he squawked, rearing back on his heels.

"Shhh!" cautioned Timothy. "We don't know that for a fact."

"Unfortunately, we do," said Theodosia. "Brooke is a jeweler and expert gemologist. If she says this cameo is a fake, then it's probably a fake."

"How could this happen?" asked Drayton in a shocked tone. "Was some sort of switch made in Italy? At the Lugori Museum?"

Theodosia was trying to process this strange revelation. "Wait a minute," she said, putting a hand on Timothy's sleeve. "Didn't you tell me the jewels were photographed a couple of weeks ago?"

"Taken out for all of five minutes," said Timothy. "Then locked back inside our vault at the Heritage Society."

"Who handled the photography?" asked Theodosia.

Timothy paused for a long moment. "Thandie McLean."

"Thandie's reputation is impeccable," said Drayton. "At least I think it is."

Timothy held up an index finger. "Along with a fellow by the name of Julian Bruno."

"Oh my," breathed Theodosia.

"What?" snapped Timothy.

Now Theodosia's mind was reeling. "There's a possibility Julian Bruno stole your cameo," she told Timothy.

"What?" he howled again.

Theodosia drew a long breath, before she continued. "And then there's a chance *I* stole it back again."

Now there was a collective "What!"

*   *   *

Theodosia explained how she'd noticed Abby wearing the cameo the day of the shooting. Then told them how she'd once again come across the cameo at the visitation. And while Drayton eyed the ceiling, looking decidedly embarrassed, Theodosia delicately recounted her little theft.

"You're a bold one, aren't you," said Brooke with a wry smile once Theodosia had finished her story.

"What an exceedingly strange tale," muttered Timothy. "You're telling me you simply had a *feeling* about the cameo? A suspicion?" He took a step back and stared at her.

Theodosia nodded. She realized the whole thing did sound awfully weak. And incredibly strange.

"Theodosia's a very suspicious person," added Drayton.

"Thank you, Drayton," said Theodosia. "I think."

"The thing is," said Timothy, "what to do now?"

"We have to call Detective Tidwell," proposed Theodosia. "After all, he's part and parcel of the Abby Davis investigation. And he does head Charleston PD's Robbery-Homicide Division."

"Agreed," said Timothy, still looking shell-shocked regarding the possible theft of his cameo. "But we must keep this completely under wraps. Not a word to anyone."

"Mum's the word," said Drayton.

"So we should maybe give him a ring right now?" asked Theodosia.

Timothy glanced over his shoulder at the cameo in the jewel case, then grimaced. "Make the call."

Theodosia, Drayton, and Brooke slipped out Timothy's back door and hurried over to the Indigo Tea Shop where Tidwell had reluctantly agreed to meet them. Once they arrived, Theodosia hustled upstairs and grabbed the cameo from its resting place inside her jewel box.

When she came back downstairs, she found that Burt Tidwell was already there. Drayton had hastily brewed tea and was pouring cups for all of them. Tidwell, sitting lumpishly at a table with his back to her, was chatting quietly with Brooke.

"Miss Browning," Tidwell said expansively when Theodosia circled round the table. "I never pegged you for a jewel thief."

"It was more like part of my investigation," said Theodosia.

"So," said Tidwell, "you were suspicious about Abby Davis wearing costume jewelry, in light of all the expensive pieces her husband had gifted her with."

"Yes," said Theodosia. Her speculation had felt shaky. But now it looked like she might be proven correct.

"Then let's get to it, shall we?" said Tidwell. "Let's have a look at this mysterious cameo."

Theodosia set it on the table. The carved figure and the jewels surrounding it sparkled enticingly in the low light.

"A gorgeous piece," declared Drayton, peering at the cameo. "I'm thinking this one has to be authentic."

"Ah," said Tidwell, poking at the cameo with a fat finger, then leaning back in his chair. "That is where we look to Miss Crockett to enlighten us." He inclined his head toward Brooke. "Could you do an analysis? Give us a quick lesson in cameos?"

Brooke was happy to comply. "Cameos are typically carved from conch shells, coral, lava, and hard stone, especially agate and onyx," she told them. "As you probably know, Wedgwood also crafted some beautiful cameos. The older pieces are hand-carved, usually from prominent carving centers such as Italy or Germany. The newer ones, the contemporary cameos you see today, are pretty much done by machine."

"Okay," said Theodosia. She was finding all this fascinating, but wanted to cut to the heart of the matter.

"This particular cameo," said Brooke, as she picked it up and studied it, "appears to be Diana, the Roman goddess of the hunt. Carved from onyx and surrounded by a gold bezel set with red and purple stones. This sort of piece was very popular during the Victorian era."

"And the stones are authentic?" asked Drayton, who prided himself on having a good eye for art. "This piece is from the Lugori Museum set?"

Brooke studied the cameo again. "Probably . . . no."

"No?" said Theodosia. This was a shock!

Brooke shrugged. "Much like the piece on display back at Timothy's house, this piece is basically costume jewelry. It's worth at most a couple of hundred dollars."

"Huh," said Tidwell in a noncommittal tone.

Feeling somewhat deflated by Brooke's pronouncement, Theodosia wrinkled her brow. And thought hard about the first time she'd seen the cameo on Abby. That terrible Sunday when Abby had looked so white and cold and the jewels had looked so elegant and shimmering. On the other hand, Theodosia knew that she'd also hit her head. Maybe that slight injury had contributed to the otherworldly feeling of that whole episode.

Drayton's brows arched as he stared across the table at Theodosia. No words passed between them, but she knew what he was thinking. She'd stolen a piece of jewelry that had been dear to Abby and had been meant to be buried with her.

A pang of guilt pierced Theodosia's heart. What had she done in the name of sleuthing? "I . . . I've made a terrible mistake," said Theodosia. "I owe apologies to more than a few people."

Her stricken glance met Drayton's once again.

There was a screech of chair against wood floor as Tidwell rose.

"I'm sorry," Theodosia told him. "I really didn't . . ."

Tidwell held up a hand. "Not so fast."

Theodosia gazed placidly at him.

"Julian Bruno isn't quite off the hook," he told the group.

"He's not?" said Drayton. This was news to him.

"He may still have made off with the cameo."

"Huh?" said Brooke.

"I'm not following you," said Theodosia.

Tidwell stroked one side of his face with a giant paw. "It's possible Julian Bruno switched cameos during the photo shoot."

"Wouldn't Thandie have seen him do that?" asked Drayton.

"Not necessarily," said Tidwell. "Not if he's skillful."

"Are you serious?" said Theodosia.

"You were the one who thought Abby and Bruno were romantically linked," said Tidwell.

Theodosia continued to gaze at him. "Yes."

"So imagine this scenario, if you will," said Tidwell. "Bruno steals the cameo because he has sticky fingers, crushing debt, or some such thing. Whatever his problem, he intends to sell it and make a killing. But he's also a man who's ego-driven and a show-off. So perhaps Julian Bruno commits a cardinal error by showing the cameo to Abby Davis and then allowing her to wear it. Or perhaps Abby sees it and begs to wear it. Of course, Bruno needs the cameo back in rather short order. He's made plans to sell it, or maybe he suddenly decides he's playing with fire—someone's going to notice this swell cameo pinned to Abby's blouse."

"So he murders Abby to try to get it back?" asked Drayton.

"Or hires someone," said Tidwell. "Then sets up his air-tight alibi by giving a lecture at the Gibbes Museum."

"But I came riding along," said Theodosia. "So the murderer couldn't grab it."

"Next time Bruno sees his prize cameo, it's pinned to Abby Davis's corpse."

Brooke gave a shudder.

"Bruno shows up at Abby's visitation, hidden among the crowd, and steals the cameo," Theodosia said in a harsh whisper, "and . . . what? . . . replaces it with one that looks practically the same?"

"Because he probably has a good inventory of costume jewelry cameos," murmured Brooke.

"And then Theodosia steals the fake one," said Drayton.

They were all silent for a few moments, thinking, glancing at each other.

"It sounds . . . plausible," said Brooke. But she didn't sound all that sure.

"No," said Tidwell, "it's only supposition. Certainly not something I could build a case on." He exhaled loudly. "Do we know where Julian Bruno is right now?"

"No idea," said Theodosia.

"He's at Timothy's party," said Drayton in a strangled voice. "I noticed him just before we all tore out of there."

"Good heavens!" exclaimed Theodosia. "Who brought *him*?"

Drayton threw her a pained look. "Delaine."

*   *   *

"I feel like an idiot," said Theodosia, as they slipped back into Timothy's party. She and Drayton huddled in the back parlor as Tidwell and Brooke went off to deliver the news to Timothy.

"Don't feel a single pang of regret," replied Drayton. "You were just doing what you do best."

"And what's that?" asked Theodosia, still feeling slightly foolish.

"Investigating," said Drayton.

"I haven't done a very good job of it so far," said Theodosia.

"That's because you're caught in the middle," said Drayton. "First Detective Tidwell badgered you into making a few discreet inquiries, then Jory turned up like the proverbial bad penny to ask for your help."

"I shouldn't have agreed to help either one," said Theodosia.

"I don't think you had much of a choice," said Drayton, in a kindly, agreeable tone. "Your natural instinct is to be helpful. Plus, you do have a keen sense of curiosity." He put a hand on her shoulder. "Hang on, here comes Parker."

"Where were you?" asked Parker, slaloming up to them through a throng of people. "I looked everywhere!" He turned his worried, slightly accusing eyes on Theodosia. "I thought maybe you ditched me."

"We were merely in Timothy's back garden looking at a new bonsai acquisition," said Drayton.

Parker narrowed his eyes. "I thought *you* were the one with the bonsai collection."

"I am," said Drayton, "which is why I wanted to inspect Timothy's new piece."

"Well, you're both missing a terrific buffet," said Parker.

"There's raw oysters and caviar, plus loads of smoked salmon and duck sausage balls, and some really terrific crab dip."

But Theodosia had her eyes focused on Delaine and Julian Bruno, who were standing in the hallway, chatting with a group of people. Detective Tidwell had just tapped Bruno on the shoulder and separated him from the crowd.

"Excuse me," said Theodosia, quickly slipping away.

"Theo?" Parker called after her. He threw up his hands. "Now what?"

Theodosia sped down the hallway, dodging men in tuxedos and women in elegant cocktail dresses. When she reached Delaine, she put a hand on her arm and pulled her away from the group.

"We have to talk," she told Delaine.

"I *was* talking," Delaine said, a little defensively. "In fact, I was making serious inroads for a nice donation to the Heritage Society."

"This is urgent," said Theodosia. "Something's come up and I need to . . . well, I have to ask you a couple of questions."

"What now?" asked Delaine, looking more than a little perturbed, her eyes searching the crowd for Julian Bruno, who seemed to have completely disappeared.

"How did you meet Julian Bruno?" Theodosia asked.

Delaine swiveled her head and stared directly at Theodosia. "I don't know," she said in an exasperated tone. "I . . . well, *you* were there. At the church."

"That's the first time you met him?" asked Theodosia.

Delaine's front teeth nibbled her lower lip. "Oh. Well, I guess I *actually* ran into Julian at Abby's visitation. And *then* I saw him at the church." She gave a little giggle. "And, of course, I stopped by Vianello this morning." She shrugged. "One thing just led to another."

"Bruno was at Abby's visitation?" This was news to her. "I didn't see him." *So he could have switched cameos*, she thought.

"The visitation wasn't exactly a social function," said Delaine. "People weren't required to mingle."

"Well, your date is in big trouble right now," said Theodosia.

"What are you talking about?" demanded Delaine.

"He seems to be connected to this Abby Davis thing."

"What?" howled Delaine. Her face suddenly assumed an uneasy, pinched look. Now it was her turn to grab Theodosia's arm and give it a little shake. "You're saying Julian is a *murderer?*"

"No charges have been made on that count yet," said Theodosia. "But he could be a jewel thief."

Delaine pulled her face into a frown. "What exactly has he been accused of?"

"I'm not the one making accusations," said Theodosia. "But Julian Bruno is with Detective Burt Tidwell right now. And they're on their way to Bruno's shop."

Delaine's mouth flew open, but no words came out. Only a surprised gasp.

"It looks like Bruno may have switched cameos," explained Theodosia.

"Cameos," breathed Delaine. She seemed to have been knocked for a loop.

"There's more," Theodosia told her. "It seems Julian Bruno might have been having an affair with Abby Davis."

Delaine stared at Theodosia in disbelief.

"And he was with Thandie McLean last night." Theodosia hated to hurt Delaine's feelings, but she had to know.

"Oh," said Delaine, and some of the anger seemed to drain from her. "Maybe he . . ."

"The other night at the McBee house, Drayton and I witnessed two thugs trying to beat him up. I think Bruno owes money to someone and they were trying to collect."

Delaine took a deep breath, blew it out, then took a step backward and regarded Theodosia with slightly hooded eyes. "Now that you mention it, dear, Julian Bruno does seem like slightly damaged goods."

Twenty minutes later, Drayton approached Theodosia and Parker. Theodosia had given Parker an abbreviated version of what was going on and he wasn't one bit happy. He glowered, asked questions, ground his teeth, and gazed at Theodosia like a puppy dog who'd been betrayed.

"Timothy just received a call from Detective Tidwell," said a breathless Drayton. "They found a jeweled cameo stashed in the safe at Bruno's shop. It appears to be the genuine article."

"So it's over?" asked Parker. He looked like he certainly wanted this little episode to end. "Theodosia doesn't have to chase all over the place searching for clues and criminals?"

"Mystery solved," said Drayton. He dusted his hands together, looking pleased.

A long silence spun out and then Theodosia spoke up. "Not quite. There's still the matter of Abby Davis."

24

$\sim$

Before she headed down to Savannah that Saturday morning, Theodosia swung by the house where Jory's aunt Marie and uncle Otto lived. It was where he was staying.

When Jory opened the door, barefoot and looking slightly disheveled in a light blue T-shirt and gray sweatpants, Theodosia pressed the cameo into his hand.

"I owe you an apology," she told him. "In fact, I owe your entire family an apology."

He stared at the cameo. "This was Abby's," he said in a quizzical tone.

"Yes, it was," she told him. "And I made a horrible mistake." Theodosia backed away from the front door. "I'm so sorry. I really shouldn't . . . see you anymore."

"Hey," he called, balancing the cameo in his outstretched hand, looking a little stunned. "You want to explain this?"

"I really can't," Theodosia said over her shoulder. "There's no good explanation for what I did. No excuse at all."

*   *   *

On the drive down to Savannah, Theodosia focused on clearing her head. Tried to forget about the thieving Julian Bruno, the murdered Abby Davis, and everyone else who had become implicated, betrayed, or peripherally involved.

She bypassed Interstate 95 in favor of the smaller roads and was rewarded with a relaxing, pretty drive filled with twists and turns through pine forests, along quiet waterways, and through swampland that spun out to either side of her like a great green carpet.

When she arrived in Savannah, certainly one of her favorite cities, Theodosia grabbed her printout from MapQuest and gave it a cursory glance. She'd never been to Forsyth Park before, but knew the city well enough. Figured if she navigated over to Bay Street and then headed down Bull Street, she'd probably find it.

Theodosia found the Romp and Run even before she hit Forsyth Park. Cars were parked everywhere along a six-block stretch and people and their dogs streamed in the park's general direction.

Theodosia drove around a bit, finally found a parking space, then hiked four blocks back to Forsyth Park. She passed by the Fragrant Garden for the Blind, headed past a spectacular two-tiered fountain that featured a statue of a classically garbed female figure, and headed for the myriad of colorful tents.

Ten minutes of exploring and petting the occasional dog led her to the KSAV-TV tent. Kay Lorillard was seated behind a table, consulting a clipboard, and handing out neatly printed nametags. She was early forties, trim in her white slacks and Romp and Run T-shirt, with curly, blond hair and an unlined oval face.

When Theodosia introduced herself, Kay looked at her with thoughtful, green-tinted eyes. "I never for a minute thought you'd drive down."

"I had another errand, too," Theodosia told her.

Kay lowered her voice. "And you want to know about Abby Davis?"

Theodosia nodded.

Kay touched the shoulder of the woman sitting next to her. "Sylvia, can you take over for a few minutes?" The woman nodded and then Kay led Theodosia outside the tent.

"And you say you're investigating her murder?" In the bright sunlight, with hundreds of barking dogs and their owners milling about, Kay sounded skeptical.

"In a way, I am," said Theodosia. "I was the one who discovered Abby's body."

"Oh," said Kay. Now she seemed to focus her entire attention on Theodosia. "Okay. That must have been awful."

"It was," said Theodosia. "And now I'm working with the investigating detective under the auspices of the family." Little white lie there, but who's the wiser?

Kay blinked rapidly. "I'm not sure what I can tell you."

Theodosia cleared her throat. At least the woman hadn't clammed up entirely or told her to bug off. "I wanted to know about the circumstances of Abby's firing."

Kay frowned. "Why would that be relevant?"

"It might have to do with money," said Theodosia, keeping her answer purposefully vague. Probably because she was a little vague herself about what she was asking.

Kay thought for a few long moments then said, "Abby was

fired because she came across some information during the course of a news story, then withheld that information from the police."

"You're talking about the Travis McBee kidnapping," said Theodosia.

"Yes," Kay said slowly.

"Do you know what that information was?" asked Theodosia.

"Not really. She was very coy about everything. Of course, it turned into a big brouhaha between Abby and our general manager, Sam Links. And then the lawyers got involved." Kay rolled her eyes.

"But the upshot was that Abby was let go," said Theodosia.

"That's right."

"And because she wasn't employed for a full six months, she lost most of her advance."

Kay puckered her mouth, as if the recollection was distasteful. "No, Abby actually made out like a bandit in that regard. She not only lawyered up fast, she had a very tough agent. She . . . uh, ended up keeping most of the money."

"That must have caused some problems."

"Are you serious?" said Kay. "I thought Sam would have a cat!"

They talked a while longer, Theodosia asking a few more general questions. But she didn't really learn anything more. Nothing she hadn't pieced together already.

After thanking Kay and wishing her luck with the Romp and Run, Theodosia started back toward her car. When she reached the Fragrant Garden for the Blind, she paused at the gate and went in.

Constructed as a flower garden specifically for the blind,

the garden was a tangle of lovely, aromatic plants. Large wells of water edged three sides of the garden, engineered, she supposed, to help keep all the scents concentrated.

Sitting down on a marble bench, Theodosia pulled her cell phone out and punched in Tidwell's phone number.

It took a few minutes and some fast talking to get him on the line, but finally Tidwell was there.

"What?" he said without preamble.

"It's me. Theodosia. I was wondering what luck you had with Julian Bruno."

She could hear Tidwell sucking air through his front teeth and then he said. "Nothing, not a thing."

"What?" said Theodosia.

"He claims Abby must have put the cameo in his safe."

"So now he's admitting to the affair?" asked Theodosia.

"Yes," said Tidwell, "but that's all he's admitting to." He paused. "You thought perhaps Bruno would pour his guts out concerning the murder of Abby Davis?"

"Well . . . maybe," said Theodosia. "Something like that."

"Not a chance," said Tidwell. "He's a cool one. Claims he had nothing to do with it. Oh, one thing did come to light . . ."

"What's that?" asked Theodosia.

"The man has gambling debts. Crushing gambling debts, as a matter of fact."

"Doesn't that explain the cameo theft?" asked Theodosia.

"Perhaps," said Tidwell.

"And the fact that he was being pressured for repayment," said Theodosia. "Might that not suggest a certain underworld connection?"

"Where exactly are you going with this?" asked Tidwell.

"Bruno could have easily arranged Abby's death," said Theodosia.

"And what was his motive again?" asked Tidwell.

Now it was Theodosia's turn to pause. "She knew about the cameo theft? She threatened to turn him in? Seems to me you constructed a pretty powerful argument last night."

"Perhaps," said Tidwell. "But my gut tells me . . ."

"What?"

Tidwell sighed. "There's something else going on."

"Something else going on," Theodosia muttered to herself as she found a parking spot on West Congress Street, close to the City Market. "But what?"

And then she was striding down the street and into Sun Moon Tea, one of her favorite tea wholesalers.

Mr. Yu wasn't there today, but his daughter, Miss Lin, greeted her warmly and immediately shuttled her to the back counter where the teakettle was always on and the tea tasting always heavenly.

A jade oolong, from the mountains of Nantou, Taiwan, was first up. It was a clear golden-green infusion that carried an aroma reminiscent of lilacs.

"Delightful," proclaimed Theodosia.

"Also must try," said Miss Lin, pouring out a second cup.

This was an orchid oolong with a pale yellow-green liquor. And as the name promised, the floral notes were very much like orchids.

And finally there was a Nepalese black tea, grown at the base of Mount Everest. This delicious tea offered a bouquet of lotus, sandalwood, and honey.

"I'd like a pound of each," Theodosia told Miss Lin. And then promptly fell in love with some silver heart-shaped tea infusers as well as an YiXing teapot in the shape of a fish.

She picked the teapot up by its handle, an upturned fish tail, and gazed at the spout, which was a generous fish mouth. "Gotta have this, too," she murmured.

Twenty minutes later, Theodosia was buzzing back up the highway, just edging the outskirts of Beaufort. Just past the turn for Highway 21, she knew there was a little shop that served tea. Honey Creek. It wasn't a tea shop per se, really more of a floral and gift shop. But Sadie Shayne, the lady who owned Honey Creek, always had a pot of tea brewing as well as fresh-baked jumbo scones. Since it was after two and she still hadn't eaten, the place would be a welcome respite. Now, if she could just find that little strip of businesses . . .

A jumble of signs and colorful wooden buildings suddenly came into view. There it was!

Tap-tap-tapping her brakes, Theodosia swerved into the gravel parking lot and eased into a parking space.

Sadie was there today to offer her a nice steaming cup of Darjeeling, as well as an enormous peach scone and a small croissant stuffed with chicken salad.

Theodosia perched at one of three white metal tables at the back of the shop and inhaled the aroma of the lilies, hydrangeas, roses, daffodils, asters, and carnations that sat in tall, metal pots around her. Sadie also retailed a few teapots and tea cozies, as well as a small selection of tea books and tea-themed note cards. But the majority of her inventory was gifty stuff—vases, soy candles, teddy bears, cookbooks, Tinker Bell dolls, jewelry, and brocade evening bags.

As Theodosia sipped her tea, she decided to try to get hold of Miss Josette. Along with everything else that was jouncing around in her head was the image of the strange totem she'd found at the Mobley Plantation. Miss Josette had promised to ask around about Blue Root magic, but Theodosia still hadn't heard back from her.

Dialing the number from memory, Theodosia got a busy signal. So she checked her phone directory, found she'd been a digit off, tried again, and got nothing. Just a ringing phone. Apparently Miss Josette wasn't big on answering machines.

Theodosia finished her lunch, poked around Honey Creek for a few minutes, then finally decided it might be time to head back. It was almost three o'clock and the day was slipping away. True, it hadn't been a terribly productive day, but she had successfully cleared her head. Can't always output, she reminded herself, or the battery runs dry. Gotta input, too.

Outside Honey Creek, Theodosia noticed a carved wooden sign for Truffles & Ruffles, a shop that she couldn't remember seeing before. At least she didn't think she had. But when she wandered down to check it out, she found the shop closed. Too bad, because the truffles on display in the front window looked spectacular. Arranged on antique glass plates and labeled with hand-lettered cards, Theodosia fairly salivated over chocolate mint, praline and cream, raspberry almond, hazelnut espresso, and peanut butter parfait truffles. Maybe, she decided, this was a possible source of goodies for the Indigo Tea Shop.

She edged left to a triple-paned glass door and noticed a building directory hanging on the interior wall next to a flight of steps. Pushing open the door, Theodosia thought Truffles & Ruffles might have a phone number listed on the directory. Scanning the board, she was more than a little surprised when she saw a listing for the Carolina Heartland Trust.

What? Isn't this interesting.

On a whim, she climbed the staircase, then wandered down a slightly dingy hallway with scuffed gray carpeting and fluorescent lights flickering overhead. There was an insurance agent, a chiropractor, what looked to be a couple of empty offices, and an answering service. Peering through a narrow rectangle of glass on the office door for Pronto Answering and Secretarial, Theodosia could see a woman seated at the front desk.

She went in and stepped up to the desk where a woman in an electric-blue sweater and a heroic beehive hairdo manned the console.

"Hi," said Theodosia, when the woman was between calls, "I was wondering if you could tell me where I could find the office for the Carolina Heartland Trust?"

The woman smiled sweetly. "You're looking at it, sugar."

Theodosia was taken aback. "Here?"

"Well," said the woman, "we're their answering service."

"So there is no office," Theodosia said slowly. This was a little strange. She'd been expecting a bustling office manned by dedicated history buffs and American Studies students. "Do you know where I could find their executive director?"

The woman behind the desk smiled and shook her head. "Nope."

"Do you have another number for them?"

"Afraid not, sugar."

"Have you ever met anyone from the Carolina Heartland Trust?"

Again the woman shook her head. "No, but I only work here on weekends. You know, filling in kind of temporary-like. So, probably, if you came back or called back on Monday you'd have better luck."

"You think they might have moved their offices?"

"Sorry," said the woman. "I just don't know. But tell you what, scribble down your name and number and if somebody calls in, I'll have them get back to you."

"Thanks," said Theodosia, printing out her name and home phone number.

"I'll check the files, too," promised the woman, as the phones started up again. "See if I can find a contact."

On the drive back to Charleston, questions whirled like a cyclone inside Theodosia's head. Did Julian Bruno have Abby murdered? Did someone else with a powerful grudge against Abby shoot her that day? Who had chased her on the Sea-Doo yesterday? And what was the deal with the Carolina Heartland Trust? Had they suddenly received a windfall of donations and moved to better digs? She certainly hoped so.

Gravel crunched under her wheels as she finally swung down her own back alley and rocked to a stop behind the Indigo Tea Shop. Climbing out of her Jeep, Theodosia saw Haley walking toward her. Earl Grey trotted beside her.

"How was your trip down to Savannah?" Haley asked, as Earl Grey bounded toward Theodosia, pulling her along, and then circling around and hog-tying everyone with his leash.

"Okay," said Theodosia. "Not real productive in the snooping department. Got some new tea, though."

"No big insights into Abby Davis?" asked Haley, squinting at her. Then she added, "Drayton filled me in on everything today. If you ask me, that Julian Bruno guy is guilty with a capital G."

"Guilty of . . . ?" began Theodosia.

"He killed Abby Davis," declared Haley. She reached up

and removed a tortoiseshell clip from her hair, letting her stick-straight blond hair fall over her shoulders. "It's an open-and-shut case. Abby and Julian Bruno were having an affair, he stole the cameo, she threatened to rat him out."

"Rat him out for what reason?" asked Theodosia.

Haley shrugged. "Not sure. But neither of them were exactly model citizens. Abby was mean as a junkyard dog and this Bruno guys sounds snooty."

"Snooty doesn't mean guilty." Theodosia smiled. But Haley made a good point. The explanation could be as simple as that. She hoped it was.

"I know, I know," said Haley, "but I have a feeling about this case. It might take a little time, but everything's gonna get sorted out."

"I'm sure you're right," said Theodosia, pulling the shopping bag filled with tea tins out of the backseat.

"Hey, you know what?" said Haley, handing Earl Grey over to Theodosia. "Parker called the tea shop this afternoon. He wanted to know if it was okay to meet you at the Masked Ball tonight. He was involved in some last-minute pickle, so I told him no problem." She shifted from one foot to the other, a little unsure now. "It's not, is it? A problem, I mean?"

Theodosia glanced at her watch. It was almost six. Time was really ticking away on her and in her mind's eye she could imagine one of Salvador Dali's infamous clocks, melting into oblivion. "Actually, it's fine," she told Haley. "It's going to take a little time to get gorgeous and jump into my dress." *The dress that's still hanging on the back of my closet door in a plastic bag and probably needs pressing*, she thought.

Haley backed across the alley, jingling her keys. "Well, I'm supposed to be at the Corinth Theatre in forty minutes.

And *you're* supposed to be there in . . . what? Just over an hour, huh?"

Gotta hurry, Theodosia told herself as she clumped up the stairs to her apartment, balancing the tea tins, being dragged by a whirling Earl Grey. *Gotta get moving.*

25

❧

Theodosia's velvet cape fluttered behind her as she hurried up the wide stone steps of the Corinth Theatre. Her gold Venetian mask, worn lightly on her face, lent a sexy, anonymous air. Two ushers in white masks, red velvet capes, and three-cornered tricorne hats pulled open the massive double doors, and then she was suddenly transported into a Venetian carnival of yesteryear.

Overhead, a twenty-foot-long Italian loggia twinkled with thousands of tiny white lights. Then that loggia opened into the Corinth Theatre, which had been magically transformed into San Marco Square at the height of Carnivale.

Theodosia's initial impression was of a delicious swirl of lights, color, and music. Costumed acrobats and musicians swept past her. Palm trees cordoned off a cozy café to the left. And stretching out in front of her was a dance floor where men in elegant tuxedos and women in sparkling ball gowns glided to and fro wearing Venetian masks.

And what amazing masks they wore!

Glittering black silk masks with sequins. Masks constructed entirely of feathers. Gilded masks of silver and gold that featured long noses or beaks. Even masks dripping with jewels and strands of beads.

A tall, purple-caped man greeted her. "Welcome to Venice," he intoned, then bowed stiffly from the waist. "And welcome to *Un Ballo in Maschera.*"

Gazing up into a black-and-gold mask that revealed only its owner's kindly-looking eyes, Theodosia said, "Drayton?"

"Drat!" he answered. "You knew it was me."

She smiled. "Well, I did recognize your voice."

"You came alone?" he asked, holding out an arm.

"Parker's here somewhere," Theodosia told him. "He had some sort of catering problem, so he came on ahead." She hoped Parker wasn't still upset over last night, or else it would be a very long evening.

"Yes, yes, I've seen Parker," said Drayton, guiding her across the dance floor, steering her toward the bar. "But I didn't realize you'd be arriving solo."

"Aren't you supposed to be escorting someone?" Theodosia asked.

"Timothy is busy entertaining our group over in the sidewalk café," said Drayton, chuckling. "Holding court in his salon, shall we say." He held up an index finger to signal the bartender. "Two glasses of wine please."

"You're serving Italian wine?" Theodosia asked the bartender.

The bartender grinned, and she recognized him as the weekend bartender from Solstice. "Of course, signora."

"In that case," said Drayton, "a Soave for the lady and a Barolo for me."

They watched as the bartender poured their wine into stemmed crystal goblets, then slid them across the bar. "Enjoy," he told them.

Theodosia took a tiny sip of her wine. It was straw-colored and just slightly fruity.

"I love that the Opera Society hired actors in costumes to add to the festivity," said Drayton, as a Venetian lord and lady in vibrant silks and velvets strolled by.

"And staged such an amazing transformation," said Theodosia, gazing around at the lights and decor and costumes. "The Corinth Theatre really does look like the Doge's Palace or some lovely gallery."

"Wait until they unveil some of the actual sets and the singing troupe performs a musical number," said Drayton. "It's going to be absolutely spectacular." Looking deliriously happy, he managed a sip of his red wine. "Listen, I've got to get back to our table. Are you going to be okay on your own?"

"No problem," said Theodosia. "I plan to wander around and take in the sights and sounds of this whole thing. Probably bump into Parker and Haley in the process."

"See you later then," said Drayton, dashing off.

Feeling very elegant in her blue degradé dress and anonymous in her mask, Theodosia wandered through the crowd. She paused for a few moments to watch an Italian puppet show, enjoying the jigging little marionettes and their puppeteers, who seemed to revel in showing off their skills.

At a gold-and-silver-draped buffet table she finally spied Parker. He was fussing with the arrangement of a fresh tray of bruschetta. Haley was right behind him carrying a second tray filled with tiny white appetizer-sized pizzas.

"Hey," said Parker, when Theodosia lifted her mask to

reveal herself, "I wondered who that gorgeous contessa was." He was dressed in a tuxedo with his mask pulled down around his neck, Haley had on a long black skirt, white tank top, and narrow black mask with purple plumes at the sides.

"Love your dress," said Haley, giving Theodosia a quick wave.

Parker gazed at Theodosia with a worried expression. "I really apologize for the last-minute change in plans. I hope you're not upset that I ran on ahead." He glanced at a service door that led to a small kitchen. "Got a few problems."

"I hope you're not still angry about last night," said Theodosia.

Parker shrugged. "I'm getting over it. Trying to show a little maturity."

"Thank you," she told him, then eyed the table full of canapés. "This is a spectacular assortment. What are all these things, anyway?"

Parker took her arm and led her down the length of the table for a personally guided culinary tour. "Those are bruschetta," he pointed out, "and these little delights are individual white pizzas." He pointed again, happily, "and, of course, grilled clams and *stromboli* bites. Oh, and the little breaded things are *taradls*. Italian pepper rings."

"Your restaurant prepared all this?" asked Theodosia. "I've never seen any of these things on your menu."

"Then it's probably time to add them," said Parker, "because everything's being snapped up like hotcakes. Well, like *stromboli* bites anyway. Listen, Theo, we've got to take a whirl on the dance floor, okay? But can you give me a few more minutes?" He glanced back toward the service door again where two chefs from his kitchen were silhouetted in what seemed to be a heated dispute. He held up one hand, fingers spread apart. "Five minutes. Then I promise you my undivided attention."

"I'll be back," Theodosia told him, "to hold you to that."

As Theodosia circled around the dance floor, a voice called out, "I'd recognize that dress anywhere."

She turned as a woman in a spangled dress and elaborate silver mask swished up to her.

"Delaine?"

Delaine nodded, then pulled her mask aside. "It's me," she said with a pussycat grin. "Isn't this a marvelous ball? Isn't the decor gorgeous?"

"Great fun," Theodosia agreed as Delaine clutched her arm and swished her skirt again for full effect. "Do you . . . I mean . . . you're not here alone are you?" Theodosia asked.

Delaine spun her head sharply and gave Theodosia an irate look. "No, of course not. I have an *escort* if that's what you're wondering."

"Sorry," said Theodosia. Delaine was obviously still twitchy about last night. About her ill-fated date with Julian Bruno.

Delaine waved a hand as though the Julian Bruno incident was of no consequence to her. "I'm on my way to the bar. Walk with me, will you, dear?"

But halfway there, Delaine saw someone she knew, let loose an earsplitting shriek, and got completely sidetracked. So Theodosia found herself alone at the bar, facing the same bartender again.

"You're back," he said. "What can I get for you this time? Same thing?"

"Do you have a Pinot Grigio?" she asked. "Something a little drier?"

"Coming right up," said the bartender.

"Better make that two," said Jory, suddenly stepping up to the bar and slipping off his mask.

Theodosia jerked as though a hot wire had been suddenly run up her leg. "Jory," she said, staring at him. "What are *you* doing here?"

"Trying to talk to you, for one thing," he said. His voice was low and clipped.

"What I meant," said Theodosia, "was . . . oh, never mind." She was flustered and suddenly didn't want to be having this conversation.

"So this morning," said Jory. "What was that all about?"

Oops. Looks like they *were* going to have that conversation.

"I think you can pretty much guess," said Theodosia.

"I'd like to hear it from you," said Jory.

"I had a feeling," Theodosia told him, trying not to stumble over her words. "About that cameo."

"Cameos are a hot commodity right now," said Jory. "After you went skittering down the sidewalk this morning, I got a call from Detective Tidwell."

"Ah," said Theodosia. "So he explained everything to you?"

"Yes and no. But it would appear that, once again, your instincts were right on target."

Theodosia stared at him.

Jory dropped his voice even lower. "It looks as though . . ." He cleared his throat. "That my sister's killer might be behind bars."

"Oh, Jory," said Theodosia, emotion pouring into her voice. "I sincerely hope so. But please don't . . ."

"Here you are!" cried a tall, blond woman, sliding carefully between Theodosia and Jory, causing them each to take a step backward. "I wondered where you ran off to." She gave

Jory an absent peck on the cheek, then turned to regard Theodosia with a bemused expression. "Who are you?" she asked. "An old girlfriend?"

"Theodosia," said Jory. "This is Beth Ann."

"Nice to meet you," said Theodosia, curiosity evident in her voice.

Beth Ann held out a champagne flute and waggled it to no one in particular. "Beth Ann would like another drink please. Beth Ann is thirsty."

"Beth Ann's from New York," said Jory, as if that explained everything.

"I wanted to come down for the funeral," Beth Ann told Theodosia, rolling her eyes at Jory. "But this one wouldn't hear of it. Wanted to be among *family*, he said." She shook her head. "Southerners. Big on family, I guess."

"We're big on tradition," Jory said through clenched teeth.

Beth Ann turned to face him. "Where is it written that a fiancé leaves his beloved behind? I would have *adored* meeting your family. Seems to me this was the perfect time."

"Believe me, it wasn't," said Jory.

Theodosia inclined her head toward Beth Ann. "You're Jory's fiancée," she said brightly. "We heard there was a special woman in his life."

"Oh, we're on again, off again," sang Beth Ann. "You never know what's up with us. That's why I flew down here this morning to surprise him."

"I'll be you were quite a surprise," said Theodosia.

"You have no idea," murmured Jory, taking a long pull of wine.

"Anyway," said Beth Ann, "it looks as if Jory's poor sister, God rest her soul, is finally at peace. The police have arrested someone, I understand?"

"They have a suspect in custody, yes," said Theodosia. There was a small part of her that was starting to enjoy Jory's discomfort with the somewhat outspoken, slightly drunken Beth Ann.

Beth Ann reached over and patted Jory's arm, which did nothing to hearten his expression.

"So nice you could make it to the Masked Ball tonight," Theodosia told her.

Beth Ann glanced around. "Yeah, this is all pretty cool. I told Jory I wasn't going to leave until he took me to some sort of dinner or fancy shindig."

"How did you two meet?" asked Theodosia, fascinated. Although her interest was slightly akin to a mongoose squaring off against a cobra.

"I was tempting at his law firm," said Beth Ann. She suddenly put a hand to her mouth and laughed hysterically. "I mean *temping*. Anyway, Jory and I hit it off right from the start."

"We have to go now," said Jory, suddenly clutching Beth Ann's shoulder.

"We do?" said Beth Ann.

"Yes," said Jory steering her away. "We're going to dance now."

"Okay," said Beth Ann. She executed a little wave at Theodosia over her shoulder. "Bye."

"Bye," said Theodosia. She turned back to the bar, decided she really didn't want another drink, then slid a five-dollar bill across the counter. "Thanks anyway," she told the bartender, who winked at her.

As she wandered through the crowd, Theodosia suddenly started chuckling. Jory's girlfriend, Jory's fiancée, if that's what she really was, was almost a slightly younger version of

Delaine. Outspoken, pushy, slightly over the top. But . . . a little strange, too.

Was that the type of woman Jory was attracted to? she wondered. Because Beth Ann didn't seem in character with the Jory she knew. On the other hand, people changed. People . . .

A man in a black velvet cape and white *Phantom of the Opera* mask suddenly blocked her way. "Care to dance?" he asked in a smooth, baritone voice.

"No, thank you," Theodosia told him, still puzzling about Jory, wanting to find Parker as soon as she could. She wanted to tell him . . .

"Come on," insisted the man, grabbing her hand, pressing an arm around her waist. "Just one little dance."

Theodosia resisted slightly. "Do we know each other?"

"We most certainly do," said the man.

Not wanting to be rude, figuring this had to be a customer or supplier or friend of Drayton's from the Heritage Society, Theodosia let herself get pulled into the swirl of dancers. The orchestra was playing a waltz now and she let herself relax and go with the flow.

Her partner, whoever he was, was a good dancer. Very agile and light on his feet, and she told him so.

"Thank you," said her still-masked partner. "You're quite lovely yourself."

"Why don't you take off your mask," suggested Theodosia. With the evening well under way, at least half the guests had discarded their masks. And she was getting more and more curious.

"Tell you what," said her mysterious dance partner. "I'll give you three guesses."

"Let's not be coy," said Theodosia, who was beginning to

tire of his little cat-and-mouse game. Customer or not, Heritage Society board member yay or nay, enough was enough.

The man let loose a hearty laugh. "You're probably right, it's time we chatted face-to-face." He waltzed her over to one of the sets of French doors that had been embellished with tangled grapevine and tiny white lights. They stopped and Theodosia took a step backward, her shoulders suddenly pressed against the cool of the glass doors.

Theodosia cocked her head and stared at him as one hand moved to his face. He grasped the corner of his mask, paused for a second, then pulled it off slowly.

Her eyes widened and her stomach lurched. An electrical shiver passed through her. "What?" she gasped.

Theodosia had more than a passing familiarity with the face that stared back at her. In fact, it was the same face that had smiled out from a silver picture frame on the second floor of Truman McBee's house.

"You're . . ." Studying the fleshy face, reddish hair, and slightly sagging jowls, Theodosia suddenly knew this was also the man who'd chased her yesterday! This was Travis McBee, Truman McBee's missing son!

26

"You've been doing too much investigating, lady," Travis told her, twisting his cupid's mouth into an ugly snarl. He clapped one hand across Theodosia's mouth, then reached the other around behind her, sprang the door handle, and bulldozed her backward onto the stone portico that ran the full length of the building.

He finally let her speak when they were outside, the door closed, cool air engulfing them. "Stop it!" shouted Theodosia. "I don't know what you want, what you're trying to do, but this nonsense is about to come to a screeching halt!"

"What's the trouble?" barked a male voice from out of the darkness.

Thank goodness, Theodosia thought. Someone had heard her yelp. Someone must have stepped outside for a cigarette. Relief flooded her brain as she turned to face her gallant rescuer.

"I specifically told you *not* to play stupid games," said Drew Donovan as he oozed quietly out from the shadows.

"Drew?" said Theodosia in a small voice. Drew was here? Drew was her rescuer?

Drew took another step forward. "You fool," he snarled at Travis. "You were supposed to stay under wraps!"

Theodosia's hopeful look withered on her face.

Travis gave a harsh laugh that sounded like a bark. "Yeah, yeah, make up your mind, pal. First you want me to stay hidden in the Bahamas—then you invite me back here to do your dirty work!"

Theodosia's head whirled from Drew to Travis and back to Drew. And a cold trickle of fear ran down her back. This wasn't good. They were . . . could they be . . . in collusion?

"Travis, my man," said Drew, with false heartiness, "you got your three million dollars fair and square. Plus your spiff from the condos I built."

"Yeah," snorted Travis. "Using my old man's money!"

"Enough with the whining," said Drew. "You'll be rolling in it once I subdivide the Mobley Plantation and build luxury homes."

"What?" squawked Theodosia. Now Drew and Travis were talking as though she wasn't even here. Except for the fact that Travis had his giant hand clamped firmly—painfully—in a viselike grip on her shoulder.

Drew finally flicked his eyes down at Theodosia. "You didn't really fall for that Carolina Heartland Trust story, did you?" Then, seeing the shattered expression on her face, gave a low chortle. "Oh, you did! Gracious me, aren't I just the boy wonder? And all we wanted was some cooked-up crap to make Abby's generous donation seem more palatable."

"Yeah," echoed Travis, "until she fell inconveniently out of love with my so-called business partner here. Cuckolded him, in fact."

Theodosia opened her mouth to scream just as Drew's hand snapped up fast. He held a gun, an ugly gray .38, pointed in the general direction of her heart. "Enough!" Drew ordered, his anger radiating to Theodosia as well as Travis.

But Travis continued his semi-maniacal giggle. "Of course, the Carolina Heartland Trust will conveniently go out of business but still manage to deed the land back to Drew."

"You killed Abby," said Theodosia, staring at Drew. "You murdered your own wife!" She shook her head in despair and disbelief. All his professed grief . . . just crocodile tears."

"Believe me," said Drew, pursing his lips and blowing out a glut of air, "she wasn't that much of a prize."

Theodosia shifted her accusation to Travis. "And your coldhearted disappearing act deceived your entire family!"

Travis gave an elaborate shrug. "Yeah, well, me and the old man never did see eye to eye."

"What about your mother?" asked Theodosia.

Travis's face sagged for an instant. "Leave her out of it!"

"Shut up, both of you!" ordered Drew.

"You won't get away with any of this," Theodosia snarled, turning her attention back to Drew.

Drew raised a single eyebrow. "I already have."

Travis's evil grin floated above her like a rotting jack-o'-lantern. "Now we're really gonna clean up. With nobody the wiser."

"Jory will know," said Theodosia. "He'll figure it out."

"Jory will be back in New York," said Drew. "By the time he finds out it'll be too late. The land will be in my name, the wetland drained, and construction begun." He gave a disdainful snort. "Besides, Jory's got problems of his own."

"And the great thing is," said Travis, giving an elaborate wink, "we can always take care of him if we have to."

"Shut up," snapped Drew. "We've got business to deal with right here."

"Now's the fun part," Travis told Theodosia as Drew led them all the way down the stone portico.

Theodosia gazed around helplessly. She saw only darkness, trees, and land sloping away to a parking lot filled with empty cars. Only a round gibbous moon floating on a black sea of clouds looked impassively down upon her. A silent witness.

Drew turned the handle on the last set of French doors and they all stepped inside. That's when Theodosia realized they were in the backstage area of the Corinth Theatre. It was dark, musty, a little too warm. Props and sets loomed large everywhere you looked. A tangle of ropes hung overhead like an elaborate spider's web.

They picked and bumped their way slowly through the inventory of props, Drew still leading the way. Finally, he paused.

"I think . . . this one," Drew murmured in a low voice.

Theodosia raised her head, focused her eyes, then stared in horror and disbelief. Drew's hand rested on the crossbar of a sinister-looking wooden gallows. Probably the prop from the Gallows at Midnight scene that Drayton had spoken excitedly about. The thing was . . . was it a working gallows? She didn't really want to find out.

"No," gasped Theodosia.

"You're in no position to give orders," snarled Drew.

Reaching into his jacket pocket, he dug around, and Theodosia heard a faint clank. Metal against metal.

Oh no!

A pair of silver handcuffs seemed to materialize before Theodosia's eyes. "No!" she protested again. But Travis had already snaked a chubby but well-muscled arm around her neck and bent her over backward in a painful pose that brought her up almost on tiptoes. In that uncomfortable position she could hardly resist.

Theodosia's brain seemed to be shutting down; her thoughts were in free fall. *Not the gallows. Not this way . . .*

As Theodosia raised her hands to try to pry loose his grip, Drew snapped the cuffs tightly about her wrists, then clicked them closed until they cut painfully into her flesh. "Kneel down," he barked.

Legs shaking, knees practically knocking together, Theodosia stared defiantly at him. "No."

"You heard the man," Travis told her in a hoarse whisper. "Get down!"

Theodosia felt Travis loosen his grasp slightly, then his knee slammed painfully against the backs of her legs, eliciting sharp darts of pain and turning her legs to jelly. She dropped to the floor hard.

Oof.

In the dust and the gloom, Theodosia bent her head forward slightly and prayed silently, waiting for the end to come.

And when the pfft of the silencer sounded in the dark like a dull, dead pop, she could almost feel the bullet enter her head, hot and fast, just behind her right temple.

Until Travis dropped to the floor next to her, hitting hard like a sack of potatoes.

What?

Drew was suddenly scrambling on his knees next to her, smacking a piece of blue sticky tape across Travis's mouth. Then Drew reached under Travis's armpits and hauled him upward.

Theodosia watched in mounting horror as Drew, grunting and shoving, positioned Travis in the wooden gallows, then strung the wire noose around his neck.

"I thought . . ." Theodosia's throat was so parched and dry from fear, her words were barely audible.

Drew glanced down briefly. "You thought Travis and I were partners? Not anymore," he snarled. "Looks like that position is about to be terminated. Things just weren't working out."

Travis's head lolled sickeningly as Drew tightened the noose.

"Is he dead?" Theodosia croaked, appalled at Drew's total lack of emotion.

"Not yet," said Drew, in a cool, distant voice. "But as he loses blood and his respiration slips, chances are excellent he'll slump forward and strangle himself."

Drew Donovan is a maniac, Theodosia told herself. *A cold-blooded sociopath.*

"What are you going to do when Truman McBee finds out you murdered his son?" Theodosia managed a dry hiss.

Drew's lips curled in an ugly, mirthless smile and he focused dark, lifeless eyes on her. "He's not going to find out. Because now I'm going to take care of *you*."

27

Gun poked rudely against the back of her neck, Drew pushed a stumbling Theodosia out the back door of the theater and marched her across the parking lot. When they reached his car, a dark green Jaguar XK, he waved the gun in a menacing gesture and forced her into the narrow backseat. Once she was crouched on the floor, he took another set of cuffs and tethered her hands to the metal seat-belt loop that poked out from behind a rubber mat. Then, as Theodosia kicked and fought and snapped at him, Drew covered her mouth with a wide hunk of sticky tape and tossed a dirty blanket on top of her.

The drive was agony for Theodosia. Chained to the floor, her world in total darkness, she tried as hard as possible to remember how many left turns Drew was making, how many right turns. After a while it all became a dizzying blur and she finally gave up trying to figure out directions.

But she didn't stop trying to get the tape off. She dragged

her mouth against the back of the seat, finally prying up a corner of the tape. From there she lowered her face between her hands and pulled the rest off. She laid there, breathing a little easier now. Thinking. Scheming how she could get herself out of this appalling mess.

Thirty, maybe forty minutes later, the Jaguar rocked to a stop. Even though the heavy blanket muffled sounds, Theodosia could tell that Drew was just sitting in the front seat. Waiting for . . . what? Didn't matter, she decided. The thing to do was try to open a dialogue with him.

"Let me go," she said to him in what she hoped was a calm, rational voice. "Let me walk away from here right now and I promise to help you any way I can."

A long silence spun out and then Drew said, "Help me?"

"Absolutely," said Theodosia. "In fact, I'll vouch to the Charleston police that you're not guilty of engineering your wife's death by reason of insanity. Think about it, Drew. Because you *will* get caught. You can choose to spend your days finger painting and weaving plastic lanyards in a state mental hospital or sit in a six-by-ten-foot cinder-block cell at Ridgeville Prison awaiting death by lethal injection."

Drew ignored her for a few moments. Then he climbed from the driver's seat, leaned over her, and hissed, "You're in no position to bargain. You're completely expendable."

She kicked at him then, hard. Might have even caught him with her heel, before he slammed the door shut. She could hear him swearing softly outside, then the other door, the door right by her head flew open. Drew unfastened the second set of manacles and jerked her from the car.

Theodosia slid out, fighting hard all the way, and hit the ground with her elbows.

Ouch!

Then her knees slammed the ground with another bone-shaking jounce. Before she could even register pain, Drew was on top of her, jerking her roughly to her feet. With moonlight casting dappled shadows on his face, making hollows of his eye sockets and mouth, he looked positively menacing. Like some sort of half monster, half man. A darkling.

Another jerk and Theodosia was dragged swiftly through knee-high weeds until, finally, a familiar landscape came into view. And she realized where Drew had brought her. The old plantation house! Mobley Plantation!

"Bad plan, Drew!" Theodosia spat out as he pulled her up onto the front porch. He kicked open the front door, jerked her again, then spun her around. Before she could cry out again, she was slammed up against the basement door.

She knew what he was going to do then. Drag her downstairs into the dreaded basement!

Theodosia let loose a bloodcurdling scream. "Nooo! Don't you dare . . . !"

Shut up!" barked Drew, shoving her so hard against the basement door she saw stars. "Shut up right now or, so help me, I'll tape your mouth and your nose shut! Then I'll tape your hands to your sides. I'll wrap you so tight you'll look like an Egyptian mummy. You won't be able to draw a single breath!"

Theodosia stopped screaming. She allowed Drew to march her downstairs into the darkness. When they hit the basement, she swallowed hard and said, "The police will know it was you."

"No, they won't," he replied. He set his flashlight down,

then shoved her toward the gaping hole in the center of the basement floor. The hole she and Delaine had dragged themselves out of two days earlier. The hole where Colleton County's coroner had removed a skeleton. "I'm not stupid, you know," he hissed. "I gathered a few cigarette butts from that silly little one-horse town a few miles over. I'll toss 'em in the weeds so the fire marshal will figure it was kids or some homeless guy who set the fire. If they get tricky and try to do DNA shit, they'll be looking for someone local."

Once again, his cool delivery chilled Theodosia to the bone.

"Fire marshal?" she said, her mind stuttering back to those seemingly crucial words that jarred a kernel of fear in her brain.

"You're not too smart, are you?" Drew muttered. "Not nearly as smart as Jory thinks you are. Course, he's not exactly into brainy women these days." Drew stuck a key into the manacles and pulled them from her wrists.

Quick as a cat, kicking and screaming like a banshee, Theodosia clawed at Drew's eyes, pummeled him with her fists. Her fingernails drew blood from high up on his cheek, but Drew didn't seem to register pain. He grabbed her arm, gave it a painful wrench, and shoved her closer to the dreaded hole.

"Another skeleton among the ruins," he crooned softly in her ear. "That's all you'll be. You drove out to have another look and had a terrible accident . . ."

"You can't . . ." she began. And then Drew gave her a tremendous shove that tipped her over the edge and sent her cartwheeling downward.

Just like the time before, Theodosia clutched at wood, mud, anything that might break her terrible fall.

Her descent felt like a freaked-out slow-motion somersault

and then, suddenly, her eyes and mouth filled with a fine spray of dust and her body slammed to a jarring halt.

Dear Lord, what did I land on? What broke my fall?

Slowly, tentatively, Theodosia stretched her hands out and felt around.

The old bed. I fell into the web of ropes that formed the hammock for that old bed.

She let out a rattling, shaky sigh and then her still-whirling mind suddenly flashed, *Sleep tight, don't let the bedbugs bite.*

Sleep tight, she thought. Right. It was a lucky thing those ropes *had* held tight.

She listened carefully then, heard Drew clomp up the basement stairs and slam the door shut.

Extricating herself gingerly from the tangle of ropes, Theodosia forced herself to stand up. Tried to quiet her breathing and listen. For a clue, for anything that would tell her what Drew was really up to. A minute later she heard a faint clank. What was he doing?

She remained still for another few minutes until she finally heard a faint whooshing sound high above her head. And was suddenly confronted with another fear.

"Fire," she breathed, the word lighting up like orange neon inside her brain.

She listened again, now detected the stealthy hiss of flames. Dangerously close. Maybe even right overhead.

Got to get out of here. But how?

The old ladder lay askew on the basement floor above her, where they'd left it. There was nothing down here to climb on except the old trunk. The coroner, after collecting the old bones, had left it in the middle of the tiny subbasement room, the top thrown back.

Theodosia stared at the trunk and bit her lip. In her long

blue dress with the subtly faded colors, she feared she'd end up just like the old bride!

No, she told herself, mustering inner fury. Bag that thought!

Quick as she could, Theodosia, slammed the lid shut on the trunk and struggled to upend it. She knew the trunk wasn't nearly tall enough for her to reach the ragged edge of the ceiling above her, but she had to try!

Slowly, carefully, Theodosia eased herself onto the end of the trunk. She stood balancing for a long moment, then extended her hands over her head. Could she somehow jump?

No way. With her arms extended over her head she was still a good three feet from the lip of the hole.

Now what?

As her eyes finally grew accustomed to the dark, she gazed at the tangle of ropes that had formed her landing pad.

Would those work? Could she unthread them, reknot them, and somehow attach a makeshift grappling hook? Somehow pull herself out of here?

Red light seemed to sift down from above.

And could she do it before the fire took hold and the entire house, which surely had to be tinder dry, came crashing down around her?

Theodosia gnashed her teeth together and let out a snarl. Like a wildcat. An animal cornered. An animal not about to go down easy.

Shaking her head furiously, she fought to clear her mind, to *think* her way free of this. And as she shook and batted her arms angrily, the tips of her fingers brushed against something.

Huh?

Theodosia gazed up. A thin layer of white smoke seemed to hover above her now.

She coughed, narrowed her eyes, and looked again.

And saw . . . the end of Delaine's leather belt. Still hanging there, but fluttering just out of reach.

Hope streaked through Theodosia's heart like a hawk taking wing. This was it. This was her chance. Jump up, grab the end of the belt, pull herself up.

Could she manage that kind of acrobatic?

Theodosia shook her head again, felt the fullness of her auburn hair stream out around her shoulders. Felt the power within her. She *had* to do it.

In one fluid motion, Theodosia dropped into a tuck position, then sprang upward, like a basketball player jumping for a rebound. Her feet left the solidity of the upended trunk, her hands grasped desperately for the leather belt.

She caught it, slid an inch or so, was halted by the belt buckle.

Thank goodness Delaine tied it so the buckle end dangled!

But now there was the matter of pulling herself up.

Could she pull herself up, hand over hand?

Theodosia didn't think so. A summer of tennis lessons had made her arms and shoulders strong and flexible. An autumn of horseback riding had strengthened her core muscles. But not enough for her to pull herself up hand over hand.

So . . . then what?

Almost without thinking, Theodosia raised her knees to her chest and pressed the balls of her feet against the wall of the little room. Like a pendulum, she swung back instantly.

Ah.

She let herself swing back, smacked the wall again with her feet, and pushed even harder.

Again she swung out, only this time she swung a bit higher. This time, her eyes were able to peek just above the rim of the hole.

Theodosia let herself swing back, slammed against the wall, and put everything she could into it. Leg muscles, knees, and thigh muscles tightened like wire coils, then released.

And this time she swung even higher, her head and shoulders rising above the hole.

This is it!

This was the moment! Twisting her entire body in midair, she threw a leg up onto the mud-crusted basement floor, while at the same time, she scrabbled for purchase with her hands.

And it worked, sort of. She teetered precariously on the edge, her hips in danger of slipping over and pulling her back into the subbasement, her arms and leg muscles shaking from the effort.

Like an inchworm, Theodosia eased herself up toward safety, fighting hard for every small bit of real estate. Her shoulders cried out, the muscles that crisscrossed her back protested, her legs quivered. But she persisted.

Five minutes later, she'd worked her way completely out of the hole. Was lying on the muddy, scummy basement floor with flames beginning to flicker overhead. Thinking how lucky she was!

Struggling to her feet, shaking with fear, choking from smoke, Theodosia crab-stepped her way up the stairs. At the top, she placed her hands flat against the door. The wood was warm. No, it was hot. Really hot.

No good. Got to find a better way out.

Theodosia descended the wooden stairs again, carefully skirting the hole in the middle of the cellar floor. She had an idea. When they were trapped down here before, she'd told Delaine there was probably a root cellar at that other end. And another way out.

Now she was going to find out if she'd been right about that. Or if her words had only been wishful thinking.

Batting at cobwebs, inching slowly across the cellar, she pushed past an old spinning wheel, some kind of rotting dresser, and yet another old trunk. Reaching the back wall, Theodosia inched her fingers across rough wood, feeling for a door.

And found it.

Heart quickening, her hands slid down to grasp a metal handle. She pulled hard. Nothing. She pushed. No way. The door held fast.

Fear drove her now. She had to figure a way out. Smoke was beginning to seriously drift down and fill the cellar.

Theodosia leaned a cheek against the filthy door, and took a breath. Slowly, she slid one hand up the door, feeling around, hoping. Her fingers touched a latch.

Will it work?

The latch gave a dry click and then Theodosia was pulling the door open and tumbling into a small, windowless room.

Which wasn't a root cellar at all, but a coal bin.

Pawing blindly, she shuffled around, finally located a square metal door. Maybe three feet by three feet. The coal chute.

Would she fit? Did she even have a choice?

As Theodosia cranked open the door, she was struck by a

billow of decades-old soot. Blowing, spitting coal dust, hating the dirt and stench, she mustered all her courage and dove headfirst into the chute.

Scrambling, pushing, clawing her way, Theodosia discovered the ascent wasn't as difficult as she thought it might be. Lying on one side, she adopted a kind of sidestroke crawl, pushing with her knees, clawing with her hands. Heart pounding inside her chest, she felt like a terrified rat skittering through a dark tunnel. But still, she seemed to be making headway.

Then, ten feet up, edging sideways, leading with her head and left shoulder, she hit a barrier.

What? The outside door? A compacted hunk of coal? Something else?

She wasn't sure.

Fingers explored tentatively, then grazed metal, as she struggled to figure a way out. And finally found another catch. Only this one was rusted shut.

"No, it can't be," she told herself. She jiggled the catch, jarred it, cajoled it. Still the door wouldn't budge.

Pulling herself into a tight ball, she wiggled and shifted her body completely around, praying she had room for such contortions, hoping she had the strength to make one final push.

Finally, feet flat against the door, Theodosia let loose a mighty kick.

And like Houdini uttering the magic word, *shazam*, the door shrieked a protesting creak and flew open! Freedom!

When Theodosia crawled out, covered head to toe in soot, her first thought was, *Lights? Somebody turned on the lights?*

Then she heard the roar of flames above her and knew the entire house was engulfed in fire!

Limping away from the house, Theodosia felt intense heat radiate off her back. When she was a good thirty feet away, almost at the edge of the yard where swamp blended with woods, Theodosia spun around and took a good hard look.

Mobley Plantation was a tornado of fire. Red and orange flames licked off the corner turrets, danced off the gabled roof. Great gluts of smoke swirled skyward like an angry white tornado.

Got to get help, was Theodosia's first thought.

As she backed another few feet into the cover of the swamp, almost mesmerized by the flames, she was stunned to hear soft footfalls behind her!

Whirling fast, fearful Drew was still lurking, Theodosia was utterly stunned when she saw the questioning face of a young African American man.

"How did . . . ?" she began. And suddenly realized a dozen more African Americans were slowly emerging from the woods.

The Gullah people? They've been watching this place?

And then, before Theodosia could even voice her question, she recognized another face.

"Miss Josette?" said Theodosia, her voice a papery whisper.

"You poor thing," said Miss Josette, wrapping her arms tightly around Theodosia.

Turns out, some of the Gullah people *had* been watching Mobley Plantation.

"I didn't know it," Miss Josette explained to her, "but Dexter's been keeping an eye out here. He noticed more and more people around the old place and got an idea in his head that somebody might be fixing to drain the swamp and cut down some of the forest."

"That was the plan *exactly*," Theodosia choked out. "That's what Drew Donovan would have done." She coughed again. "Does anyone, uh, have a cell phone?" She had to call Parker at the Corinth Theatre and have him free Travis from the guillotine. Get the paramedics there. Oh, and then call Detective Tidwell about Drew Donovan!

Dexter extended a big paw that held a silver sliver of phone. "Here. Use mine."

28

Dexter, Miss Josette's nephew, was a real peach. He drove Theodosia back to Charleston at breakneck speed, letting her yack on his cell phone the entire way.

Now she was talking to Drayton, who was filling her in on the rescue of Travis.

"Parker dashed backstage," said Drayton, sounding a little breathless, "just in the nick of time. And another fellow, an ER doctor who was attending the ball, also helped with the rescue. Travis lost a serious amount of blood and was only semiconscious when the paramedics hauled him out, but it looks as though he's going to make it."

"That's good," breathed Theodosia. She'd glossed over the exact details of her own trauma, not wanting to throw Drayton into a complete tizzy.

"So you'll come directly to Timothy's?" Drayton asked.

Theodosia glanced at Dexter. "Can you take me to Timothy Neville's house?" she asked.

Dexter nodded. "Just tell me what street to turn on."

Forty minutes later they pulled into the side portico of Timothy Neville's mansion. Timothy, looking dapper in his tuxedo, came bounding out to greet them.

"Theodosia, my dear! Are you all right? Goodness, you're absolutely *covered* in dirt!" Timothy spun around excitedly and extended a hand to Dexter. "Pleased to meet you, sir. My supreme thanks for bringing our girl back home."

Theodosia found more surprises when they all trooped inside.

Drayton, Detective Burt Tidwell, Parker, and Jory all clustered around to greet her.

"I was so worried about you," said Parker, putting a proprietary arm around her shoulders.

"Hello," said Theodosia in a small voice, feeling a little overwhelmed at having an audience.

Henry, Timothy's butler, appeared out of nowhere and offered Theodosia a damp towel to wipe her hands and face. "I've a pot of tea brewing," he told her in a kind voice. "Some lovely Russian Caravan."

She smiled at him gratefully. "You've been hanging out with Drayton."

Timothy waved his arms about magnanimously. "Come sit down, we have *news*." He took his place at the head of the table while they all settled in around him. Theodosia noted that Jory took a place directly opposite Parker.

"Actually," Timothy continued, "Detective Tidwell is the one who can fill in the blanks."

Theodosia gazed across the table at Tidwell. "You caught him," she said. "Drew."

Tidwell nodded. "The minute Parker called, we got word out. Didn't take long. Easy to spot a car like that. Plus, he had a few things working against him."

"Like what?" asked Jory.

"Insanity, to start with," replied Tidwell.

Theodosia put a hand to her chest. "Thank goodness it's over." She glanced down at her grimy nails, suddenly dropped her hands into her lap. "I'm a mess," she muttered.

Parker snuggled closer to her. "You look great to me." He flashed a slightly triumphant glance at Jory.

Feeling a tug of sympathy, Theodosia gazed at Jory. "Your family's house burned down," she said. "I'm so sorry."

Jory waved a hand. "That land should stay the way it has for a couple of centuries," he told the group. "In fact, first thing Monday morning, I'm going to see about putting it in trust for the Gullah people. That's where it came from, that's where it should stay. And I'm talking about a real, legitimate trust this time."

"That's . . . that's wonderful," said Theodosia. She glanced at Dexter who gave a smile and an approving nod.

Henry came in then and set a bone china cup and saucer in front of each of them, then carefully poured out tea.

Theodosia took a sip and felt the tension slip from her shoulders as the hot, steaming liquid fortified her from within.

Tidwell cleared his throat self-consciously. "There's still an issue regarding a sizeable sum of money," he said in a gruff tone.

"What are you talking about?" asked Drayton. "Real estate profits from Drew and Travis's company? Ill-gotten gains?"

Tidwell's jowls sloshed as he shook his head. "I'm sure that will be in court for years to come. No, I'm talking about the reward for information leading to the recovery of Travis McBee."

"What reward?" asked Jory.

"The one Truman McBee put up last year," said Tidwell. "One million dollars. It still stands, you realize."

"Someone's going to get it?" asked Parker.

"Part of it," said Tidwell, swiveling his large head and focusing his beady eyes directly on Theodosia. "In fact, a rather substantial portion will be awarded to Theodosia."

Theodosia just stared at him.

"What!" squawked Drayton. "Are you serious?"

Tidwell nodded. "Absolutely."

Still too stunned for words, Theodosia sat for a long moment with a dazed expression on her face. Finally, she managed to squeak out a single word. "Really?"

"Really," said Tidwell. "When I spoke with Truman McBee about his son, whom we *will* press charges against, I assure you, I strongly suggested to him that Theodosia be awarded a portion of that money."

"That's . . . amazing," said Theodosia, suddenly grasping the magnitude of Tidwell's words.

Jory smiled softly at Theodosia and murmured, "I'm happy for you."

"But what on earth are you going to do with the money?" asked Parker. He seemed more stunned than any of them. "Maybe . . . invest it?"

Theodosia angled her head to the left and met Drayton's intense gaze. A subtle smile seemed to pass between them.

"I do believe she has a plan." Drayton chuckled.

"That so?" said Parker, leaning toward Theodosia and frowning slightly. "Because she sure cooked it up fast."

"No," said Theodosia, finally managing to speak in a clear, coherent voice. "It's something I've actually given a lot of thought to recently. I'm going to buy . . ."

They all leaned forward slightly in anticipation.

Theodosia smiled. "I'm *finally* going to buy the cottage of my dreams."

The Indigo Tea Shop

Strawberry Cream Cheese Tea Sandwiches

1 small box strawberries, reserving 2 for garnish

8-oz. pkg. cream cheese, softened

1 Tbsp. cream

4–6 slices bread

¼ cup walnuts, finely chopped

WASH and stem strawberries, then pulse in food processor with cream cheese and cream. Spread mixture on your favorite bread—crusts removed, please. Garnish with a sprinkle of nuts and a slice of strawberry and serve open-face.

Vegetable Egg Strata

1 Tbsp. butter
1 small onion, diced
1 small zucchini, sliced
¼ cup red pepper, diced
2 cups cubed French bread
⅓ cup shredded cheddar or Monterey Jack
4 large eggs, beaten
¾ cup milk
Salt and pepper to taste

MELT butter in large skillet and sizzle vegetables until tender. Add bread cubes and mix quickly, then pour mixture into greased 8-inch-square pan. Top mixture with cheese. In bowl, mix eggs and milk, then pour over mixture in pan. Bake at 375 degrees for approximately 45 minutes.

Chocolate Sour Cream Scones

2 cups all-purpose flour
⅓ cup unsweetened cocoa powder
⅓ cup brown sugar, packed
2 tsp. baking powder
¾ tsp. baking soda
⅛ tsp. salt
½ cup butter
1 beaten egg yolk

8-oz. container sour cream

½ cup miniature chocolate chips

MIX together flour, cocoa powder, brown sugar, baking powder, baking soda, and salt. Cut in butter. Add egg yolk and sour cream and mix. Add chocolate chips and stir until soft. Spoon dough (about 2 Tbsp. worth for each scone) onto a cookie sheet covered with parchment paper. Bake at 375 degrees for 10 to 12 minutes.

Pineapple Tea Sandwiches

2 cups crushed pineapple, drained

1 cup sugar

1 cup chopped walnuts or pecans

8-oz. pkg. cream cheese, softened

1–2 Tbsp. milk or cream

COMBINE pineapple and sugar in saucepan and bring to boil. Stirring constantly, cook until thick. Cool, then stir in nuts. In separate bowl, mash cream cheese, adding enough milk to make cream cheese a spreadable consistency. Add cream cheese to pineapple-nut mixture and combine. To serve, spread on thin bread to make sandwiches, trim crusts, and cut into triangles.

Southern Corn Casserole

15-oz. can cream-style corn

8-oz. container sour cream

2 large eggs, beaten

Jiffy cornbread mix

1 stick butter, softened

½ cup cheddar cheese, shredded

MIX together corn, sour cream, beaten eggs, cornbread mix, and butter. Pour into lightly greased 9-inch-by-13-inch baking dish, then sprinkle cheese on top. Cover with tinfoil. Bake at 350 degrees for 45 minutes, then uncover and bake for another 15 minutes. Slice just as you would cornbread and serve hot or at room temperature.

Green Tea Granita

3 cups water

1 cup sugar

3 tea bags, green tea

DISSOLVE sugar in water over medium heat. Remove from heat, add tea bags, and let steep for 10 minutes. Remove tea bags and pour mixture into a shallow bowl and place in freezer to chill. Every 20 minutes or so, break up ice crystals with a fork. Mixture will turn solid in about 5 hours. To serve, scoop granita into dishes and garnish with your favorite combination of whipped cream, fruit, or dollop of lemon curd.

Honey Mustard Egg Salad

8 eggs
½ cup mayonnaise
½ tsp. prepared mustard
2 tsp. honey
2 Tbsp. shredded cheddar cheese
¼ cup red or yellow pepper, chopped finely
Salt and pepper to taste

PLACE eggs in pan and cover completely with cold water. Bring to a rolling boil over high heat, then reduce heat slightly and cook for 10 to 12 minutes. Cool, peel, and chop eggs. Place eggs in medium-sized bowl and add mayonnaise, mustard, honey, cheese, and chopped pepper. Mash until smooth, add salt and pepper to taste. Chill until ready to use.

Cinnamon Muffins

1½ cups flour
½ cup white sugar
¼ cup brown sugar, packed

2 tsp. baking powder

½ tsp. salt

½ tsp. cinnamon

1 egg, beaten

½ cup oil

½ cup milk

SIFT together flour, white sugar, brown sugar, baking powder, salt, and cinnamon. In a separate bowl, combine egg, oil, and milk, then add to dry ingredients. Stir just enough to moisten. Fill greased muffin tins about ⅔ full and bake at 400 degrees for 16 to 18 minutes.

Chilled Asparagus Soup

8-oz. pkg. frozen cut asparagus

1 slice onion

½ cup boiling water

1 cup milk

½ cup half-and-half

½ tsp. salt

Pepper to taste

COOK frozen asparagus and onion slice in ½ cup boiling water (per pkg. directions). Cool slightly, but do not drain. Place cooked asparagus, onion slice, and liquid in food processor. Add milk, half-and-half, salt, and pepper, then blend mixture until smooth, 30 to 40 seconds. Chill soup for 3 to

4 hours, then stir before serving. Garnish with a dab of sour cream, a wedge of lemon, or fresh herbs.

Southern Chocolate Chess Pie

1½ cups sugar

3½ Tbsp. unsweetened cocoa powder

½ cup butter, melted

1 can (5 oz.) evaporated milk

2 eggs, beaten

1 tsp. vanilla

¾ cup pecans, chopped

9-inch piecrust, unbaked

MIX sugar, cocoa powder, and melted butter in medium bowl. Stir in evaporated milk, beaten eggs, vanilla, and pecans. Pour mixture into unbaked pie shell and bake at 400 degrees for 10 minutes. Then reduce oven temperature to 325 degrees and bake for an additional 30 minutes.

Drayton's Favorite Buttermilk Dressing

⅓ cup mayonnaise

⅓ cup sour cream

⅓ cup buttermilk

3 Tbsp lemon juice

1 tsp. onion powder

½ tsp. garlic powder

Salt and pepper to taste

MIX all ingredients until well blended. Use as salad dressing or vegetable dip.

Timothy's Crab Dab Dip

6-oz. can crabmeat

8-oz. pkg. cream cheese

1 ½ Tbsp. lemon juice

¼ cup sour cream

⅛ tsp. cayenne pepper (optional)

¼ cup scallion, minced

¼ cup green pepper, minced

1 Tbsp. cream

COMBINE all ingredients in a food processor and blend well. Chill mixture at least 2 hours. Serve as a dip for fresh vegetables or crackers, or make tea sandwiches by spreading mixture on rounds of bread and garnishing with a tiny bit of fresh dill.

TEA TIME TIPS

from Laura Childs

Book Lovers Tea

Since reading and tea are so complementary, why not invite your friends in for a Book Lovers Tea? Everyone can bring a favorite novel and do a mini review, or you can discuss a preselected book. Make your table look like a writer's studio by piling leather-bound books in the center, then adding candles and a crock of flowers. Color-copy and enlarge book reviews to create your own distinctive placemats. Serve a fruity oolong tea or a robust Russian blend. Tea sandwiches might be white cheddar and green olives on dark bread, or crostini topped with curried chicken salad or mushroom pate. Favors might include bookmarks or a copy of the *New York Times Book Review.*

Dessert Tea

Late afternoon, evening, or even a holiday works beautifully for a Dessert Tea. You can even simplify your entertaining and do a buffet. Arrange an assortment of petit fours, brownie bites, truffles, mini chocolate scones, ladyfingers, pecan bars, and lemon bars on your prettiest footed cake stands or three-tiered serving trays. Include bowls of Devonshire cream, whipped cream, jam, and sliced strawberries. Select a tea that complements sweets, such as an Indian Nilgiri, black currant, or cinnamon orange spice.

Mothers Tea

Invite your mom, grandma, favorite aunt, or even a neighbor whom you designate "mum" for the day. Decorate your table with white linen, your best china, and polished silver—aim for a slightly old-fashioned atmosphere—and when it comes to flowers, opt for mums. Put on your CDs with music from the forties and fifties and brew up a pot of fragrant jasmine tea. Food offerings might include almond scones, ham and apricot pinwheels, and cucumber and cream cheese tea sandwiches.

Chinoiserie Tea

Pull out all your Chinese-inspired napkins, placemats, plates, teapots, and lacquer trays and arrange them atop a gold or red tablecloth. Think *The Last Emperor* and make your table as sumptuous as possible, even adding bamboo floral arrangements or Chinese pots filled with peonies. Scour craft and party stores for Chinese lanterns, chopsticks, fans, and paper dragons. Call your favorite Chinese take-out restaurant or whip up your own Chinese noodles, dim sum, and Chinese chicken salad. Serve China's finest oolong, pouchong, or Keemun tea and don't forget the fortune cookies!

Progressive Tea

Pull together three or four friends or neighbors and enjoy a Progressive Tea. Start with scones and jam at one house, move on to sandwiches and savories at another, and end with dessert at a final house. Of course, a different tea is served with each course!

Knitters Tea

Cover your table with an afghan, pile colorful balls of yarn into a wooden bowl for a centerpiece, and lay out a patchwork of plates, teacups, and saucers. Invite all your friends who knit, and make sure they bring a project to work on! This tea should be casual and fun—after all, you're weaving the bonds of friendship. Serve chocolate chip scones, Devonshire cream, deviled eggs, and popovers stuffed with curried chicken.

Golden Hours Tea

Love that languid, late-afternoon time of day? Celebrate with a Golden Hours Tea. Think golden scones, brandy snaps, or apple cake, along with peach tea or golden-red Darjeeling with honey. Let your tea table (or tea tray if it's tea for one) glow with shades of gold and pale yellow. Classical music and golden prose from Shelley or Byron can only enhance the mood.

For great pictorials and informative articles on tea, be sure to check out the many tea magazines available such as *Tea-A Magazine* (teamag.com), *Tea Time* (teatimemagazine.com), and *The Tea House Times* (theteahousetimes.com). Also check the Ladies Tea Guild (glily.com) and TeaRadio.com.

The poem quoted in this book was selected from *Tea Poetry* by Pearl Dexter (teamag.com).

A Special Invitation to Readers

Eggs Benedict Arnold

When Ozzie Driesden, Kindred's local mortician, ends up on his own slab, the ladies from the Cackleberry Club launch their own investigation. But as friends become suspects, one suspect turns traitor.

This is a mystery with tea, recipes, quilting, knitting, cake decorating, a dash of spirituality, and a rollicking good time with three women who are over forty and proud of it. Come on, ladies, this is your kind of mystery!

All my best,
Laura Childs